UNCERTAIN MAGIC

As he stood on the dais above the battle, Oliver the wizard made a magnificent figure in his magenta robes. He traced the slow figure of an Ultimate Spell, calling the force of Wild Lightning down on those who had burst into the banquet hall intent on ending Haldane's betrothal with the stroke of a sword.

The last words were spoken. Oliver stood with arms spread, waiting for the white tongues of flame that would lash down and destroy these wolvish swordsmen and himself.

But nothing happened. Nothing+ The one-sided slaughter continued as though Oliver had spoken not a word.

Haldane's lips moved through the last automatic mumble of the one spell he knew, the Pall of Darkness. A shuddering wave of cold passed through him and he was invisible to the eyes of men, though the gods might see him still.

Men smeared themselves with the red blood of those who had fallen, painting themselves in glory. They turned to the scattered gold of the dowry that had been Haldane's so briefly in search of prizes. But their work was not done.

"Make sure of Morca's cub!" their leader commanded. "Kill him!"

That was Haldane. Haldane then disappeared. Haldane who was invisible in their midst.

A sudden shattering hand fell on Haldane's shoulder. . .

ACE Books
by
ALEXEI PANSHIN

RITE OF PASSAGE
The Anthony Villiers series:
STAR WELL
THE THURB REVOLUTION
MASQUE WORLD
with Cory Panshin
EARTH MAGIC

Earth Magic

Alexei & Cory Panshin

ace books

A Division of Charter Communications Inc.
A GROSSET & DUNLAP COMPANY
360 Park Avenue South
New York, New York 10010

EARTH MAGIC

An ACE Book

Cover art by Boris

First Ace printing: October 1978
Second Ace printing: November 1978

Printed in U.S.A.

For our fathers
Alexis J. Panshin
Ralph F. Seidman

PART I: ESCAPE

1

The dun of Black Morca, War King of the Gets and as much of a ruler as Nestor could boast, lay out of sight behind the rise of two grassy hill shoulders. In this country, in these times, that was dangerously far.

It was a cool day in mid-spring, a Libera's Day that fell in that month when the sun was in the sign of the Wurox, Libera's Beast. It was a few hours after a freshening rain and the sky still held to an even gray. In the long hill grass at the edge of an oak wood a hunting pig cast back and forth for the scent of a rabbit. Following afoot, arrow nocked on string and eyes alert, was a boy of sixteen named Haldane—nearly a man, but not yet a man —the one son of Black Morca.

He had been warned to stay within sight of the tower as he had been warned not to hunt alone. There were times when he did both, but this was not one. He was empty-handed so far, and he would not be. He was ranging far for a Get on foot, chancing the end of daylight, as vulnerable as any Nestorian cowherd to a meeting with Get baron or Nestorian outlaw. More vulnerable. If he was alert, it was for more than rabbits.

He waved and whistled the pig left, up the hill

slope, there where a dolmen stood sentinel, one great rock balanced on another, placed so by men of olden times for purposes that no man of today could name. Slut, the pig, was small, black and quick. Men of the Western Kingdoms might use dogs for hunting, but the Gets held to the brighter animals they had used since long before they seized this land. On a thong around his neck Haldane wore an amulet, a boar's tooth marvelously graven, which he prized. He had kept the tooth to remember the boar by and paid for the graving. Grunt, an excellent dog killer.

Slut's trotters dug small divots as she coursed the hill, snout to the ground. She was only a pig for small game, but she loved the hunt. The sight of a strung bow delighted her until she fairly wriggled with pleasure. A beautiful black little darling. Ivory tushed.

A light wind toyed with the grass, the young leaves on the oaks, and the boy's brown hair. The light was starting to fail and the wind to quicken, and Haldane was reluctantly thinking of calling the pig in. It would be dark in little more than an hour. If he were back in sight of the stockade before dark, his father would never hear, but if he had to be looked for, Morca would be told and he would have to take his buffets.

Morca was gone now with a raiding party into Chastain, smallest of the Western Kingdoms. Some two weeks past, Morca had gathered barons and fighting men, lean and restless after a long winter, and led them not for the close and easy border with Palsance across the Trenoth River, but south toward the Nails and Chastain.

Haldane had been left. Haldane had been embarrassed. Haldane had been left. He had the size, the skill. He was ready. He could place arrows with half the party and at worst he could handle a sword better than Hemming Paleface, who was half a Nestorian anyway. Since Morca's departure, Haldane had gone hunting alone every day.

Sometimes Haldane hunted on horse, more often on foot with only a single pig for company. Morca had drawn the limits of Haldane's world exactly. On horse he might ride to the forest verge beyond the village in the valley, the farthest point a man could see clearly from the tower. On foot he might walk to the crest of the first hill. Haldane respected the first rule and was careless of the second. He hunted on foot because it made his small world larger.

He had decided to start for home and was raising his fingers to whistle when Slut stopped abruptly and raised her head. Her ears perked. She strained and trembled, testing the air with her flat pink nose. Haldane lowered his left hand to the bowstring again and drew the arrow back.

Haldane waited. The breeze joined him, holding its breath. The leaves on the oaks hushed to listen. There was no sound, no movement except the suspicious craning of Slut's head. Then Slut slowly trotted forward. In an explosion, not a rabbit, but a hen pheasant, plump, brown and sudden, burst from the grass and rattle-winged toward the oaks.

Fingers tight on familiar leather, string pulled taught, and arrow released. A dart speeding to overtake the bird. A good shot, well-aimed. The aspen shaft struck the pheasant like a skewer, and brought it to the ground just inside the verge of the forest.

With suspense ended, the tableau over, the watching world went back to its work. The wind blew coolly, raising goosepimples. The leaves whispered privacies to each other. Slut trotted rapidly after the bird, and Haldane followed down the slope. He was pleased with his shot. He did not enjoy returning to the dun with nothing in his bag. He wished to recover the hen and be on his way. The sooner the better.

Slut passed into the twilight wood, her dark shape merging into the shadows. Haldane followed the sound of her eager grunts, but before he reached the trees, she gave a startled squeal and burst out of the brush. When she reached the protection of his heel, she pressed close and bared her tushes at the wood like a true braveheart.

"On, Slut. Fetch," said Haldane, and waved her toward the wood, but she stayed close. She knew where she wanted to be.

Haldane touched his boar's tooth. He took a last look at the hill, and then set a new arrow to his bowstring. He shivered as he passed between the first trees. It was colder under their dark locked arms. Slut followed, grunting rapid little comments to herself.

His arrow was fletched in brown and white. He saw the feather and then the angled shaft. Haldane glanced quickly at Slut, still close at his heel, and then at the pheasant.

It doubled in size and glared at him with eyes like flaring sparks. Haldane drew his bowstring tight. The cat hissed once, leaped sideways and was gone up a tree like a black mystery.

Haldane continued to hold his arrow ready. His heart was racing and there was a trickle of melting snow in his chest. He walked to the arrow. It stood alone among dead leaves. No pheasant and no remains of one. Haldane loosed the tension on his bowstring. He squatted, laid his bow across his knees and pulled the grounded arrow free. There was no trace of blood on shaft or point. He smoothed the feathers and flicked away the crumbs of dirt on the arrowhead. He looked at the tree the cat had climbed and then put the arrow into his quiver.

"Well, boy, did you lose something?"

The voice came from behind him. It was old and it spoke in Nestorian which he had learned from his nurses before he had learned Gettish. He heard only the words, not the language.

Haldane lunged forward, aiming for the cover of the nearest tree. Slut squealed as he half-tripped over her. He lost his balance but kept his forward momentum. He tumbled and rolled, ending behind the tree he had started for. Slut huddled and grunted forgivingly to him.

He skritched her once to calm her fears, but who would do the same for him? He put arrow to string and checked his position. It was only now that he had time to think that he was sure he had been spoken to in Nestorian, the language of cattle, peasants and outlaws. His heart galloped. He felt his horn, which was his from his grandfather Arngrim, but he would not blow it for help unless he had no other choice. He preferred retreat if it was possible.

The voice laughed. It was old and cracked. He peered cautiously around the tree bole, prepared to jerk his head back. It was no Get-hating Nestorian bandit ready to bury a blade in his back that he saw, but an ancient woman appreciating him and herself.

"Did I frighten you now?" she asked. "I merely wondered if you had lost something."

He started up with the intent of unstringing his bow and thrashing her out of the forest for her laughter. It is no business of slaves to frighten their masters or to wonder overmuch about their affairs. But her figure, by some trick of the eye, suddenly seemed the person of a giant trollmother. Framed by oak she was, that ancient dolmen rearing high on the hillside behind her like a giant mushroom of stone against the sky, and she leaned heavily on her staff. But when she raised it, thunder threatened. The black cat, smug in its knowledge, sat on its heels by her side. And Haldane was afraid and stopped short.

He recognized her. He had been told of her too often not to know who she was. That was why he was afraid and that was why he stopped short. Since the Battle of Stone Heath, when the unleashed magic of the West had struck the Gets a cruel stroke, lone Gets were wary about thrashing even solitary witches and wizards. They had no wizards of their own and magic was strange and terrifying to them.

The boy was more used to magic than most Gets. He had even learned a small spell, the Pall of Darkness, and had suffered the costs of using it— though all that was behind him now. It did not occur to him to invoke the spell any more than he would have dared to bare a sword in the presence of Black Morca. Indeed, his hand sought the comfort of his boar's tooth, not for the contact with Grunt, but for the securities lent by the gravings, his clan markings.

"That's right," she said, gesturing with the staff. "Come close, boy."

The name of the witch was Jael. She was ugly with her years. Her nose was like a stripped chicken bone, her skin a withered weathered mushroom, and the veins on the back of her hands were as thick and blue as the yarn in Haldane's winter cap. She had been old when Haldane's nurses were virgins, many many years past. But her hair blowing wild about her face and shoulders was blacker than Morca's.

He approached warily. Nestorian though she was, he was ready to be polite. He wanted nothing more than for this moment to be done so that he could be off over the hills, pig at his heels, before light failed. This felt very much like an interview with Morca. His mind was a tortoise, his heart a hare. But he had had practice in hiding his fears.

"Who are you, boy?" she asked.

He lifted his head. With some pride he said, "Haldane, son of Black Morca, King of the Gets."

"Oh," she said. "Yes. I believe idle tongues have wagged somewhat of Morca to me. What do you do here in these woods of mine, walking abroad with only a pig for company?"

"This is Nestor," said Haldane. "The Gets rule in Nestor and Morca rules the Gets. This is Morca's land. Why should I not walk abroad?"

"Morca's land, Getling? There were people in Nestor before the Gets were ever heard of. There are people now in Nestor of whom the Gets have never heard. They remain, living in Nestor, and will in that day when the Gets are only a name."

Jael spoke, not with vehemence, but with a simple mocking assurance that disconcerted Haldane.

"A distant day," he said. "We. . ."

"A day soon to come," the witch said. "The Goddess is awake and walks again in the West."

Haldane's hand went back to his gravings. The Gets had left all their familiar gods behind when they first circled out of their high home plains of Shagetai. Here they had no gods to stand with them and they were wary.

"I know no Goddess," he said.

"Never fear, the Goddess will know you, and that is all that is necessary. Her passage shakes the land and her portents are everywhere."

Haldane said, "I know of no portents."

"Have you asked the plain folk? You don't know enough to follow sheep, little one, but you will learn. Haldane Hen-Heart. Haldane Left-Behind. Haldane Dribblenose."

"Those are not my names!"

Slut trembled at his passion. But those were not his names. He had no earburner, for good or ill, except sometimes Haldane Hardhead, because he was stubborn and could take a blow. He didn't really mind that one. But he didn't want these as presents.

"The wake of the Goddess is marked by change. Read the changes in your life, Haldane Libera-

Liege, and you will see portents in plenty. The Gets will meet a bloody end on Stone Heath, and you will be the instrument of the Goddess."

Haldane was a free Get, and son of Black Morca. He would be no one's instrument. Who was Libera? The name of a day, the name of a wandering star. But this day was one of Libera's. He was frightened.

"I won't be!"

"You will be! When you are ready, when you are ripe, the Goddess will come and snatch the soul from your body. You are hers to take. Libera—"

She raised her gnarly staff in her gnarly hand and gestured widely so that Haldane's eye was compelled to follow, there where she seemed to point, where rock balanced on rock. Her movements were slow and grand. And then, suddenly, unexpectedly, she brought the knobbed end of the staff down with power and precision and rapped Haldane smartly on the noggin. It set him on his heels and flaked a tooth and blurred his vision like wind-ruffled waters.

"I mark you," he heard a distant crabbed voice say. "Libera's liege. Serve her well and faithfully.

"And if you wish a portent to chew on, Haldane Eggsucker, your father awaits you now in his dun. He has brought you a foreign bride to wed."

Haldane blinked to clear his vision. When his eyes were clear again the witch and her cat were vanished, stolen away by magic. The forest was empty.

The trees began cool conversation about the approach of night. Slut whuffled anxiously.

2

There was but one road to the top of Morca's hill. From the point it left the last trees on the far side of the Nestorian village in the valley, through the settled fields and up the hill where nothing taller than a berry bush was allowed to stand, the road ran under the eyes of the tower in the corner of the palisade. Both dun and tower were there before Morca.

It was not because the hill was high and the fort safe that Morca had taken possession of the dun, nor yet for its sweet spring or its closeness to the Western Kingdoms. There were higher safer forts on Breakneck and Crow's Nest and Little Nail, other duns with sweet clear springs, other duns closer to Palsance, Chastain or Vilicea, and he might have had any of them. On Morca's Hill there was room for the largest dun in Nestor, and Morca had plans to extend his walls, plans long-nursed.

Haldane met the road at the hill foot beyond the last field. Only then, in twilight but at last in full sight of the palisade, did he pause for breath. Slut had been pressed hard, poor pig. Her sides were heaving. She had been as anxious as Haldane to be away, even if her reasons were now forgotten. She nosed at his feet and grunted of her bad dreams.

Haldane, his reasons better-remembered, looked back at the darkening country and shivered.

He explored the bump on his head with a finger, and he worried the rough edge of his chipped tooth with his tongue. One pain connected the two.

A bloody end on Stone Heath? Stone Heath was long ago when Morca still hung in a cradleboard on his mother's back, before the Gets lived within walls. There wasn't a word that he had heard that he liked, from talk of a Goddess to talk of marriage. He touched the tooth with his fingertip. The finger confirmed what his tongue told him. It was a flake shorter than his other lower front teeth. Hardly a war wound to boast of.

Yes, and Morca home, so the witch had said. He took a deep breath and started up the road to the dun. Slut followed at his heel.

He slowed his pace before he reached the dun. The gate of the stockade stood wide. The men at guard were not the men Haldane had left on watch. Morca was home. The carls at the gate, Morca's men, grinned at Haldane as they saluted him.

"You're home late, fuzzface," old Rolf said. He was still wearing his leather war jerkin, but he vaunted no fresh wounds and he showed more signs of travel than war. Still, as proof of the raid he wore a fork with a bone handle, lashed to his dagger sheath with a piece of light cord so that everyone could see them. "Your command has been lifted, Haldane, and you out walking a pig."

Haldane bid Slut stay. "Does Morca know of your fork, Rolf? Fingers are good enough for you. Fingers are enough for him. He'll make you give it up."

Rolf shook his sturdy head. "Oh, na," he said. "He has a fork of his own now. You should have seen the place we took. Stone walls as thick as a man." He held a hand over his head to indicate the width of the walls. "Forks everywhere. A trayful. Morca said I could take two if I wanted, since there were so many, but one is enough. My left hand is not so cunning as my right."

The other guard, Hemming Paleface it was, laughed and said, "You'll stab yourself yet, Rolf."

"I'll stab anyone who gets between me and the spit. My arm is too short. If I had a second fork, someone would have it from me in no time, and then where would be my advantage? And admire the cord. Isn't that fine? I think of one use for it and then another. For now, I'll just delight to play with it."

Haldane said, "Take my bow and bag, Rolf?"

"So you can escape Morca's hand? I'm on duty here. I cannot help you. But you are just on our heels. Slide the pig back to the swinery, nip through the back of the hall and meet Morca in the yard tying the strings of your trousers as though fresh come from the outhouse."

Hemming Paleface said, "Any game in your bag? A freshly dressed rabbit would make Morca sweet." He had no wounds to boast of, either.

Haldane had few words to spare for Hemming Paleface, who was not so much older, and not as good with sword or bow, but who was allowed on raids. But he would not appear small, so he forced himself to say, "Nothing. The gods of Nestor were not with me." And groaned inwardly as he remembered how much they had been with him.

"No matter," old Rolf said. "We've brought you a sweet little partridge from out of Chastain."

Both carls laughed. Haldane didn't laugh, but he did smile and show them the safe side of his hand, and they returned his salute.

He led Slut by the collar into the courtyard. Truly it seemed he was on the heels of Morca's party. The mud of their tracks had not settled. How had the witch known? How could she have known?

The yard was a tangle of movement. Get barons, those Morca had raised, and their carls. Nestorian serfs. And a party of strangely dressed fighting men standing aloof between a wagon piled high with spoils and a heavy traveling carriage at a lurch in the spring mud. Fighting men with all their weapons. What did Morca have in mind? Who were these armed strangers in his home camp?

Morca himself, the full height of a Western bow and more, dark and hairy, black-bearded, black-visaged, stood by the painted carriage talking to a painted man. A small man, a stranger to Haldane. The mixed colors of his clothes were an offense to Haldane's eye. Haldane had never seen a Western man before, except for Oliver, Morca's wizard, and even Oliver did not dress this way. Oliver wore red, or on great occasions magenta.

The buildings of the dun were set in a hollow square within the larger square of the stockade walls. The stables on one side were large and sturdy. Directly opposite across the yard stood Morca's hall, even more magnificent. It stood a full two stories high, built of great rough-hewn timbers and fronted with a balcony, with room within to hold all of Morca's men. It was a luxurious building, visible sign of Morca's ambition even for those who knew nothing of his plans to enlarge the dun.

Haldane looked one way and then another, the pig he held straining in his grip. Before greeting Morca, he needed to rid himself of all the visibles of his disobedience. He caught the arm of a serf plodding past.

"Here, old man," he said. "Take the pig to the swinery."

"Yes, Lord Haldane."

The serf seized the pig, but Slut was in no mood to be penned. She squealed and tried to wriggle free, but the serf held her by collar and ear.

That was easy enough, but bow, quiver and empty game bag could not be passed like the pig to a Nestorian. To enter the hall unseen, Haldane must do it from the rear. He looked after the old man, dragging the pig away by force of arm.

"Hey, hold," he said. "I have a question."

"Yes, lord?" The old man tried to make his respectful gesture and keep his grip on the pig, and did badly at both.

"I'll walk with you a distance," Haldane said, pointing to the swinery tucked in one corner of the dun out of sight of the courtyard. "You'll do better to loose her ear. She doesn't like that."

"Yes, lord."

"What. . . What portents have been seen of late by the *plain folk?*" He used the Nestorian phrase, Jael's phrase, rather than the Gettish word that came most easily: cattle.

"Portents, lord?"

"Signs. Strange occurrences. Omens."

"Omens. It's strange that you should ask of

omens, lord. Lon, the son of Witold the Woodcutter, saw a wurox in the forest only two days
past. So he says to anyone who will listen."

"Simple Lon? The boy who wets his smock?"

"Ah, well, yes, lord. He does, but he is a good
boy. He saw a cow, he says, and he is very positive."

"What is this wurox? Of what is it a portent?"
Haldane knew the wurox only as the name of a sky
sign. It was no more real to him than that other sky
beast, the pard, sacred of Jan.

"Why, lord, it is the wild bull of the woods in all
the old stories. Libera's kine. Travelers say they in-
habit the great forest beyond Lake Lamorne, but
none has been seen here in Nestor since my
grandsire's grandsire's time. They drop stones
rather than normal turds. I have seen them myself,
great stone whorls. But the wuroxen are gone. Until now."

Haldane's tongue went back to his flaked tooth.
The edge was rough. That one little tooth edge
dominated his mouth.

His heart in arrest, he said, "Does this mean that
Libera is here in Nestor?"

The old man sucked his breath and nearly lost
his grip on Slut. "I hope not," he said. "Veton preserve us."

He meant Veton preserve himself, for Veton was
his god, and not Haldane's. Haldane had seen the
old serf often enough standing in his gardens, shar-
ing his wine with Veton, a great swallow for
himself, a dollop on the earth for the god.

They reached the swinery and the swineherd
came hurrying out to take the pig.

Haldane said, "If these wuroxen have not been

seen in living time, how comes Simple Lon to know one?"

"Why, Lord Haldane, I've never seen a wurox and I would know one. They shit stones, as I told you. I've never seen the great bird of the sea with a wingspan twice your father's height, but I would know it if I saw it. Wouldn't you?"

"I suppose I would," said Haldane.

Haldane's attention was taken by the approach of a bearded barefoot man of middle years, short, stout and wrapped in a red robe. His name was Oliver. He was the only wizard in all of Nestor, one of Morca's luxuries, evidence of Morca's ambition. Great kings keep wizards. Morca kept a wizard. He slicked and slid his way over the rain-muddied ground from the weathered board steps at the rear of Morca's hall. It was usually muddy there. No shoon and his woolen red robe billowing about bare shanks. That mud would be cold between his toes and he made no practice of cultivating discomfort. His spells and experiments made sufficient demand on his health without him courting indisposition, he would say, often said, and he did his best to keep his feet dry and his belly full. He didn't fight, either.

Oliver hailed Haldane and danced to spare his feet contact with the mud. His unbelted robe had the appearance of a flapping half-pitched tent. In the usual way of things, his feet were shod, his robes were in place, his pockets were full of secrets and his head full of answers beyond Haldane's patience to bear. At the moment, however, nothing was in place.

He said, "Your father wishes your immediate

presence. He is holding me accountable for your coming. They arrived in a sudden hour," he said, to explain the self-evident.

The boy wasn't sure how much he liked Oliver, who wouldn't fight. He thought of leaving him floundering there while he passed through the hall, dropping bow, arrows and bag, and found his father by himself. At last, however, he hooked his bow over his shoulder the way Morca had taught him to carry it, and said, "Let us go to my father."

He had an automatic clout to take, Morca's price for disobedience, but he was ready for it. He had bargained for as much, slipping away to hunt alone, but his head had already been broken once today and still ached. He touched his chipped tooth with his tongue and his boar's tush with thumb and forefinger, and he shivered.

"Is all well with you?" Oliver asked.

"Just the evening breeze," Haldane said. "I wonder that you don't feel it, Oliver."

"I do," said Oliver. "Let us get out of the wind." And he pulled his robe into an imitation of order and tied the belt.

As they passed between buildings into the courtyard, Haldane said, "Who are these strangers?"

"Have you no eye for panoply? A Get raider should be able to gauge wealth and value like a clerk lest he fetch trash. You have much to learn. Your father has for company Lothor of Chastain."

"A King of the West here? In the land of the Gets? Why not be satisfied with his head?"

"Ah, as to that, I cannot say. I was in my cell collecting my thoughts for an hour or two when your father arrived so suddenly. He sent no messengers to warn of his coming, and in these minutes he hasn't seen fit to take me aside for consultation. Perhaps he intends to roast Lothor for the company and wished to keep the meat fresh. Proper spits are not easily found in Chastain, so there was nothing to do but bring him home."

If Haldane disliked Oliver, it was in large part for his tongue which could deal blows no man in Morca's Dun could ward, save only Morca—who was only rarely put to the test. Men were wary of the wizard.

Oliver had appeared suddenly out of the West with an eye to his backtrail when Haldane was only a boy and entered Morca's service, valued as much for his tongue as for his magic—as long as Morca was not put to the test too often. And he was not, for if Morca had use for a sharp-tongued wizard, Oliver had need of protection. He had been a younger son, and then a younger brother, his family of some power in Palsance, and he had filled his days with magic and other study. His pride being great, he had allowed himself enemies to match, until at last he had aimed a successful spell at too great and powerful an enemy and found his overmatch, not in magic, but in politics, and been forced to flee.

He told the story well, leaving the best parts to the imagination, and he told it rarely enough that it kept its flavor. Haldane had heard it only twice from Oliver, though other men might tell it more often. Oliver never named his enemy, but men around their campfires who claimed to know spoke of the childlessness of Richard, King of Palsance, and nodded.

In other days, Haldane had been in closer company with Oliver than he was wont to be now and liked him better. Not at first, of course. Oliver was far from Haldane's idea of what a Get should be—he was not Black Morca. He was a left-behind, a member of the train with the women and children, no fighting man, but only a counselor, and content to be; a strange, plump, remote figure, a man who wore glass in front of his eyes to help him to read his book. And then, when Haldane was twelve, Morca informed him that he was to be placed in Oliver's hands to learn letters and number, magical figures on paper that no self-respecting Get would know. Haldane naturally resisted the idea. Black Morca was Black Morca without knowledge of these cabalisms.

Haldane said as much. A solid thumping—how else are impressions to be made?—altered his thinking.

"Learn," Morca said. "Train your arm. Train your eye. Train your wits. A king must be more than other men."

A king—Haldane a king? It was a new idea, a new possibility. Morca's father, Garmund, and his uncle, Garulf, who had died leading the Gets at Stone Heath, had each been War King of the Gets in his own time, but this was not the West where crowns were inherited. Among the Gets the strongest baron was king, and if there was any lesson Haldane had learned, any one thing that Black Morca had impressed upon him, it was that he was not the man his father was. Haldane a king? Was it possible?

And so into Oliver's hands he went and learned to read and cipher, and it was a strange, exhilarat-

ing world he found there far outside the ken of any
man in Morca's Dun, a world that could be shared
with no one but Oliver. Oliver talked of Palsance
and the great tourneys held under the eye of King
Richard at the stone castle of Fomoria on Clear
Lake where the best and strongest were given bid
to enter Richard's service and stand behind him to
face the threat of the Gets. Haldane laughed at
that. The fighting men of Palsance were butter to
Morca's knife.

Oliver spoke of the trading ships of Vilicea with
their sails of blue and red and white, coursing the
Bay of Whales to Grelland in the north, faring
south along the Brenadine Coast of Palsance where
the old mountain trees stand high, narrow and naked with strange scales for bark, hoving round
South Cape to the Isle of Orkay and to Jedburke in
Pellardy that paid tribute to the Gets. And he
spoke of the dead and wasted ruins of Nestria at
the mouth of the Blackstone, the old city of the
Kings in the West, the legend of which was so powerful that it had carried even to the far high plains
of Shagetai.

"And you saw this yourself?" Haldane asked. "I
thought the city of Jehannes was only a story."

"And the Three Kings, too?" Oliver asked gently. "No, little one. I myself have walked the broken streets of Nestria and seen the monkeys at play
on the toppled statues of the Three Kings. All that
remains of the old glory is bare ruin and empty
desolation. There is a mindless village tucked up
against the last standing wall of the city and
barefoot boys shy stones at the head of Leonidus,

the Poet King. His bust has had five hundred years of the abuse he merited in life. Remember that, and leave no statues. Or rule well."

"I'll waste no time in making poems," Haldane said. But in his secret heart he was pleased that Oliver should recognize the stuff of kings in him. It made him feel that it might really be there.

So, in time, as he learned, he and Oliver came as close to being friends as a wizard and a boy can. Not truly friends, but they might talk to each other when there was no one else.

And then Oliver began to teach Haldane magic. Not the magic of simple figures reeling in the dance of multiplication and division. Not the magic of words on paper that could bring the dead voice of Leonidus, more poet than king, to life again after these five hundred years. True magic. The Pall of Darkness.

Haldane had balked. Haldane had questioned. But Oliver said, "Did your father not put you into my hands to learn? The things I have to teach you can serve a king as well as any man. The things I have to teach may serve a king better than other men."

So Haldane had followed Oliver. He learned the signs of hand and the words, nervous all the while, fearing, uncertain, unsteady. And failed, as magic will fail those who fail magic.

And he tried again, until at last once and then twice he pulled the cold curtain of night over himself while the sun still held the day. His touch was uncertain—the second time the spell succeeded, the veil of invisibility covered Oliver as well as himself. His count was slow and far from smooth. And yet, the spell did work.

Nonetheless, he felt he was doing wrong. Arms, not magic, were the Gettish way. Force of arm was clean and honest, the mark of the superior, the road of those who rule. Spells and sorcery were the dirty tricks of the weaklings of the West, the cowards who had struck from secret at Stone Heath.

Fortunately for his peace of mind, the aftermath of the spell was nausea and weakness. Magic always exacts a price from those who woo her, a bride price: blood, weakness, disease, and even death for power. And the day following his successes, Haldane was too weak to swing his sword or sit his horse under Morca's eye.

"What's the matter, boy?" asked Morca. "You fail and faint."

"Nothing," said Haldane. "The sun is too hot. It makes me dizzy."

Morca shook his head, but then he said, "Rest under the tree until your head returns."

But the sky filled with clouds and Haldane's weakness did not pass and the story came out. Morca's anger darked the day more than any spell and his fists blacked both Haldane's eyes and left him sore as well as weak. Morca's temper was a well-used tool, but Haldane never saw him angrier than at that moment when he left the boy in a beaten heap and went to search out Oliver. What passed between Morca and the wizard, Haldane had never learned, but he was taken forever from Oliver's hands and after that, for the first time, Oliver's sharpness began to be directed at him as much as any other man. After that, they were no longer friends.

There was compensation of a sort. From that day, Morca publicly called Haldane his lieutenant, his second. It was a good name and it filled Haldane with pride, until he found it hollow, a word without power. Hemming Paleface knew how much it meant. Nothing. Morca might say once and again that he left Haldane in command, but when he raided, he raided without him. Even when he promised, swearing before men, swearing lightly, he raided into Chastain without Haldane.

Now, as he and Oliver walked past the great hall into the tangle of the courtyard to face Morca returned from Chastain, as the witch had said, Haldane tried questions in his mind.

He craved answers, but he would not say too much, not to Oliver. He would not tell Oliver of the witch's words: nothing of portents or Stone Heath, or a foreign bride, or his soul, his, Haldane's, torn from his body by this Goddess, this Libera. But in this moment when he could ask, he must have at least one answer.

They passed the high loaded wagon with heavy carved doors lashed one to a side like elaborate shields. Morca had been looking for a proper set of doors for two years.

Haldane shot a look at the huddle of foreign men out of Chastain and then he asked, "Does magic cost a witch pain?"

3

The men of Chastain they paused near were a
lean lot, leaner than Haldane, although Haldane
was lean for a Get. Their hair was of an unmanly
length, and though they wore their weapons well-
displayed, it was all in show because they gave
Haldane and Oliver ground. They burdened themselves in hauberks of chain mail, shoulder to knee,
and they held their helmets by the noseguards like
clumsy bludgeons or tucked under their arms like
men waiting their turn to bowl at the jackstone.
Haldane wondered if they would flee in a herd if he
stamped his foot.

Oliver looked at Haldane. These days he must
even look up. No apparent matter to him that with
the parting of the men of Chastain, they were in
sight of Black Morca.

"Magic always takes its price without excep-
tion," Oliver said. "It is the one thing I know about
magic. What commerce would you have with
witches? Do you seek a new tutor?"

"No!" said Haldane. "I saw the old witch Jael in
the woods as I hunted today. She made a pheasant
for my arrow with magic and then laughed. And
she disappeared before me with the aid of a spell
like your Pall of Darkness, but other. I wished to

know if her tricks cost her pain."

"Ah, no doubt," said Oliver. His beard was white and cropped to the outline of his face. His lip and cheeks were bare and ruddy. His hair was gray and wild. He ran his hand through his hair and left it wilder. "But I wonder their meaning. Did she speak?"

"She laughed," Haldane said.

"It must have been to hide her pain," said Oliver. It was his way of closing the question. He indicated Morca with a lift of his chin and a wag of his beard. "Your father waits."

Serfs began to light the courtyard torches against the darkness. Odo the Steward directed hands to the unloading of the high-piled wagon. Odo sent a serving woman across the muddy yard to show the knights of Chastain to their quarters. The gates of the dun were swung shut, a solid door for the wild night to rap at for entry.

As Oliver and Haldane approached, Morca caught sight of them. He pushed past the painted man, raising an arm. Morca was a dark, overpowering giant. He had charm and a rude wit, but lacked grace. His subtleties were crude, and even his whispers were loud. His hand was heavy.

His son was little like him, except perhaps in owning wit and lacking subtlety, but he would never be as obvious a presence, never as tall, never as strong, never as whelming. Haldane's hair was a neutral brown. Morca's was a black and curly bush. Morca's hand could cover and hold Haldane's two fists.

Haldane readied to take his blow, but Morca swung his arm around his son's shoulders and pulled him close, saying, "Hey, Lothor. Here is Haldane, my son and second. My little brown bull to match your little brown heifer. Bring your daughter out and we'll introduce them. Introductions before weddings, hey?"

Haldane was staggered by the blow that did not fall. His heart was felled by the words that followed. Morca was in his gay and unpredictable mood. He was manic in his half-played game. What now? The witch's sight had been true—Morca's return had brought change indeed. Was he then to be Libera's brown bull, her wurox? Was he to be dumb-eyed sacrifice to a goddess he had asked nothing of? He felt himself a helpless hand-tossed die, spun for others' pleasure. At that moment, for that moment, he wished to be simple. He wished to be nothing, almost nothing—a house-carl. Still a Get, but not a king.

Lothor tugged his cloak into place as though Morca had set it awry with his violence. He held a brown-and-white dog, as neat and small as a puppy. His hair was white to his shoulders and he wore a fur cap a-jaunt. He wore tight hose and he stood on heels strapped to pattens to keep him above the mud. He on his heels and Oliver in his bare feet in the mud were much of a height.

He said, "In Chastain, only one of equal rank would presume to ask to be presented. Marriage is hardly sufficient excuse. But since you were willing to forego your long-tried Gettish customs in favor of ours in the matter of a dowry, I suppose we must be equally civil."

He was no older than Morca, but he seemed older. His days as a leader of fighting men, if ever

they existed, must have been early and brief. His
voice was boyish thin, his face was paled with
powder and brightened with rouge, and he carried
a dog—and who would follow a man like that?

His traveling carriage was decorated in strong
shades of yellow and red, and the drawn leather
curtains that masked the interior were painted with
gilt flowers. Lothor tapped at the door of the carriage with the head of his scepter, his thin stick of
power.

"Marthe," he said, "You must come out now."

He spoke of matters beyond Haldane's knowledge. His tongue was a twisted Nestorian that had
more in common with the difficult language of
Leonidus, the Poet King, five hundred years dead,
than with the country speech, plain and simple, of
the boy's nurses or with the Western speech Oliver
had brought with him out of Palsance. Still,
Haldane understood him. His tone was clear if his
words were not.

Lothor must surely be a king. Morca did not
bother to understand him, as he would have understood any lesser man. The dog watched all, silent
but eager.

The door of the carriage opened and a girl, a
woman, a princess, Lothor's little brown heifer,
stepped down into the mud of the yard with some
difficulty. It was impossible to tell if her clumsiness
was the result of shoes raised and protected like her
father's. Her great dress of white and gold hid her
feet. The heavy sleeves of the dress were a series of
puffs and every puff wore a modest skirt of its own.
Her face, underneath her broadbrimmed hat, was
unappealing, sour and painted.

"Odo!" Morca bawled, calling like a herdsman, as she stepped to the ground.

She flinched at the roar of it and seemed to teeter, and was steadied by her father's hand.

Odo the Steward, the Nestorian of highest rank in Morca's service, who might even order house-carls to come, go or stay, ceased his directions and overseeing as he heard his master call. His exhortations and movements of hand were no more needed than sideline signals to a squad of well-drilled horse on parade. The work continued smoothly without him as he came off the porch of Morca's hall and out into the yard.

"Yes, Lord Morca?"

"Unload the carriage," Morca called. "It is empty now." He turned back to Lothor. "Ha. I said if breakfast was early and cold, we should make our dinner here in the comfort of home."

Odo began to draft serfs from the earnest ant line waiting to carry away what it was handed from the wagon of spoils to Morca's storehouse within. Or was the wagon the dowry Lothor had spoken of? Trust Morca. For years, until men had drifted back to calling him Black Morca, he had been known as Morca Bride-stealer, the man who paid no bride price. In these days, unlike the better ones of old, the name was no sully. Men had laughed and leapt to follow him.

The serfs hurried to the carriage. One bounded up a-top and began to unstrap royal baggage.

Haldane studied the girl. His bride? Her hair under the hat was some shade of brown and pinned in draping curls. In this light, that was all that could be said. Her nose was long and straight and her face was round. He thought she must be older than he, all of twenty or more. And stunted, shorter than her father. Shorter than the Nestorian women he knew best, the nurses, serving maids and cooks of the dun, or those he saw in the villages. Shorter than Get women, though he knew none of these, never having traveled, except once to his grandfather's when he was a child, and it being Morca's rule that men might marry but that married men might not serve within his walls. But the Get women of his mind and the Get women of his memory were taller than this.

The boy thought though he might marry this princess of Chastain, he wouldn't like her. He would close her away in a tight room and turn his back on the door. She deserved no better, and she would get from him only what she deserved. Men might see him with her and laugh.

Morca said, "This is Lothor of Chastain. The king. And this is his daugh . . ."

"No, no," said Lothor, changing the lapdog to his other arm. "Let me make the introductions. This gaping lurdane, my dear, is your husband to be. Haldane, the son of Black Morca. My youngest daughter, the Princess Marthe, the spring of my old age. You are not fit to lay eyes upon her, but I grace you with her hand. I do not know this barefoot man."

"Embrace her, boy," said Morca. "This is Oliver, my maker of magic. Oliver from the Hook of Palsance. Did you know I had a wizard? Would you care to try his skill?"

Lothor said, "It is a large place to be from. And the name is unknown to me. Call him wizard if you like. We have no barefoot wizards in the Western Kingdoms."

"Embrace her, boy," said Morca in Nestorian.

"But she's painted," Haldane said. He spoke in Gettish.

"Embrace her. You can wipe it off after."

Oliver stood silent. He did not speak to Lothor, but stood toes a-squelch in the mud and looked steadily at him, as though his sheer presence spoke against all doubts. Men here knew him if Lothor did not.

At his father's continued urging, Haldane finally stepped forward and put his arms around the stranger princess. The material of her dress was thick rich brocade, stiff and heavy under his hands. She must have been a-teeter on pattens because he threw her off balance and only saved her from falling by seizing her shoulders. She pressed at him to be free and, balancing, struck at him, knocking his bow off his shoulder so that it hung at his elbow by the string.

"Don't touch me," she said. "You have grimed and soiled my dress. Do you understand Nestorian?"

"My little bull," said Morca.

"I'll teach her to speak Gettish," said Haldane. Speaking Gettish.

"Let us go in," said Morca. "At dinner, I'll have Oliver prove his magic for you. An Ultimate Spell, if you are willing to try your courage. Stone Heath in reverse."

"If you have so many wizards to spare," said Lothor.

"Wizards are of nature economical," said Oliver. "We suit the size of our spells to the occasion. We do not waste ourselves idly. But tonight I will show you magic."

"Odo!" Morca called. "Show King Lothor and Princess Marthe to their apartments. We meet at dinner, Lothor. Bring your fork."

"And you bring yours," said Lothor.

"I will. I will." And Morca held his new fork high, finer than Rolf the carl's, and he waved it. As he saw Lothor and Marthe led away, he said, "Come, you two. Follow me to my rooms. We will talk before dinner."

4

Morca led the way to the hall followed by Oliver at one heel and Haldane at the other. Within his dun, Black Morca was first. That is what it means to rule. Morca was never late. Other men clocked themselves by him and nothing began until he gave signal. Whatever he commanded was done. Whatever he chose to want was his. He was served first and ate sweetest. When he walked, he was followed. Where he walked, way was made.

A careless serf, too intent on the heavy brass-bound chest he helped to bear to realize his mistake, stepped backwards onto the portico and into Morca's path. Morca informed him of his error with a casual backhand blow that separated him from the chest and sent him tripping over his feet and into the wall. The chest became too much for the other man and he was jerked forward. He dropped the chest and it landed on his toes, sending him into a painful dance.

All laughed at the joke but Morca who was content to grin hugely. Once when he was drunk, Morca had won a bet by breaking a door with a slack serf, a dropper of food and spiller of ale, lifting the Nestorian in his two hands and carrying him forward like a lance as he yelled his slogan,

"Alf Morca Gettha!" The serf was broken as well as the door. Men still marveled at the thickness of wood that was smashed and the proofs of Morca's strength.

Morca said to the serf he had struck, "You'll never rise to serve within the hall if you continue clumsy."

"Your pardon, master," said the serf, first in Nestorian and then again in rude Gettish. "Please."

Odo the Steward rushed past them and began to strike the man. "Is this the way you see your lord home? There will be no meat for you tonight."

Odo looked to Morca for approval. He was still beating the shrinking serf when Morca, Oliver and Haldane passed inside the hall.

After the cool evening air, the main room of the hall was warm. There were fires in both fireplaces and the air was moist and heavy with the odors of dinner seeping through from the kitchens behind the dais. Arrases, some of Gettish fashioning, some taken from the West, hung before all the walls and kept the warmth and homey smells well-contained within the room.

The great dinner boards were being unstacked and laid across their trestles to make tables for the company. Barons joined with carls to make light of the work. It was honest work for a man to do. With Morca gone, three tables had been sufficient to serve the dun, and with so few to sleep in the hall, the tables had never been struck.

The three tables had already been increased to five and more were being laid. The benches were being carried into place. There was but one chair

within the room and it was Morca's. It stood behind the main table in the center of the dais, solid,
great and heavy, as tall as Morca and wide enough
to seat two ordinary men. Morca's father, Garmund, had seen it one year in the West, known it as
better than his own, and returned for it the next
summer with a wagon and the strength to take it
away.

"Hey, by damn, when do we eat?" asked Morca,
his voice filling the room.

"Within the hour, Lord Morca."

"Ale for all. Let's have the dirt well-washed from
our throats. A good raid deserves a good end."

"What about our guests?" called a baron, raising
laughter.

"Send them all the water they will drink," said
Morca. "I'll have my ale upstairs."

He took the stairs by the wall to his rooms
above, followed by Oliver and Haldane. No Get
was allowed above except at Morca's bidding, and
no one at all was allowed to walk the upper porch
above the portico but Morca. His wife had had
permission while yet she lived, but since her fall
and death, no one.

At the head of the stairs, sitting on a three-legged
stool, was an old man, the oldest man within the
dun. His name was Svein. He was one of the few
who had been a man at Stone Heath and lived, one
of the very few who yet lived these many years later. As his proof of the battle he carried a red lightning scar on his right cheek. For as long as the boy
could remember, his hair had been white, but in
other days he had been known as Svein Half-White
Half-Right. He had served as Lore Master for Gar-

mund, remembering the old ways, the songs, the stories, the sayings, the wisdom the Gets had brought west to Nestor, and applying them to these new times and new ways. Now he sat his stool before Morca's door, guarding the stair in Morca's absence and remembering for himself all the things that younger men did not care to know. He rose when he saw Morca.

"Woe," he said. "Woe to you, Morca. You overreach yourself. You wish to be king in more than war. You would turn Nestor into the fourth Kingdom of the West. Your father was a good king, a right and proper king. He held to the old ways and bowed to the will of his peers."

It was the sort of thing he was wont to say. As the last of those at Stone Heath, he was allowed by Morca to say what he would, however rude, however contrary. Morca had that much respect for the old ways.

"Have you been downstairs again?" Morca asked.

"No, I have not," the old man said and plunked back onto his stool. "I have no need. I've been sitting my stool and minding my business as I should, but I can hear of your alliance to Chastain well enough from here. What your father would have thought!"

Svein pointed an accusing finger at Oliver. "It is his fault. You were a good boy until he came and now he has filled your head with gross ambitions. Garulf overrode the word of his barons and bought the Gets Stone Heath. What will your appetites buy?"

Morca said, "Be at peace, old man. You excite

yourself. Sit your stool and watch my door well.
When my ale comes, pass it through. There is ale
for you, too, if your watch is good and your tongue
ceases its flap."

"There is?" Svein rose and went trotting halfway
down the stair. "Ale," he called. "Ale for me.
Morca said I might have ale."

A fire had been laid and started on Morca's arrival. Nestorian serfs might pass within the room
under Svein's watchful eye to do their work and
leave again. The rules did not apply to them since
they were not people. The stair was the distance
between Morca and lesser Gets, but the distance
between any Get and the Nestorians who served
them was so great and obvious that it needed no
emphasis.

Haldane sat him down by the fire on a three-
legged stool the match of Svein's. Oliver closed the
heavy door on the din from belowstairs.

Morca said, "Woe, woe, woe. It is all he can say.
He eats and shits and sits his stool now in Nestor,
but his mind dwells in Shagetai that we left fifty
years before he was born. If it weren't for the respect I bear my father, I would cut his throat. That
is a sense of tradition for you. I'm an old-fashioned
man and he gives me no credit for it."

"You're a generous man, Morca," Oliver said.
"If the world only knew. But what will your peers
make of this marriage? You said nothing of this
before you left. If you had told me what you in-
tended, I would have advised against it."

"I know," said Morca. "That is why I did not
tell you. That is why I am a king and you a wizard
whose spells of occasion fail. I dare. You do not. I

have no peers. I am king here and I will act the king. That is why you sought me out. Do you remember? With what other man among the Gets could you dare to practice your art?"

"None other. But I wish to practice it longer. I am your man, Morca, but what good is my advice to you if you will not hear what you have no wish to hear?"

"I will not be told what I cannot do! Study your book and be prepared to help me hold what I have taken. That is your business."

Oliver pointed at Haldane who was sitting by the fire, hands clasped, elbows on knees, listening tight to every word. His head did not move, but his eyes flicked from one to the other.

"You make the boy your pawn," Oliver said.

"That is his part. He is a pawn as I am a king and you a wizard. But he is a pawn who will be made into a king."

"Tell him of your intent. Let him know what risks he runs."

There was a knock then at the door and Morca crossed to open it. It was a serf bearing Morca's ale. Morca took pitcher and leather jack and bade the man wait outside for further call.

Oliver moved toward the door as Morca turned.

Oliver said, "Did you know that the witch Jael was seen in the woods today? Where she appears, trouble trails after. She is a bad omen. Kings and witches—too much power stirs about us. I will study my gramarie as you suggest. It may yet take an Ultimate Spell to keep what you are taking."

He closed the door behind him. Morca looked after him and shook his head. It was his bad habit to speak of others when they were not present.

"He frets too much," he said. "He lacks guts. He doesn't do, he dances. Give him a sword and a man to kill, and he would wash his hands."

Morca poured ale from pitcher to tankard and took the whole in one draft as he crossed the room. He set jack and pitcher down on the table that stood in one corner, swiped his beard, then turned and belted his son with the same backhand blow he had shown the serf. Haldane was knocked from his stool and stretched at his length upon the floor.

Morca shook an admonishing finger at him. "That will teach you to listen and mind. You are a pawn. Mine. Learn to do as you are told."

Haldane nursed his head. One blow added to another, and now he had a headache, a throbbing pain behind his right eye. The blow had come when he had ceased to expect it and he had been unprepared. He picked himself up from the floor and took his seat again, sitting silently, shaking his head to clear it, ceasing to touch it, doing his best to ignore the pain he'd earned.

He didn't grudge Morca the blow, for why should he? It was Morca's right. It was merely unexpected. The blow was far from the first he had taken, and he thought it fairly purchased. It was the price of hunting alone.

But then in an outrush, he let his reasons go. "You promised in the fall that I should ride on the first spring reaving! When will you count me man enough? I was called Haldane Left-Behind today. Men begin to laugh at me, and yet I can outdo Hemming Paleface. Why should he go and not me? I begin to envy men their scars. When the carls return I look to see their fresh-won honors."

And then Morca began to speak in a tone new to Haldane and Haldane could only stare up at him in wonder. Morca was a man who could no more easily call Haldane "Son" than Haldane could call him "Father". He was as bluff and rough in private as he was in public. This was the boy's secret and he told no one. He would pretend otherwise. Even in that moment when Morca had first called Haldane his lieutenant, he had been rough and bluff.

But now he said in a softer voice than Haldane had ever heard, "I know. I know. You shall have scars enough before I am done making you. But you must have patience. You are man enough to be left in charge. You are my reserve, as Garmund was Garulf's reserve at Stone Heath, and Garmund became king. Would you have me waste you lightly, boy?"

He clapped Haldane on the shoulder. "You are my strength. Without you, all my plans come to nothing. I need you. I would not use you too soon and lose you."

"But I am strong now," said Haldane. "Use me." But his heart was trembling on the edge of the jump to jubilation.

Morca said, "I do owe you a reaving. And you shall have it. It is time for you to prove yourself." He put his hand almost tenderly on Haldane's biceps and tested the muscle. "My son. Be all that I need you to be." His voice was intense.

Haldane could only look at him, Morca, the distant, dominating sun he followed, who ordered and denied, and numbly say, "I will." He was too filled to say more. His head was spinning. Morca was admitting of a need for him.

Then abruptly, as though the intimacy were too much for him, Morca rose and turned to the table where stood his pitcher and jack. He did not break away completely, but he poured and finished his second tankard and then stood about patting himself on the stomach until he delivered a satisfactory belch, and only then did he speak again and it was in his customary hearty voice or something like it.

"It was a beautiful raid," he said. "Oh, it was fine. If Richard of Palsance were as simple as Lothor of Chastain, the West would lie open to any man's hand. There would be no need to draw the barons together behind me as one. Anyone could rape the West."

"And you would raise the barons? All the barons as in the old days?"

Haldane might well ask. Since the Gets had recoiled into Nestor to rule there after Stone Heath, the barons had been united in nothing. They had been arrogant, grasping, quarrelsome, careless of law, unmindful of clan, jealous of privilege, and unruled.

"What do you think a King of the Gets should be?" Morca asked.

"Leader of the Gets in war."

That was the simple, well-known answer. Svein's answer. Morca said as much. "These are new and modern times. We are no longer in Shagetai. What was does not rule what might be. I will rule the barons in peace as in war. I shall lead those that can be led. I shall inspire those who would be in-

spired. I shall beat those who must be beaten. And
when I am ready, I mean to take the West. All the
West, from South Cape to the Hook, Chastain and
Palsance and Vilicea. From Orkay to Grelland.
From Lake Lamorne to the sea."

If Haldane was one of those who must be inspired, truly this was inspiring talk. It filled him
with visions of Morca leading a great army into the
West with Haldane at his right hand. He watched
Morca in awe as he spelled out his full flashing vision.

"King of the Gets?" asked Morca. "Why not
King of the Get Empire, master of greater territory
than the Empire of Nestria ever knew? Why not all
the world if a man can seize it?"

The Morca that Haldane knew did not like questions he could not answer. Haldane risked a blow
to ask. "What of the wizards of the West?"

Morca waved the question aside as of no im-
portance. "What of them?" he asked, roaring on.
"They are dead. They died at Stone Heath and
those that are left are small men, more theoretic
than our Oliver, whom I can provoke to perform.
Why else should I tolerate a man of magic? We
were too weak to take the West after Stone Heath
and the West lay helpless, too weak to defend itself.
In our weakness, we did nothing. In their
weakness, they survived. Our weakness is now
strength—we have a new generation of Get fighting men. What does the West have? Still nothing.
Lothor thought himself safe behind his mountains
and his guarded passes. We spent a week crossing
through snow and high rock on our mission of
state, and Lothor still wonders from where we

came. Give me an army and the West is mine. And yours after me."

Morca paused, for the moment talked to an end. He poured the last of the pitcher of ale into his leather cup, sipped and looked upon Haldane to gauge the effect of his words.

Haldane jumped up and seized Morca by the sleeve. "Call the Storthing together," he said in excitement. "Please, father, tonight. Let us raise the barons and go take the West!"

There had been no Storthing in Haldane's lifetime, none since Morca's election as King of the Gets. That gathering had been marked by quarrels and blood and Morca had prevailed only with the aid of his good friend Arngrim, who had been lieutenant to Garmund, though barely older than Morca. That was before Morca had taken Arngrim's daughter Freda and paid no bride price for her, opening a breach that had taken years to heal. In the meantime, though parties to this quarrel and that had changed and changed again, the quarrels had hardly grown fewer.

Morca pushed the boy away with his great hand, forcing Haldane to loose his fierce grip. Morca's cup was never in danger.

"Not yet," said Morca. "Not yet, but soon. I will call the Storthing when I command the barons. If I am to hold the West, the Gets must be united behind me. I will have my homage. I am not nice about the reasons. I will have some through love and some through lealty, some by command of their land or life. But I will have my grip."

And he finished his cup and the last of the ale. As though his habits were well-known and taken

into account, which they were, the door opened
and the serf outside announced that Morca's dinner was served. While he stood with his hand to the
door, the serf was brushed aside by Svein come
pellmelling up the stairs.

"I heard them talking," Svein said. "That Princess Marthe is in the hall with her father. She ex-
pects to eat at the High Table. No one knows what
to say."

Morca's table and dun were celibate, it being
Morca's rule that no man should keep what Morca
did not. Those of Morca's men who cared to marry
were encouraged to establish steads of their own
under Morca's protection.

Morca said, "Go down and tell them that the
girl is to be served privately in her rooms. The custom of my hall is not to be disturbed. Call me for
dinner when all is settled."

Svein turned and went out with a glancing look
at the serf at the door. In the old days before there
were serfs, a Get carl did his own labor and was
proud. Svein was proud.

Haldane said, "When you speak from the
balcony before a raid, you always say that women
are to be taken where they are found and not
dragged back to the dun. Do you intend to send
this woman and me out to start our own home-
stead, our own dun?"

"What is a custom in the face of an opportunity?" said Morca. "By damn, you have no sense!
This marriage is part of my brightest planning.
Men will follow you. They like the thought of long
tradition. You there, Rab," he said to the serf holding the door open yet. "If you were a Get would you

follow Lord Haldane and Princess Marthe?"

The serf nodded, "Oh yes, master, I would. Yes."

"See, and thus with many. If I had not made a vow to your mother never to keep another woman, I would marry the girl myself. A daughter of the line of Chastain and Nestria mated to the ruler of the Gets. It is an epic."

"The woman is painted."

"Her age washes off. She is but fourteen. She has more spirit than you might think. She threatened to kill me at first. And listen to the roar she is causing. Your mother tried to kill me four times before we came to terms. See the girl tomorrow. You may find you like her better. And if you don't, we have rooms enough to keep her in. The story needn't suffer. Come along, boy. Let us go down for dinner."

Before they were out the door, Morca said, "If I had only known before the softness of Chastain, I would not have spent these many years in wading the Great Slough and other adventures. When Lothor is well-returned to Dunbar, you and I will rape an estate or two in Chastain. Mind you, we won't tell the girl. We'll spare her feelings."

Morca started forward down the stair calling, "Remove the girl. It is my order, Lothor."

Haldane followed at a slower pace. His tongue touched his chipped tooth and he shivered and wasn't quite sure why.

5

Haldane was exuberant in the morning. Far out of sight of Morca's dun and Morca's tower, far beyond the huddled Nestorian village and the edge of the wood, Haldane galloped the cool forest avenue alone. He was loosed from all the limits and responsibility he had suffered in Morca's absence, and he recked for nothing. He felt like a true Get again.

The mist that had held the dun when he left that morning had been blown away. As he rode the natural lane, the wind nipped the boy's back and harried him onward. His horse drummed the mold and his heart raced to the drum beat. He could not be slowed. He could not be stayed. He ducked the reaching branches that lined the forest gallery as though they were enemy broadswords slicing over his saddlebow and laughed though he lost his head fully five times to the cold wet kiss of steel.

Hemming Paleface, his guard and companion, sent by Morca to heel after Haldane, lay lost somewhere on the turning Pellardy Road behind him, unable to stand the pace. He had called to halt, to slack a little, but Haldane had not heeded. Why should he? Let Hemming explain to Morca why he could not keep up to a proper Gettish pace. If

Morca would listen. Haldane could keep up.

Once again, Haldane saw himself riding beside Morca, leading the Gets into the West. Being Gets as Gets should be, bleeding and being bled, trading blow for blow, squeezing the throat of the world in a hand. No, not at Morca's elbow. Morca at the head of one army, he at the head of another—Morca's reserve. Vaulting the Trenoth River into Palsance, overspreading the West.

But this beautiful vision was spoiled by a thought. Suddenly looming in front of the progress of his armies was a plain. The boy had never seen the plain, but he knew it instantly. It was Stone Heath. Stone Heath lay in Palsance on the other side of the Trenoth River. Out of the stories of his childhood, he had conjured a picture of the place in his mind. It was an open landscape, a series of plains and cliffs, carelessly bestrewn with great rocks shaped like eggs and lit by wild and dangerous lightnings under black clouds. It was a deserted place of death and danger. And in Haldane's mind the two armies, Morca's and his, galloped headlong down onto the plain and disappeared into a sudden crevasse.

Haldane's gelding swerved at a bridle tug, but it served no purpose to dodge destiny. The army in his mind was gone and the plain stood empty under deathly skies. Haldane was abruptly sobered and drew rein. He looked to see if he were watched. If he had seen outlaws he would have killed them then. He would have cut them down for seeing him.

He felt it was unmanly of his mind to return to the witch's words and to dwell on them. Either he was a silly old man like Svein and Oliver, haunted by thoughts of woe and doom, or he was a Get, Morca's son, Morca's own man. To harry the West was not to meet a bloody end on Stone Heath. It need not be. Stone Heath could be ridden by. Cast the thought out, Haldane, and revel in your fortune.

But in the moment before he dismissed his fear, Haldane had a premonition, a vision that he knew not whether to heed. He saw himself returning home to find Morca ready to lead the Gets again to Stone Heath. Haldane closed the thought determined that should the vision prove true—which he would doubt—he would warn Morca no, whatever Morca said.

He halted his horse on the hill above the New Bridge, back on the Pellardy Road once more. At the ford just upstream from the pilings of the fallen bridge there were two Nestorians in gray smocks kneedeep in the chilly water. They bent and searched slowly in the water with their hands, but he thought they watched him, as he would have watched himself if he had been they. He sat taller in the saddle and looked back down the road for Hemming Paleface. Ear served better than eye on the tree-closed road, but there was no more sound than sight of the carl. So much for him.

Haldane set his horse down the road slope and trotted past the bridge pilings standing bare-kneed. He remembered New Bridge on Rock Run when the bridge still existed. He and his mother had passed over it as they traveled the Pellardy Road on their visit to his grandfather in his dun on Little Nail. Of that journey he remembered two things—

the bridge and his steel grandfather Arngrim.
When they had left Little Nail Arngrim gave him
the horn that he still carried, though it was years
before he could blow it.

He had wondered that a bridge so old could be
called new and had been told not to fret about
things Nestorian. But that was all very long ago. It
was before Oliver had appeared from the West,
before his mother's fall, and even before Morca's
hall was built with its second story and its balcony.
It was long ago when Haldane was a child and
nothing had yet happened.

He reined his horse at the bank of the stream
close by the wading men. He waited for respect.
Haldane was armed and the Nestorians were not.
He sat tall and dry on a handsome gelding while
they paddled with the river bottom. He was a Get
and they were cattle. For all these reasons he expected to be given attention.

The peasants straightened and touched their
foreheads with dripping muddy fingers. It was funny to Haldane. Their fingers left smears. One
peasant was old. The other was younger and larger
and stood in need of a shave come market day.
Like many Nestorians, he had a dull and stupid
face.

Haldane was curious to know for what purpose
they waded. "What are you doing?" he asked in
Nestorian.

"Gathering clams for our dinner, lord," the old
man said. He pointed to shells looking like damp
shale on the river bank.

Would they really eat shells? These peasants ate
many things like roots and mushrooms that a Get
would know enough to kick aside as he walked.

"Mussels, too," the younger one said, grinning foolishly.

Haldane shook his head. "How do you eat such stuff?"

"In a broth with fish and vegetables," the old man said. "It is a very good meal."

Haldane waved the answer away because it was not to the question he had asked. The *plain folk* misunderstood much that was said to them. Odo the Steward was a rare man. Most of his fellow natives understood only the plainest of Nestorian country speech, spoken slowly and clearly, often repeated, often rephrased.

The foolish one said, "We will give you some to take home, lord." And he proffered a shell smeared with mud.

Not to be misunderstood, Haldane said, "Your food is unclean. It is not fit to eat. Now, what late signs or portents have you seen or heard tell of?"

"Nothing, lord," the older one said.

"Nothing?"

"Yes, lord," said the old man. He danced a little shuffling dance in the water as he spoke, shifting from one foot to the other as though he found it cold to stand. Then he balanced on one foot, drawing the other from the water and setting it a-drip against his knee.

"What?"

"Nothing, lord." And he shook his head.

"No signs at all?" said Haldane. "Have you heard aught of a wurox being seen in the forest?"

"Oh, that. Yes, lord. The woodcutters do speak of a wurox they have seen. I have not seen it myself."

Haldane gestured with a questioning hand. "Is

that not a portent? Bud-Month is the month when
the sun is in the sign of the Wurox."

"No," the old man said. "No, lord. There used
to be many wuroxen in the forest. Many, many.
They have been away. Now they return."

"Ah, but if that is not a portent, then what is?"

The old man shook his head again. He was
almost as slow a head as the other.

"I don't know, lord. I have seen no portents."

"Is that a portent, lord?" the great lout asked.
He pointed past Haldane.

Haldane turned in the saddle. It was Hemming
Paleface caught up to him at last. Hemming
Paleface, a portent? Hemming was too familiar and
small to be anything more than himself.

"I know him," said Haldane, "and he is not important."

Hemming reined his chestnut mare in on the
slope above the bridge pilings. He waved and
called to Haldane.

"Hey, ho, Haldane. Come."

Haldane waved back. "Come here yourself," he
called in return.

But Hemming did not come. He sat his horse
and waved again to Haldane.

Haldane was angered. Who was Hemming that
he should refuse him before these peasants?

The wind blew overhead, scudding heavy clouds
across the sky, and the light altered frequently. A
sudden shaft of light picked Hemming out as he sat
his horse on the slope. And they below were in a
cloud shadow. In that moment, Hemming looked
very like a portent. Or meat for an arrow.

Haldane brought his horse around. His jaw was
set tight.

"When will you be putting our bridge back up, lord?" the simple peasant said.

Haldane looked back at him. Fords were made before bridges as any fool knows, and a Get had no need for more. The Gets were careless of bridges. Bridges that fell in Nestor under Gettish rule would stay fallen.

"Continue to wade as you are used to do," Haldane said shortly, clapped heels to his horse and rode up the hill.

Hemming Paleface was two years Haldane's elder, but no bigger or stronger. He was not yet finally grown and his paleness was marred by the red remains of pimples nipped young. He was always pinching at himself. He was a dogged unquestioning would-be-good and only half a Get. Haldane meant to have him left behind in the tail when he and Morca raided into Chastain. He had thought on it over night.

Haldane rode up the slope determined to throw Hemming Paleface from his saddle before the eyes of the shell gatherers. He meant they should know Hemming for a Nestorian. Haldane guided his gelding with one hand and uncumbered his bow with the other and when he reached Hemming he slipped the bow behind his leg and tumbled him. It was an unfair trick fairly played. Haldane laughed at Hemming sitting surprised on his rump on the damp Bud-Month roadway. By his hand a solitary daffodil waved with the wind.

"Pick a bugleflower," Haldane said and rode beyond the hill.

But he checked there and waited until Hemming came riding to join him. In his hand Hemming held the lonely bugleflower. It was not what Haldane would have done, or perhaps it was.

The carl said, "Haldane, you shouldn't have thrown me. I wouldn't throw you."

"Couldn't," said Haldane. "Why would you not ride closer when I called for you to come?"

"I don't like me here so far from the dun. Morca said we two should ride together on account of outlaws venturing out with the springtime. I didn't know those peasants. Where were they from?"

"I never ask those things," Haldane said.

"As ready as peasants, they might have been some outlaws," Hemming said. He was called Hemming Paleface in the same manner that Haldane was Haldane Hardhead, but he heard his earburner more often. "If they were outlaws, it wasn't meet to dump me on the road. Here is the flower you asked me to pick."

Haldane took the flower, pale yellow trumpet-mouth, white star, green stalk, belated harbinger of spring. He held it gently.

"They were but peasants gathering shells for dinner," he said, believing that he made his point.

"Outlaws must eat, too."

Haldane knew what outlaws would do because he knew what he would do if he were an outlaw. He had only two standards, himself and Black Morca, and Morca was only to be compared to Morca. He knew outlaws as he knew Hemming, and both of them were much like himself.

"But not shells," he said. "Outlaws would have too much pride. And those two sad cattle were no outlaws. They wouldn't be allowed."

Hemming bowed to Haldane's authority and

agreed to judge as Haldane judged. That was because his standards, too, were Black Morca and Haldane.

"Na, Haldane," he said. "Don't ride away from me. My mare will not keep pace with your gelding."

"Why should I stay for you?"

"I'm your man now. It wouldn't look right to the others if I were not to ride into the dun with you. They would think it strange. And if you were killed on the road before me, I could not tell Morca. You are my clan, Haldane."

Hemming laid a hand on Haldane's arm, their horses standing nose-to-tail, wind gusts whipping. He spoke earnestly.

The old clans of the Gets, the Eight, were blurred in the long passage west and broken on Stone Heath. Morca enlisted men without regard to their grandsire's clan, which other barons might also do, and dealt outside justice, for which he was resented by some. Haldane was a Deldring. Hemming's father had been a Maring. The gravings on Haldane's amulet, his boar's tooth, which he would sometimes study, were Deldring marks. Hemming knew less of Maring.

Haldane tapped Hemming's nose with the bell of the flower. "You are not my man. I am not responsible for you or anything that happens to you."

Hemming spread his hands. "I am your man. I will hold your horse. I will fight for you. I will follow where you lead me. Keep me close."

"Why would you follow me, Hemming Paleface?" Haldane's mind trembled. He wanted to be followed, but by the right men and for the right reasons. He was not yet like Morca, who only wanted to be followed.

Hemming said, "Morca has ordered me to."

"He ordered you to follow me this morning."

"Na, Haldane. He ordered me to be your man. But I like it. I will do better with you than with Morca."

Haldane was angered. There was none of the rightness he wished in having his men tossed to him by Morca as Lothor of Chastain tossed scraps to his dancing lapdog. Not one at a time. Not Hemming. And then Haldane suddenly realized that there would never be a time when he could choose those who would follow him. He could only choose among them. That was more the way Morca would see it.

As though he were taller and stronger, more powerful and more certain than he was, Haldane asked, "How loyal would you be to me, Hemming? What trust could I place in you?"

"I will be your man, Haldane, in all things. I will do what you tell me. Then, as your fortune increases, so will mine."

"Win my love. If Morca says for you to stay and I say for you to go, what will you do?"

"What do you ask of me? Morca would wring my neck. And yours, too."

Haldane leaned to fix his bow in place beneath his leg, still holding the spring flower in his right hand. When he straightened, he looked at Hemming and said, "I wanted to know if you would follow me. Well, if you will not act on my word before my father's, then return to Morca and tell him you would prefer to follow him."

"No, no, Haldane. I will follow you even if Morca wrings my neck." And the carl touched his throat wonderingly.

"Then dismount," Haldane said. And he brought his leg over his black gelding's neck.

The two stepped out on the sward, their tunics whipping about their thighs like drying laundry. The light was pale and green. The trees overhead seethed and boiled, cursing like kettles. Haldane bade Hemming kneel before him. Hemming sank to both knees and Haldane addressed him.

Haldane knew nothing of the ancient Western forms of fealty. He knew only Morca's practice, and tags of clan oath from childhood games. But he knew how to bind a willing man:

"Hemming, son of Wermund, if you serve me truly in all things, following my word whether I am king or whether I am carl, I will make you a main man of mine. I will see to your welfare. I will lead you to your profit. But if ever you play me false, your life is mine. I will kill you where I find you. So I do swear."

Haldane kissed the bell of the daffodil. He held it before him.

"Now, if you swear to serve me, and offer me your life as your earnest, then kiss this bugleflower and wear it as my badge."

When they two, Haldane followed by Hemming, rode through the open gates of Morca's Dun harried by a wind turned cold, there were horsemen gathering in the yard. Haldane thought of his resolve to tell Morca not to venture onto Stone Heath, and his tongue touched his chipped tooth.

No one had remarked on the tooth but his tongue knew that it was rough and shorter, and worried. But it was not Morca, only Ivor Fish-eye and a party.

"Where are you to?" Haldane called.

Ivor was among Morca's barons, a narrow dark thinking man who would hide himself behind his dead white eye, then peep round the corner and flash his good eye blackly. His party was bundled against the gathering chill of the day and well-armed. Among the party were two of Lothor's men of Chastain.

"We are off to hunt the wild cow in the woods. I will show these foreign men how a Get kills. I'll have the horns. What is that flower in your shirt?"

"It is my badge he wears," Haldane said. "He is my army."

"Are you a baron now to have your own army, Morca's Haldane? Will you match your army against mine?"

"Not yet," Haldane said. "After I am married."

Ivor hid behind his eye. "Perhaps you are right," he said. "I should force you now while you are small." He laughed, gathered his party with a hand and said, "Let us leave to seek and kill the unknown beast."

It was the most lightly spoken Haldane had found Ivor. They were not familiars. The hunting party rode out into the bite of wind and Haldane and Hemming into the warmth of the stable. Haldane left his horse there in the care of his army and crossed the yard to the Hall.

6

The main room of Morca's Hall was set for hearing. Morca sat alone on the dais in his great chair, ankle cocked on knee, hand on ankle, enjoying his singularity. Before him, within a circle of crowded benches, stood a little baron, Aella of Long Barrow, pleading some case.

Fires burned warmly in their places. With breakfast long past and dinner a rumbling dream to be quieted with kitchen filchings, the boards and trestles were stacked by the walls. Barons and carls sat the circled benches listening to Aella and watching Morca, or moved about the room talking low amongst themselves, or perched atop the stacks, legs swinging. All but old Svein, conning the room from his staircase.

Haldane's ears and cheeks were heated red in the new warmth of the Hall. He spied Rolf the carl leaning against the dinner boards. He joined him and asked with an inclination of his head, "What progresses?"

"Nothing," said Rolf. "Aella seeks leave to withdraw. He says he has present occupation at home."

This was news of small interest to the boy. Aella was a minor man befitted best for long dull errands.

"Where is your fork?" Haldane asked, for he saw that Rolf's fork was missing.

Rolf looked chastened. "I should have taken two when I had the chance. I lost it last night to a stay-at-home. Ludbert Lead-butt won it from me at dice and he will only give it back in trade for my cord. I'll kill him and take it back, I think."

From the dais, Morca said, "Go then, Aella. You have my leave. But return for the betrothal banquet one week tomorrow and witness the sealing of Haldane to the Princess Marthe of Chastain."

"I will an I can, Morca. I will do my best," Aella said, and smiled. He bowed deeply and withdrew.

Before Morca could signal for another to come forward, Haldane made his way to the dais, conscious all the while of men's eyes upon him. It was more attention than he was used to, the result of this marriage of politics. He walked the straighter for it.

Morca saw him coming. In his great roaring voice he said, "Hey, Haldane, you have affairs to attend to." He waved to a Nestorian serf, one of Odo's go-fetches. "Go tell Lothor to prepare his daughter to receive a wooer."

Men laughed, led by Morca. Haldane stepped up to the dais and went to one knee by Morca's elbow. He wanted Morca to know what he had done.

He said, "Hemming and I have been riding. I have made him my own man now." He spoke low, for Morca's ear alone.

Morca replied publicly, making their business common property. "I know," he said. "It is just as I ordered."

"No," Haldane said. "Hemming follows me now. I have bound him to me by oath." He wanted Morca to know that Hemming was in truth his man now, and not Morca's. No longer Morca's to order. "He is the first man of my army and he moves by my word."

"Well and good," Morca said smiling. "And I will give you more men later."

He left the boy in doubt whether he did understand or no. If experience were the judge, he did not. He would not. He put his great hand on Haldane's shoulder and bore him down, bringing him to both knees.

"Here, sit by me now until your bride is ready to see you." He signalled for the next piece of business.

Haldane took his place at his father's feet. He had never been in battle but his heart bore scars. He looked out over the assembled men and like a good Get warrior showed nothing of his wounds.

He did not know the man who stepped forward next. It was a stranger to Morca's dun. But Morca knew him.

"Well, Soren Seed-sower, what business do you have with me?"

Old Svein, sitting his stair, knew him, too. "He is a Farthing, Morca," he called. "His great-grandfather was your uncle's enemy. Beware. Never trust a Farthing.

Morca stood in sudden anger. He waved an arm like an ax blade. "Up the stair, old man! I tire of you, Svein All-White All-Wrong. You've lived too long. Open your mouth to me again and I will break your neck."

And he sat him down again as Svein scurried up the stair to his stool and safety. Morca winked at Soren. "Say on."

Soren was a soft plump man. He was no danger to anyone, Farthing or not, great-grandson of a strong and dangerous man or not. Haldane did not know the man, but he knew his name. He was an example often spoken of. He was called Soren Seed-sower because he had settled to the land like a Nestorian. No one wanted to be called a Soren Seed-sower.

"I ask your help again, Morca. Furd Heavyhand still harries me. Now he has taken five pigs and my fourth daughter back to his dun. I want my pigs back. I want Furd to cease his lazy raids. Let him raid West like everyone else if he must raid."

His tone made it plain that he had better things to do than raid the West or anywhere.

"The price is the same price you would not pay before," Morca said.

"My oath?"

"No," said Morca. "Your life if you break your oath."

Soren shook his head. Haldane could not understand why Morca would want the allegiance of such a man. Should strength ally itself with weakness? If he were Morca he would have gone looking for Furd Heavyhand. Better one of Furd than five of Soren.

Soren said, "What will you do to Furd?"

"I will make him cease his raids and return your pigs. And your daughter, too, if you like."

"That isn't necessary. Let him keep her. She will make a sober man of him," Soren said. "All right. I will give you my word, Morca."

He was bending his knee before Morca when the serf returned from Lothor.

"Hold," said Morca to Soren, and waved the go-fetch forward.

Soren, fat as a brood sow ready to drop a litter, was left half-bent. He had to make the decision to rise, set, or remain halfway in-between, and he bobbed indecisively, raising a laugh from these on-lookers who were ready to find a laugh in him. He flushed, but then apparently decided that since he was to end on his knees eventually, he might as well do it and be done, and plopped down awkwardly.

The serf spoke to Black Morca. "Lord Morca, the little foreign king says his daughter will receive Lord Haldane now. She waits him in the small room."

Morca nodded, waved him away to his corner with one hand and nudged Haldane with the other.

"There's the signal, boy. The Princess Marthe waits for you. Go on, now."

"I would as lief not go. I have met the girl. I know already what she looks like."

Morca clenched his great right fist and showed it to Haldane. "You are marrying the girl," he said. "Don't you think she deserves a second look before you are betrothed?"

Haldane said hastily, "Oh, all right then."

As he left the room, Morca called after, "Don't let her make a sober man of you." And there was laughter.

Haldane paused outside the door of the small room where the princess awaited him. Lothor's little brown heifer. His price for becoming a king and living an epic. He counted to five and to five again, and opened the door.

She stood waiting opposite the door, Lothor's little dog in her arms, a tirewoman at her elbow. The dog yapped to see Haldane.

Marthe was shorter than he remembered. Today she wore no hat and bore less paint, but again she wore a dress that swallowed her. The sleeves were puffed and slit. Her dresses all seemed to have puffed sleeves that made her appear chubby and graceless. Gold chains hung down over her tight, jeweled bodice. Her hair was golden brown, her face was round, and her nose straight and high-bridged. She looked more the younger girl Morca had made her.

Last night after Lother had retired, it had been recounted how Morca's party had halted well short of the dun at Lothor's insistence so that he and the Princess Marthe might change from their traveling clothes. They wished to make a grand appearance at Morca's dun. They wished to impress all the important people waiting there. The Gets had let them, laughing to themselves.

"But why did they do it?" Haldane asked. If he changed his clothes once in a twelfthnight he counted it often. More like once in a month. And every man who mattered in Morca's dun was with the party. "Who was it for?"

"Well, it must have been for you," said Morca. "And Oliver. And the pigs. And the kitchen women." Everyone laughed as he worked his way down the scale. "Were you impressed?"

"No," said Haldane. "As for the kitchen women, you must ask them."

Now looking the girl over, he still was not impressed. As he closed the door behind him, Marthe handed the dog to the tirewoman who retired a step or two, not so far that she couldn't hear all that was said, but far enough to remove herself from the affairs of her betters, at least by implication. The dog was a trembling fragile thing and it strained futilely to be free. Grunt would have been ashamed to kill it.

Still without a word—for what did he have to say to her?—Haldane walked around Marthe, taking advantage of the opportunity to see her from all sides. That, after all, was his reason for coming. As he passed her, the tirewoman backed even farther as though to give him all the room he could demand and an extra margin for her own peace of mind. She was a grey woman dressed in grey—greyness compounded.

The young princess of Chastain tried to turn to continue facing him, but her skirts were long and heavy and allowed no freedom of movement. To turn without tangling she must stoop and lift her skirts free. She refused to stoop and she would not tangle herself so she stood still, wrestling with fury, while he looked at her. It pleased him to make her angry because there was nothing else about her that could please him and he craved some satisfaction.

"Have you stripped me with your eyes to your content, you barbarian pig?" she asked.

It was a well-turned nastiness in the narrow Nestorian spoken by the high-born of Chastain, but in the distance between them the nuance was lost. Haldane heard only, "Have you seen your fill?" He did not recognize the word "barbarian". It was not a word used by peasants, by Oliver or by Leonidus the Poet King. And pigs smelled far sweeter to him than they did to her. He came very close to hearing a compliment. Only her tone saved her meaning.

He surprised her by replying in his simple country Nestorian: "That I have. My fill and more." She clearly hadn't expected to be understood at all, but had been speaking bravely for the tirewoman to hear. He turned his back and walked to a chest by the door which he took for a seat.

"So you speak Nestorian," she said.

"That I may talk to serfs and my orders be understood," he said. "But I will teach you Gettish."

"I will not learn it!"

"Please yourself. You may sit in this room and face the wall until you die if that is what you like. You may mumble Nestorian to yourself as you do."

"I will entreat My Lady Libera to strike me dead and burn this place with fire after me."

Haldane's hand went to his boar's tooth. He was afraid, struck to the heart by her words as he would be by any mention of the Goddess. But he would show none of it. Was she kind of the Goddess? Was the witch's hand in this? No matter. He forced a lifted chin, a laugh, and light words.

"Tell me more of your Libera and what she will do."

But she shook her head a sudden and determined no as though she felt she had said too much. And then she just stared at him, her eyes great and round. There was a long and numbing silence.

"Say on."

But she said nothing.

"Say something."

At last she said, "Do you wish me to speak of the weather?"

"If you like."

"I like it not at all. It has been nothing but

clouds and cold and rain since we crossed the
Nails."

Haldane said, "It is spring." But she was speaking and not listening.

"Or health? I am bruised and sore from traveling
over fallen roads." Marthe spoke intensely.
"Would you like another subject?"

"An you wish," Haldane said.

"I wanted to have a bath last night and they told
me I must wait until we are betrothed. Is this a
Gettish custom?"

The tirewoman gasped. In a small voice she said,
"Oh, my lady! You told your father you would not
ask."

"I am asking. Must I stay travel-dirty until we
are betrothed?"

"No," said Haldane. "You must stay travel-dirty until bath night. That is Cel's Day coming, the
day we are plighted."

She turned away and looked upward. In a desperate voice she said, "Oh, my life! Am I lost? Am
I lost? Oh, if I were only home again where life
is right. What must I forego next?"

Haldane said, "You are much too nice. I'll
wager my father's treasure that when you shit you
have a servant standing ready to wipe you. You are
a heavy price to pay for ambition. You should have
stayed at home with your own in Chastain and never entered my life."

This stung the girl. Her head snapped round to
face him. Her eyes widened in outrage. She opened
her mouth to speak and no words came. She hit the
air with her fists in frustration.

Finally she managed to say in pain and anger, "I

had no choice! Your butcher father has dragged me here to marry you against my will. If I could I would kill him and you, too."

Haldane shrugged. "Sheep are made to be shorn."

"A sheep?" the girl asked. She reached into the folds of her skirt and brought forth a knife. It was no plaything. It was narrower in the blade than Haldane would have liked, but yet it looked to be a mean stinger in the hands of one who could use it. If this girl was one.

"You have brought me here," she said. "You may marry me. But mind yourself. If you ever lay a hand on me, I shall kill you."

On the instant Haldane was off the great chest on which he sat and across the room. He lifted his left hand and struck the small princess of Chastain a smart slap on the cheek. The dog in the tirewoman's arms yapped sharply. The girl slowly touched her reddening cheek as though to confirm the blow.

"There," Haldane said. "Now I've laid a hand on you."

When Haldane returned to the Hall, it was to find Morca's audience concluded and the room emptying of men. He saw Oliver in his red robe, his spectacles on his nose, crossing the room slowly to accost Morca at the foot of his stair. Oliver looked to be suffering the hobbles for his successful display of magical craft before Lothor at dinner. Haldane had not expected to see him abroad today.

Morca raised a palm to Oliver. It held him at bay. "Put out your pipe if you please to talk to me. I will not be smoked to death."

Smoking was a strange and filthy habit Oliver had brought with him out of the West. He said it was a necessary part of his magic. The yellow weed he smoked smelled worse than a singed chicken. It was another reason that men were wary of him. When Haldane had studied magic so briefly, the prospect of having to smoke had dismayed him. He had not studied so long that his dismay was tested.

Oliver put his palm over the bowl. "I was in my cell studying my book for you and your benefit, instead of sleeping as I would, when I heard that yet another baron has craved leave to depart. How much reason to study my book will you give me?"

"It was only Aella of Long Barrow."

"Don't say only Aella. If you followed my advice you would let no one leave until the betrothal is made and Lothor returned to Chastain. There are too many who will not like this marriage."

"Aella will return for the betrothal. And today Soren Seed-sower has joined me. He likes this marriage fine. And his brothers will follow him shortly into my hands, or so he swears." Morca waved Oliver away. "Put your fears to rest, return to your cell and have your sleep. Nap until dinner."

"I do not speak of lackweights like Aella and Soren. Larger men than they care what you do. In times like these, with witches and kings all about us, outlaws in the forest and enemies a-plenty, it is folly to keep an open gate. 'The man who walks barefoot does not plant thorns.' "

"Have you been talking to Svein to be learning his tired saws?" Morca asked. He called up the stair. "Svein, have you and Oliver been hunched together?"

"No, Morca," said Svein from the dark at the top of the stair. "But for once, your foreign man is right. Soren is a Farthing. His great-grandfather was your uncle's enemy. It is folly to let a man like that come and go."

"Enough of this," Morca said. "I will have my way. Hey, Haldane, you are hurt. You are wounded. Did she bite you?"

Haldane touched the bloody cut above his wrist. "She stung me only, but I have pulled her fang."

He reached behind him and brought out her knife. He flipped it in his hand and caught it by its wellworn black leather haft.

Morca roared at that. "I told you she had spirit. Your first war wound. When you have her in your marriage bed you can trade her stroke for stroke and wound for wound.

But Haldane's tongue knew his first war wound better. It touched the rough edge of his chipped tooth. His life was a knot, a chaos of wants and fears, but at the moment he was sure of one thing.

"I have no wish to marry this fat little foreign girl, father," Haldane said. "She does not know Garmund from Garulf."

"You have no wish," said Morca. "My wish is your wish, and my wish is that you marry."

The moment of certainty passed. Morca stared at his son so dominatingly that the boy's resolve broke and drained away.

"Hear me all of you!" Morca shouted. "I want no more argument. It is settled now! The sealing will be a week tomorrow and that is the end of it."

Haldane said, "Bath night." His submission.

Morca said, "Is it? So it is. We'll have our baths

in that morning, before the betrothal." His acceptance.

"But first we have to speak with Furd Heavyhand. Make yourself ready, Haldane. We ride to find him come morning."

7

The banquet in celebration of the betrothal of Princess Marthe, youngest and dearest to Lothor of Chastain of all his daughters, a child whose father's fathers were Jehannes and the Three Kings of Nestria, but whose mother's mothers were even older, to Lord Haldane, son and second to Black Morca, who would be a prince if the Gets had princes, was an early success. Men drank from full stoups and ate from full plates in the same great hall where they had bathed in the morning and witnessed the beginning of an epic in the afternoon. The banquet was the capstone of the day.

An ox fit for best guests turned over one fire. On the other spit hung a wild boar returned by Ivor Fish-eye's hunters. The chief tumult of platter filling was over and men were well-settled to their meat and drink.

The dowry Morca had brought back from Chastain as his price for allowing his son to marry the Princess Marthe lay on display before the dais. All but the great doors, which had been fitted and hung while Morca pursued his business with Furd Heavyhand. Men admired the treasure for its bulk and Morca for his nerve. Morca Bride-stealer. Ho, ho. At his work again.

From his great chair at the table on the dais

Morca could see his new doors. He ate beef and sopped his plate with bread. He wore pink ribands braided in his beard for the occasion.

At the table with Morca were other great people. At Morca's right hand, telling him stories to keep him amused, was Oliver, his strange and formidable maker of magic, visible evidence for all the room of Morca's control of powerful forces. Oliver had shed his usual serviceable red woolen for magenta robes of cloth that dazzled the eye.

At Morca's left hand was Lothor of Chastain, cloaked in blue brocade. He pecked at his food and did not laugh at Oliver's stories, even though they were told in Nestorian. He was without his dog tonight, but between bites he fondled the scepter that lay beside his plate, symbol of the slender power of Chastain, as he always did in the presence of the Gets.

Between Lothor and Haldane sat Princess Marthe, the only woman who ate in all the room. Morca had allowed her to eat this meal at the table to give Lothor reason to leave light-hearted. Marthe wore pale blue and white, the colors of ice. Like her father, she was silent except when addressed.

Haldane sat in Morca's second chair, brought downstairs from Morca's quarters. He cut Marthe's pork for her with a new narrow knife he had. His chair, much smaller than Morca's, framed him neatly. Morca had given it to him after the betrothal. Like so much else that had happened in this last week, it was evidence of his father's favor.

Barons and carls and knights of Chastain spilled ale on the rushes and stuffed their guts with meat and savory kitchen dishes. A serving woman carried a trencher new-brought from the kitchen to Svein All-White All-Wrong on his stair and let the oldster breach the pottage. At the next table, Rolf the carl sat with his again friend Ludbert, who had gambled for his fork and won. The fork had a new owner now and these two ate with their knives, spoons and fingers like regular Gets.

Elsewhere, together sat Soren Seed-sower and Furd Heavyhand, both Morca's men now. They ate bite for bite and drank drink for drink and haggled bride price. Companions at another table were Ivor Fish-eye, eating of the boar his party had taken while they hunted the wurox but found only its stone turds, and Aella of Long Barrow. Aella had returned to Morca's Dun as he had promised. If he had been too late for bath and betrothal, pellmelling up just before the gates were to be closed at nightfall, yet he had been in time for the banquet.

And, at the end of the table below Haldane, sat Hemming, his army, keeping him constant company with his eye. When Haldane—son, Get, story prince, new baron, new washed, new clothed, new betrothed, well-filled and happy—set forth for the outhouse half through the banquet to relieve himself of too much ale and excitement, Hemming Paleface rose and followed at his heels through Morca's splendid new doors and into the night.

Haldane stepped off the porch and into the yard. He breathed the comfort of the night. The air was cool after the close warmth of the hall, and smelled of the living spring. The wind whistled light nonsense through the stockade walls, her merry syrinx.

It was a gay time to be alive. The crescent moon had bedded early and the stars were lightly veiled. It was quiet here. The voices within were muffled by the new doors.

"Well, where are we to?" asked Hemming Paleface at Haldane's elbow.

Haldane clapped him on the shoulder. Fiercely, he said, "We are off to the outhouse. Are you game to try, though they be as thick as sand fleas all about us?"

"Who?" asked simple Hemming.

"Why, the enemy. The enemy." Haldane put his hand to his sword. "Will you strike down any man who prevents us from our goal?"

Hemming laughed and nodded. "My head is giddy from craning and from drinking black ale, but you are my captain, Haldane. I will have their lives for you. Oh, it is good to be a Get tonight!"

Haldane and his army bared their swords and rushed through the yard striking singing giant blows that could not be parried. They laughed and Hemming fell and they slew the night many times before Haldane had Hemming on his feet again and they won through to the outhouse and safety. They collapsed against the walls and hungered for breath. For a Get who was half a Nestorian, Hemming was a good Get.

"My sides ache so much I am near to puking," said Haldane. "I can't take this. I must stop laughing. Oh, I am dizzy."

"I owe you my life," said Hemming. "If not for you, I would have been slain where I fell."

Haldane waved it away. "It was nothing. You may have chance someday to serve me like."

The guard in the tower nearby at the corner of the stockade called to find what the hurly was about. They were laughing so loud that his call was lost and he must needs call again.

"Enough," said Haldane to Hemming. "We must be sober." He raised his voice in answer. "It is nothing.We are funning. We fight bogies."

"How goes the feast?"

"Drunk. Can we send you ale or meat?"

"Na. No need. I have eaten and I expect my relief at the first moment."

The two young Gets passed inside the outhouse to seek their own relief. When they were pissed dry, their heads were clearer. As they shook themselves and straightened their clothes, Haldane said, "Come early summer when Lothor is back in Dunbar, Morca and I mean to go raping in Chastain. There is a place in the party for you, Hemming."

Hemming had no chance to reply. As they left the outhouse, there were two men on the path. They were knights of Chastain, Lothor's men, quietly drunk for such a gay banquet. One waved a wineskin, the other a sword. They lacked only dice to be ready to duel any man they met on his own terms.

He with the wineskin said, "Hold!" and waved his hand before his companion's face. "Put your sword by. It is Lord Haldane and his man. They wait you inside to toast your bethrothal, young lord."

"Did you expect to meet a goblin in the night?" asked Haldane in Nestorian. Though all of Lothor's knights seemed as much alike to him in their sameness as any handful of chicken feed, he thought he knew these two. They were the patient adventurers who had gone hunting each day with Ivor Fish-eye.

"Oh. Yes, goblins. Nestor is full of goblins, but we are well-protected. Here, drink of our wine and arm yourselves for the walk back to the hall. It is a far distance you have come without protection. Our southern wine is proof against any horror of the night."

And in truth Haldane's head was ready to be rung again. The skin was passed from hand to hand. The wine was warming.

When the knight of Chastain had drunk, he offered the skin again to Haldane. "Here. Another drink on your marriage."

"No," said Haldane. "I am just right now."

"I will drink," said Hemming. "To you, my Haldane, my leader." He saluted Haldane and drank. Then he passed the skin back to the foreign knight.

"The field is yours," said Haldane, and they left the outhouse to the strangers.

The torches in Morca's hall flared brightly in their rings on the smoke stained columns, sending licking lights across the revelry. The air was close and warm, smelling of meat and men. There were songs and jokes and calls from table to table. As Haldane and Hemming stood in the door, making room for another of Lothor's men to pass outside, Fat Netta, one of the serving women, slipped on a discarded bone before their eyes. She dropped heavily on her round bottom and her pitcher flew from her hands to drench a carl in ale. He cursed heartily and swung around while men roared. He snatched her up and kissed her soundly, though she was as old as Morca and no prettier. She clouted him with her pitcher and retreated to the kitchen.

"Bring more ale," the carl called after her. "Earn another kiss."

The calm and quiet of the night were well enough, but this was where the excitement was. It was good to be back in the midst of things. On this night, it was good to be the son of Black Morca. This night, in particular.

Haldane strode the aisle between the tables, feeling tall, feeling himself grown and ready for marriage, war and command and all the other things of being a man and a Get. He was stopped by Rolf's reaching hand thrust out before him. The old carl swung around on his bench, licking his gravy-sopped fingers.

"Aye, don't you look good in your new clothes," he said. "You've grown fine, little Haldane Hardhead. You'll be earning yourself a new name next, and then I won't know you. To think, you a baron now, with men of your own, and I the man who taught you to sit a horse and string a bow."

"Hey, it's not so bad," Haldane said. "There is no need to cry."

Rolf shook his head. The drink he had taken made him soft. "Time passes. That's all. Time passes." And then he said, "Here, a present for you. For your wedding." And he thrust his cord on Haldane, the beautiful string he had brought with him from Chastain. And Haldane could not say no.

Haldane said, "Morca has promised me more men now. I can have my choice if I ask for it. I will.

Shall I ask him for you? I would like you to be one of my own men."

Rolf was touched. "Oh, aye. Aye. Ask him." He controlled his voice with difficulty and wiped his nose with his knuckle.

Then he said, "I've been stealing looks at your partridge princess. She's strange, but she's not so strange that she can't be improved. Just remember, boy—'It's bit and spur that make a horse jump.' Swive her well and she will be a Get in no time."

His friend Ludbert beside him said, "Will you teach him that, too?" And ducked away from Rolf's hand.

Haldane Bridegroom made his way to the dais and sat down again in his chair. His own chair. He was not yet accustomed to having a back to rest against and an arm to lean on, but he liked the chair well. It make him proud and happy. In the frame of the chair, he felt himself the picture of Morca's heir.

But after a single bite of meat grown cold, he leaned forward to see past the lesser part of his epic, eating her last meal here on the dais. Not eating. There was a slice of beef untouched lying atop the pork that he had been good enough to cut for her since she was too dainty to use her hands and he would not give her knife back to let her cut him again as she had threatened. Marthe's head hung over her plate and her hands were tucked away in her lap.

Haldane said, "What have I missed while I was gone?" He wished to know what pleasures he had traded for his swallow of Chastain wine.

"Ah," Morca said in Nestorian. "I was asking

your bride if it is true that she cannot tell Garulf
from Garmund. It is true. She has no answer. You
have much to teach her, Haldane. Start with that."

The plump child princess shook her head
dumbly. She turned her head away from Morca
into her shoulder.

"It is easy," Haldane said to the buried face.
"Garmund was my grandfather. He was king. Garulf was his brother. He was king before Garmund."

"There you are!" said Morca. "It is as easy as
that."

But the girl did not look up. She seemed ready to
cry. Where was her fire now? Haldane was disgusted. As soon as Lothor was safely gone, he
would take her away to a private room and shut
the door behind her.

Lothor glanced up then, tapped the hard knob of
his stick against palm and gestured with it, speaking in his whip-thin voice:

"They are right," he said. "You remember the
Three Kings of Nestria without confusion, my
child. Garulf and Garmund are as easy as Leon,
Leonus and Leonidus. Garulf was he that we killed
at Stone Heath and left for crows to pick over.
Garmund was the other. He would sneak secretly
into the West, rob and burn and slip away. Like
Morca, his son. Can you remember that? It is simplicity itself."

Marthe nodded without words. Haldane was
thunderstruck by Lothor's presumption. Oliver
could only stare.

But Black Morca was so angered by these words
of Lothor's that he slammed the tableboard with

his fist and made the dishes dance. Morca was so angered that he could not speak. The ribands in his beard quivered. He struck the table again and again until it rang like a bell and came nigh to cracking. A platter fell to the floor spilling good meat and juices amidst the rush-cover. The room stilled and all eyes turned to Morca at these evidences of his wrath.

Oliver was the first who was able to speak through the silence that followed. He said, "You speak bravely for one so far from home. An I were you, I would shave my tongue and be content to leave it unwagged until the hair grew back. Or I were safe again in Chastain."

"But you are not me, fat man," said Lothor of Chastain. "And I am no barefoot wizard piddling with dinner magic, Jan be thanked. Nor am I a bride-thief barbarian king. The time has come for all of us to show ourselves. We are what we are. And there am I."

He pointed to the doorway and Morca's eye followed, as Haldane had looked after the witch Jael's misleading hand. The new doors, once Lothor's, now Morca's, stood wide-flung. The room silenced. In the doorway stood two Get barons, Egil Two-fist and Coughing Romund, no friends to Morca. Behind them were a press of men, Get barons and carls. And Lothor's knights of Chastain, naked swords in hand, fresh come from killing the watch and throwing open the gates. Romund coughed in the silence and then they were pouring into the room, all sober and intent on ending Morca's pretensions in one stroke.

Old Svein Half-White Half-Right on his stair-

case stood and threw down his dinner. He yelled,
"Up! Up! Morca, we are undone! Your ambitions have brought fire down on us!"

As Morca looked to the doorway and the attackers, Lothor seized Morca's black beard in tight
laced fingers and brought the power of Chastain
down on Morca's head. But bull Morca's chief
strength was sturdier than Lothor's stick. The
scepter broke with the second blow and Morca's
head did not.

Morca reared, his great heavy chair toppling
backwards slowly. No one else in the world could
have disturbed it so lightly. He dragged Lothor to
his feet by his beard-tangled fingers. Then Morca
swung his great arm and stumbling Lothor of
Chastain was knocked to the floor senseless.
Morca was a strong man.

Black Morca spread his arms wide and in his
bull bellow he cried, "For your lives and for
Morca! *Alf Morca Gettha!*"

Men thrilled to the sound of his voice. With his
slogan still ringing, Morca drew his sword. He
placed a foot on Lothor to steady him and split him
like a log on the chopping block. The Princess
Marthe screamed to see her father so sudden dead.
With one great hand Morca the War King upset
the tableboard before him, dishes flying, kicked the
golden dowry of Chastain out of his way, and
strode down to the cutting floor red sword in hand
to wade in blood.

In the first moment, men stood throughout the
room shaking the fog from their heads and the
meat from their poinards. They drew their swords
and turned to meet the killing tide. They frantically

tried to sort friend from foe. They were far out-numbered and shock, dismay and gorged bellies made them slow.

Soren Seed-sower and Furd Heavyhand, their quarrel forgot, stood together side by side to face the weight of onslaught. They met it and held, fighting like true Gets, like true loyal men. Then they were overwhelmed and they died. They were only the first.

There was no quarter here. Egil, Heregar the Headstrong and the rest who came through the doors, Lothor's knights who followed, and Aella and Ivor, the traitors within, meant to kill every man.

Old Svein on his stair, no fighting man for twen-ty years, turned and scrambled upstairs for his stool. But not to sit, not to cower. He gripped his stool with his left arm as a shield and with his eat-ing knife as his weapon he strove to hold the stair. It was all he knew to do. And hold the stair he did against all attackers, turning them back in ones, twos and threes. They could not bring him down. Then Aella of Long Barrow, that man, leapt up from beside the stair and seized the old man's ankles and toppled him. Aella set his knee on Svein's thin old chest and showed him no mercy. He slit his throat in a stroke.

The room was bloody chaos, filled with shouts and slogans, cries of pain, and the groans of the felled as they were trampled and kicked by the standing. The torches leapt with the cool touch of night and the hot breath of battle, swaying to the surge of the dance of death, uncaring and uncon-cerned high above the fray. Some few of Morca's men sought to escape the maelstrom by following the screaming serving women within the kitchens or plunging through the doors into the night, but most stood their ground, falling back toward Morca when he bellowed his call, dying hard, earning their deaths by dealing death.

Morca was a giant. His sword was a circle of death for any who dared to close with him. He lifted fallen men to their feet. He inspired dead men to fight on. He was the center of the room. He was captain and king.

"Alf Morca Gettha!"

Haldane followed Morca down to the floor. He stood on his chair and stepped to the tabletop, for he did not have Morca's strength to push tables aside with a hand, and then he jumped down to the floor, banging one knee and rising with sword in hand.

"To me, Hemming. To me," he called, and Hemming Paleface came to him.

He and Hemming stood together and guarded each other's backs. Haldane was both thrilled and afraid. So this was battle! At last. At last. His heart resounded.

He knew their cause was dire, but how dire he did not realize. He did not know he was a dead man in his first battle with only the moment of his death undetermined. He had no time to think. He set aside his fear and fought.

He caught blows on his sword that numbed his arm and he dealt strokes that brought blood. He was wounded and did not feel the pain. His throat was raw from battle cries he never heard. There was the flavor of iron in his mouth. His sword was

tight locked one moment and he tasted the ugly
breath of the Get he fought, brown beard, yellow
teeth, one dogtooth missing: Heregar the Headstrong. No, a smoothshaven knight of Chastain.
No, another Get. In other moments his sword's
world was empty as far as it could reach. He braced
his back against Hemming, his one support, and he
braced Hemming in turn. When Morca called his
slogan, he strove to reach the sound of his father's
voice, Hemming following. And then, of a sudden,
his back was empty.

Haldane was lying against something unyielding
that pressed into his back and hurt him. He was
kicked as he lay. His mind was a sickening
whirlpool. Then he found himself on his knees.
There was wetness running into his right eye and he
cleared it with the back of his hand.

He wasn't sure where he was. What was happening? He was confused and sick.

Before him on the rushes was a dead man. Blood
ran from the dead man's nose and mouth and was
clotted in his beard and mustache. Haldane knew
him. Knew him? It was his dear old Rolf who had
taught him to ride and shoot, now beyond any use
of forks or strings. As dead as . . .

Everywhere around Haldane there was death.
The room was full of dead men, Gets and for-
eigners. Everywhere around Haldane there was
noise and tumult. War. The battle continued in
knots, but everywhere many against few. And there
lay Hemming Paleface dead, his head split, brains
a-dribble.

Then Haldane recovered some of his mind. He
knew where he was. He did not know what had

happened to him, but he knew what was happening.

Black Morca still stood, but he stood alone. He had been wounded many times, the great bull beset by wolves. He bellowed in pain and he bellowed in fury, but he was dying bravely and his dangerous horns kept the yapping giant killers at a distance. His sword sang a song of death and his poinard played harmony. But he was encircled and his end was close.

Haldane tried to come to his rescue, but he could not gain his feet. He crawled forward desperately over rushes and bodies and the scattered trash of the dowry, his dowry, dragging his sword with him. Then he saw Oliver a double armslength distant on the dais, crouched beneath a table. He was mumbling and moving his hands through the slow middle figures of a spell. And then Oliver stood, an eye-catching figure in his magenta robes, calling down the Chaining of Wild Lightning on their heads, the Ultimate Spell to kill the many, as the Gets had been slain at Stone Heath, that would kill himself, too, as the wizards of the West had perished with their triumph.

Haldane found himself mumbling, too, the only spell he knew, the Pall of Darkness, as though by chanting his little spell he could be of aid to Oliver. He remembered the words, he remembered the motions of hand, and did not know how he remembered. And he hoped for magical deliverance. Anything that would save them.

Oliver made his gestures and said his words. He was magnificent, rising, growing, spreading, becoming great. The last figure was traced. The last word was spoken. He stood with arms spread, waiting for the white tongues of flame that would lash down and destroy the destroyers. Fire that would know whom to strike.

But no flame came.

Nothing happened. Nothing!

The fighting continued as though Oliver had not spoken a word.

And Black Morca was a dead man. The wolves closing, tightening their little circle, dragged down the great bull. They overbore him by weight of number. And the finishing strokes were made by Ivor Fish-eye, the traitor. He waited his chance and when Morca was engaged he slipped in behind him and killed him with a knife thrice plunged into his back. Then he held the bloody knife high in exultation.

There were tears in Haldane's eyes and his mind was a morass. His whole world lay slain. Murdered. Dead.

He came at last to his feet, his lips moving through the last automatic mumble of the Pall of Darkness. He nearly fell. He stumbled against the dais. He finished the spell leaning against a table. The old wave of cold he had known before rolled over him again. He was invisible to men's eyes, though the gods could see him still.

The carrion wolves set up a gay savage howl: "Black Morca is dead! Morca is slain! We have killed him!"

They pranced around the body of the fallen king and made much of themselves. They leaped in to hack at his bones. Men smeared themselves in his blood, painting their faces red with his death. They vied to cut off his parts and hold them up to show. Others turned to the scattered gold of the dowry, picking up prizes to keep.

But their work was not done. Egil Two-fist, who led them, yelled, "Make sure of Morca's cub! He must be killed, too. Find him."

That was Haldane. Haldane the invisible. Haldane the disappeared.

A sudden shattering hand fell on Haldane's shoulder.

PART II: EVASION

8

The day held fair promise, should the two fugitives in the forest live long enough to enjoy it. It was as sweet a day as the spring had seen. The morning air was blithe, even in the cool tuckaway of a thicket. The sky beyond the trees was a light blue sea with a few small boats gently riding before the wind. A bird that Haldane neither saw nor heard landed on a branch above his head, tossed him a cheery good morning that he did not answer, and began to whet its bill.

Haldane was in sorry condition. His fine new betrothal clothes were bloodied and dirty, rent and torn. He had bruises everywhere, the worst of which were to knee and back. He wore his first true war wounds, the best of which was a head wound that Oliver had cleaned. It would make a scar to carry. His right eye was blackened, besides. In addition to his wounds and his broken head, he suffered from shock, confusion, fatigue and the sad effects of his small spell of invisibility, itself long passed. He remembered fighting back to back with Hemming Paleface and striving to reach Morca, but he remembered nothing but in flashes thereafter. He found things hard even now to fix in his mind. Worst, for a Get, he cried in weakness and could not help himself.

Before him on the ground were the small remains of his life. They were set out in a half-circle. His long sword. A narrow knife with a black haft. A horn. A boar's tooth graven with Deldring mysteries, strung on a rawhide cord. A length of string. And a daffodil that Haldane had added, weeping hotly and laying it beside the sword.

There was dried blood on the sword blade, though Haldane had been taught to clean his sword after use lest it rust. He was too confused to remember to do it now that it mattered. There was dirt on the point of the sword, sign of its employment as a staff through the night. That was not right use, either.

In his dizzy moments, Haldane would look at these pieces on the ground and wonder what they did there and why he cried. And then he would remember what Oliver had told him and become lost again in tears.

The bird was not disturbed by Haldane, but when Oliver returned from conning the country from secret, it flew away. The wizard, too, was nothing like his usual grave and well-arranged self. He, like Haldane, was suffering from shock, confusion and fatigue, and the differently upsetting effect of his own failed spell.

He was strange, this plump little fringe-bearded man who looked the fool, and could not help sometimes but act it, but whose tongue and wit had carried him through more difficult adventures than Black Morca. He was weak, but he dared. Sometimes he dared.

He had done more last night than he had known he could. On their first invisible dash, he had led them to his cell rather than into the night. That was presence of mind. He had snatched up nightcloaks and the dried beef he was wont to chew over while he worked at his book, and placed them in his old bag that he had brought with him from Palsance, keeping a hand on the boy all the while. Then he had broken the greased paper away and chivvied Haldane through the window. The spell had only taken them out of the dun. Then, suddenly, half down the hill, Oliver had been able to see Haldane again. Frightened every step, he had herded and harried the whorl-witted boy across the hills to the forest.

Oliver's magenta satinet bore a record of their desperate passage. It was a thin cold material, made for show and not for hard use. He regretted leaving his daily red robe hanging in his cell, but he had not dared the time to change.

His best daring was not of the moment, but in long plans. He had been planning what to do. He had told Haldane to set his things out, and not been sure he would.

He said, "Good. I see you have managed to empty your pockets."

Haldane said, "Why did I do it? It is all middle in my mind. I cannot remember. Where is Morca? Did I reach him?"

Oliver licked his fingers. He had been eating a piece of dried beef while he spied variously from the edge of the copse. He was not sorry that Haldane could not remember everything.

He said, "Do you remember the fighting?"

Haldane slowly touched his wounded temple with a hand that held a daffodil with a crushed stem. "I remember fighting. That is the last I remember. Is Morca dead?"

"Yes." Oliver had told him that many times.

"Who killed him?"

Oliver had told him that, too. "Ivor Fish-eye."

"I will kill him. I'll quarter him and hang him in the sun for crows to strip clean. I remember. I remember Aella and Heregar and Egil Two-fist. I'll kill them all. I'll be like Wisolf the Cunning and live in the houses of my enemies before I kill them."

"You have said that. And you killed Heregar last night. Enough, Haldane, enough," said the wizard in distress. "We must go now. Now."

"Is Morca really dead?" asked Haldane.

"I could only save us two. Morca was dead by then and you were struck senseless. They will be hunting for us in force. It is we who will be quartered and hung in the sun if we don't hie ourselves beyond their reach."

Haldane shook his head determinedly. He muttered the name Ivor Fish-eye over and over under his breath as though he would prevent himself from forgetting. His headshaking made him sick and he closed his eyes and yawed. But he righted himself again and exchanged flower for sword. He was not called Haldane Hardhead for nothing. He stroked the sword with his hand.

"I will stay here and kill them all," he said. Then he began to sing these words, his Carl Song before battle.

Oliver calmed him with some effort. Haldane was too lost to see the conflicts in his own words and he was beyond the reach of argument, but he could be led.

So Oliver would lead him. He returned to his plan. He brought a small box and a book from out of his bag. He took his spectacles out of the box and put them on, ran his fingers through the winter forest of his hair, and began to thumb the loose pages of his gramarie.

The two lost themselves in their own separate worlds. Haldane continued to play with his plans of revenge, remembering each of the stories of the Vengeance of Wisolf in far-off Shagetai that Svein had told him when he was small. He remembered them more clearly than the night just past. Oliver studied the book for some time, not wanting to begin his spell. Then he closed his book and put his spectacles away.

Since it and he had failed each other, Oliver was afraid of his magic. His confidence was shaken. But his plan was to make a spell, one of stronger weave then Haldane's, that would serve to save them. He closed his eyes before he started because his head was light. He tried to draw his courage together. They were a fine pair, both less than their usual selves. And Oliver knew he would be sick from the spell to come. If it worked. But disguise was their best hope of living.

For their purpose, he complected a new spell out of old pieces, as a cook on the demand of occasion might invent something new out of old simplicities like cabbage and onions. It was only when the

work was begun and the stew a-simmer that
Haldane forgot Wisolf and took notice of what Oliver did.

He came to his feet, saying, "No!" and waving
his arms. He made as though to seize Oliver's hand
to break the weave, but did not dare finally.

He said, "I want no part of your magics. Stop!"

He remembered neither Oliver's spoiled spell nor
his own success.

"What use is your magic now? You should have
plied it in Morca's behalf when it mattered."

Oliver broke off the spell. "I told you. There was
no time for great magic. If not for the spell that I
did manage, you would not be alive at this moment. Not be quiet, or instead of the weal of my
magic, you shall feel its weight. And be grateful!"

Haldane managed silence, but not gratitude. His
face was still too full of various hates, hurts and
confusions for it to show gratitude. But silence was
sufficient for Oliver.

With Haldane chastened, Oliver resumed his
spell, speaking the words of power and signing
sigils in the air with his hands. Chancing failure.
Chancing sickness for success. Haldane watched,
unaware of what was about to happen to him. If he
had known what he would become, he would not
have ceased protest.

Of a sudden, Oliver and Haldane were different
people. Oliver was still short, but no longer stout.
He was an old ugly red-haired man, hairy-nostriled
and with a cast to one eye so that he seemed to see
in two directions. In place of his robe, he wore a
brown smock. He was no wizard now, and no Get,
either.

Haldane was still a boy, but seemed shorter and younger than himself, and less pretty. He too wore a smock. He too was no Get. He was nobody he would have liked to know. He was disguised as a stupid, slope-shouldered peasant boy, a Nestorian calf.

He held his hands up and looked at them. Short and stubby fingers.

"What have you done?" he cried. "What have you made me?"

Oliver said calmly, "Until the spell runs its course, you wear the guise of a simple Nestorian. I will be Noll to those we meet. You will be my grandson—Giles, we will call you. Let us hope it keeps us alive until we are safe."

"A peasant!" Haldane shouted. "I will not be a peasant! The shame is too great."

He made to tear the smock off, but the illusion was beyond removal. Oliver seized the boy by the shoulder and shook him.

"Listen, you must do as I say! Your Wisolf played an old woman when he had need, and no one thought shame. Use your wits if you are able!"

"It was a Gettish woman that he played, and not some smock-wearing peasant. And when Wisolf departed his enemy's tent, in his basket he carried away a head."

"Use your wits if you are able," said Oliver again. "If you wish your revenge, you must stay alive to take it. There is no safety for us here in this country. We are hunted men. We must flee until Nestor is quiet. When we are safe across the Trenoth in Palsance, and friend and foe show themselves clearly, that will be time enough to be a

Get again. Now give me the things you have set aside and I will put them in my bag."

Haldane was confused. Just when he thought he had caught up to himself again, he was suddenly someone new. He did not entirely understand. He turned away from Oliver and sat with his sword and his string and his other treasures. But he did not deliver them to Oliver. He was no peasant named Giles. He picked up his horn and fondled it.

"I may be sick from my wounds so that I cannot stand, but my brains are not addled," he said. "What safety is there for me in the West? In Palsance they would kill me as quickly as here. I will stay here until they come along and then I will seek my vengeance."

"No, come with me," said Oliver. "Be Wisolf, Haldane. Use your cunning. Sick and alone as you are, you will be dead if you stay. You can play the peasant in Palsance until the times have sorted themselves. Then you can take your vengeance. But men harry the country for us now. Let us be gone. Or will you leave me to cough and hobble my way to Palsance alone? The man who saved you so that you could have your vengeance?"

Oliver coughed tentatively to show Haldane the sickness he soon would suffer, as Haldane suffered now and did not realize. There was phlegm enough for him to venture a greater cough, a hack that shook him near to falling.

Haldane turned the horn in his hands. "What is there for Oliver in Palsance but the enemies he left behind?" he asked.

What would Oliver find in Palsance? The question did give him pause to think.

A sudden sun of revelation lit Haldane's face. He put the horn to his lips and made as if to blow. Then he looked at the horn again and said, "My grandfather Arngrim is almost as close as Palsance. He will help me gain my vengeance."

Oliver said, still thinking, "Arngrim is farther than Palsance. I could not walk so far."

But Haldane was instantly set. "I will go south along the Pellardy Road to Little Nail and there I will blow my horn outside Angrim's dun until he opens his gate to me, his own daughter's son. Then I will gather a new army and return to sweep the earth clean of . . ." He could not remember all the names.

"Of Ivor and Romund and Egil."

"And every traitor baron."

Oliver said, "And what welcome would a wizard find with Arngrim?"

"I owe you my life," Haldane said. "I will be your warrant with Arngrim. If you are with me, he will accept you. No Get would turn his own away."

Oliver took out his clay pipe and filled it with yellow weed, his aid to magic and thought, his mediator. He put punk in his firepump and struck a light. It would be the last smoke he would enjoy while spell and sickness held him. His cough had been more than effect. He could feel his chest filling and tightening now. This last pipe helped serve to calm him.

"You could play the peasant until the times have sorted themselves, Oliver," Haldane said. "My grandfather will have a place for a cock-eyed tiller of the soil."

Oliver would have need of Haldane's strength as

his own ebbed. He did not like to think of walking
to Palsance alone. He thought of the life he would
find waiting in Palsance. That was a certainty he
had avoided before. He thought of the uncertainty
that was Arngrim. At last—as always, at last—he
dared.

He finished his pipe and set it down on his bag.
He said, "It seems that my adventure in Nestor is
not yet over. Let us make our way to your grandfather Arngrim."

Haldane came to his knees and gathered his poor
possessions. He was much readier to move now.
The boar's tooth he placed around his neck where
it was lost in the illusion. His knife that was
Marthe's, his string that was Rolf's, and even his
horn that was Arngrim's, he gave to Oliver who
put them away in his sack. Then Haldane made to
take up his sword. His wits might be mending, but
they were not yet mended.

Oliver told him, "No."

"I cannot leave my sword behind," Haldane
said, holding it close. At the moment he was not
man enough to wield it. "It is my sword. How can
I fight if we are discovered? We need my sword."

Oliver said, "If you carry your sword, we surely
will be discovered. Whoever heard of a peasant
with a sword?"

Oliver's objection was unanswerable and his will
was stronger on this, and he overrode Haldane.
But he did not stop with that. He made Haldane
bury the sword so that it might not be found and
point their direction.

Haldane dug a shallow grave with his sword
blade there where the bushes were thickest, and

laid the sword away with its hilt to the east, returning the good iron to the earth from which it had
come, tucking the warrior in for his final rest. As
Oliver watched, Haldane covered the sword over
with dirt and mold and leaves, and then laid the
lone daffodil with its crushed stem on the grave.

Haldane said, "Rest, Morca. You will be
avenged." And then backed out of the bushes.
There were tears again on his cheeks.

It was now well along in the morning. They were
being hunted, the son of Black Morca and Morca's
wizard. They were not safe. Safety would be
Arngrim's fort on high Little Nail, or better
Palsance. And Haldane was dizzy-witted.

Oliver grabbed up his bag and led Haldane
away. He paused at the last protection of the copse.
When he had spied the land he had seen nothing,
but he had an unbearable presentiment of danger.
He feared the Gets who lurked, waiting for them to
step from cover to cut them down. But though he
looked again, he still saw nothing, and because he
must Oliver led the way from the thicket.

They raised a deer with their first steps. It started
up, thrashing to its feet, and bounded away.

In time, Oliver's heart mended.

9

Along the forest trails they walked to find the Pellardy Road, first grandson Giles trudging, then old gnarled Noll with his bag. Their pace was slow. There was no spring in Giles' stride, the poor wounded, spell-confused peasant boy Haldane. He still was not sure of himself. And his head ached.

For all that the day was green and gold, Noll was content with the pace. He was stiff. He had spent too much of the night awake and then slept as badly as a sailor his first night on land. At his age he needed a good night's rest. The bag he carried with all their lives within was a burden. He would cough frequently but could not clear his lungs.

Haldane was still fuddled. Sometimes he would ask questions like, "I can't remember who killed Hemming. Tell me again?" Other times he would turn and look at Oliver as though he didn't believe in him and expected the stranger behind him to have disappeared. But it was Haldane who led the way, now they had found a trail to follow.

In the blind dash through the morning night to the forest and panting concealment, Oliver had taken them farther than he could recognize the land. It was as strange to him as any place three leas from his native hearth in Palsance. Since he was a boy he had always been best occupied indoors. He knew this country from what other men had let drop of it, and from an old map he had that showed all the duchies of Nestor before the Gets took the land. He knew the map well. It had brought him at the first from Palsance to Morca's Dun in the old duchy of Bary.

So, when they set out, Oliver took the map from his bag and studied it. It told him only that they were in the forest. Haldane was a silent mindspun boy and asked no questions, but Oliver was embarrassed for the map. It showed the road, but not how to reach it. By his map, but more by guess, Oliver led them until they reached a trail.

Then Oliver found he could let Haldane lead the way. Haldane had hunted all over this land since he was small and he did not need his head to be a guide. His feet knew all the trails.

It was a quiet morning with many rests. Oliver called a halt whenever he thought Haldane needed one. Haldane continued distracted. He looked often at his hands and smock and shook his head. He asked questions for his vengeance, too, but Oliver did not encourage the boy with the answers he gave him. Oliver was usually a ready talker, but today he thought much on the Chaining of Wild Lightning and was a silent gnarly red-man.

They reached the Pellardy Road near mid-day. They ate more dried beef as they walked. It was all they had.

There were many rests in the afternoon, too. Oliver called a halt now whenever he thought Oliver needed one. His chest tightened and the bag weighed heavily, a fat stone on his back as great as the stone on his mind. His price for being a red peasant.

In the afternoon, Haldane began to throw off the effects of his spell, the Pall of Darkness, or so it seemed. He was still fey, but more coherent. He continued to peer at Oliver as though to spy him out beneath his strange skin, but he needed to ask less often who killed Hemming or Ludbert or Rolf, and remembered the answers better. He remembered Ivor Fish-eye without further reminder. He spoke sometimes with great glee about reaching Arngrim and raising an army. He was often silly.

He began to inquire at his smock with his hands. At last he asked Oliver, "Do I still wear my clothes? When I forget myself in walking, I can feel my belt. But when I reach for it, it isn't there. And sometimes I feel the wind touch me through the tears in my clothes."

Haldane was still following his feet. Oliver for his part followed his map and looked about him for what the map told him he could expect to see. Wizards are fools for illusion. That is why they become wizards. Oliver followed maps and believed in them, and he could almost forget that Giles was not a Nestorian peasant boy.

Oliver said, "You still wear your belt and your old clothes. But men's eyes are led to see what they expect to see. When they look at us, they will expect Nestorians and see them. The reality is unchanged and the wind is not fooled."

"Then why can't I touch my belt? I know I can really expect it. Can't I?" Haldane added unwittingly to the illusion he wore by acting the young boy.

To silence Haldane and occupy him, Oliver said, "You can do it, but only if you clear your mind of all thoughts of yourself. When you cease to think of your belt, your hands will be able to touch it."

It was a game that Haldane could not but lose. He played it visibly as they walked along the Pellardy Road through the forest. His hands could not fool his mind. They would try to touch before he could think, and they never could. It made him angry and he gave up in disgust. But natural habit won him what concentration could not and sometime later he found himself for the briefest moment with his thumbs hooked in his belt.

"I felt my belt, Oliver," he said. "I did feel my belt."

"Noll," said Oliver. "You are Giles. And speak Nestorian."

When Oliver remembered to think of it, he worried of what would happen if they were come upon by Gets. But he had strength only to plod the road.

"Noll," said Haldane and did speak Nestorian. "Give me my knife back from your bag. I'll wear it now. My hands will know where to find it when I have need of it."

That was why Oliver continued to carry the bag, even though he plodded.

"We cannot give your hands the chance. We cannot afford to kill. We are safest as simple peasants. Besides, you could not forget yourself long enough to fix the knife in place."

"Safest. Safest," mocked Haldane in Nestorian. "That's all you can think of. What do I do when I need to unbuckle my pants?"

"If you wait until your need is great enough, you

will find it no problem. Now, by my map there is a bridge over the next hill. Let us rest there."

"We cannot rest there," said Haldane.

"Why not?"

"There is no bridge on the other side of the hill," Haldane said. And laughed as though he had made a great joke.

"By my map, there is a bridge," said Oliver, "and I believe my map." Even though it of occasion embarrassed him.

When they reached the top of the hill above New Bridge on Rock Run, Haldane said, "As I told you. There is no bridge. It fell down."

"That is bridge enough for me," said Oliver. "My map was right."

"Then you walk across your bridge and keep your feet dry," said Haldane. "I will wade the ford."

But Oliver wet his feet, too. He waded past the broken pilings standing surprised in riffling water. The two peasants threw themselves down in the sun on the farther bank to dry and rest. Oliver dropped their bag on the ground and panted and coughed. The spell had struck deep. He should not have been abroad wetting his feet.

Wild onion grew profusely around them in little clumps of green. Haldane plucked a spray. He rolled one narrow tube between thumb and forefinger until it broke, and savored the odor. He tasted it and found it good. Then he chose out shoots that pleased him best, discarded the rest, and rolled those he kept in a slice of dried beef.

Oliver was content to watch as he ate, and more content to nod.

The riders were on them almost before they knew. Oliver was struck to the heart. They were Gets. No one else in Nestor rode. The three did not pause at the hilltop as Haldane and Oliver had done.

Haldane leaped to his feet as soon as he saw them. He crammed the last of his meat and onion into his mouth. It was all that his mouth could hold. Oliver feared what he might do, but lacked the force and quickness to prevent the boy.

"Haldane!" he said, forgetting his own injunctions. "Do nothing rash!"

And then had to become more circumspect. There was no place to run or to hide. They must face these Gets. Oliver tried to become Noll in his mind.

Haldane, desperately chewing and trying not to choke on what he chewed, took no notice of the Gets. He stepped down into the water, leaving Oliver on the bank to wonder at him. What did Haldane intend?

Haldane stooped and began to grum among the rocks, fingering the stream bottom. He paid the riders no attention as they splashed by him. He forced the last of the meat and onion down his throat and came up smiling like a simpleton with a dripping bemired shell.

Was the boy being cunning like Wisolf? Oliver could scarce believe it.

The riders reined over them. It was Aella of Long Barrow and two carls. Oliver was glad Haldane lacked his knife. He was sure the boy would have dragged Aella from his horse and dealt with him as Aella had dealt with Svein. But

Haldane touched his forehead with respectful muddy fingers. Oliver tremblingly touched his forehead, too.

"What do you do here?" Aella asked. He spoke to them in Nestorian, their language. His tone was pre-emptory, as though he were an important man. Oliver knew him for an errand runner. Anyone who knew Aella knew him for an errand runner.

"We gather clams to make a meal, your lordship. My grandsire and I," Haldane volunteered. He held out his shell. He was the perfect guileless boy. "It is yours if you like, noble sir. All that we have gathered is yours."

Aella made a disgusted noise, "Faa." He waved it away with a flicking of his right hand. "We seek three on foot. A young girl dressed in white and blue. A Western girl. She is the one we want most. Morca's wizard, Oliver by name, a Western man in red robes. He is a funny little man with a round face and a white beard. And Haldane, the son of Black Morca. Have you seen any of these?"

Haldane said, "Do they travel together?"

"We know not. Have you seen them together?"

Oliver spoke hurriedly then in Nestorian so that Haldane would have no need to speak again. "No, lord. We have seen no one today. You are the first strangers we have seen."

"How long have you been here?"

"All the afternoon, lord. See, our bag is nigh to full," Oliver said, hefting his bag as though it contained clams.

"At last a straight answer from one of these cattle," Aella said in Gettish to his men. "They have been here the afternoon and they say they have seen no one. We had best return to the dun. It is no use to seek farther along this road. They could not have come so far by noon."

One of the carls spit in the water beside Haldane and did not take note of the Gettish glower in the Nestorian boy's face. "Unless these lie," he said. "I never saw a Nestorian that would talk straight when it could lie."

"Lie to us? You jest. They would not dare," Aella said, making a rooster of himself. "And they have no love for Morca or his cub. They would not lie for him."

"If they walked all night without stopping, they might have passed in the morning," said the other carl.

"Na," said Aella. "We'll find them when we set the pigs to sniffing them out. The wizard is no countryman. We'll find him under a bush. And the boy is a stubborn ass. Him we will find waving a sword in the shadow of the dun."

"Just as well," said the first carl. "If we are to find one of the three, let it be the girl. There is more reward."

They clapped their heels to their horses and splashed back across the ford. Haldane remained in the water looking after them, burned by their words.

In a rage, he called after them, "When will you raise our bridge again?"

The second carl looked back at them. Haldane bent immediately to the stream and pretended he had said nothing. He paddled in the water until they were gone, and then he straightened again, shaking his hands. He looked at Oliver, uncertain of what the wizard would say of his rashness, but proud of himself, too.

He said, "He called me an ass."

Oliver looked at him for a long moment. All the words that Haldane had spoken to the Gets, including his last call, had been in Gettish. Oliver thought the power of the spell to mislead had been strongly taxed.

He sighed. He said, "You have mud on your forehead."

10

The woodcutter's hut stood in a clearing not far from the road, close enough to be seen by tired and hungry eyes. It was Oliver who spied the thatch near about sunset when their feet were so weary they would scarce carry them from one rest to the next. Haldane saw nothing until Oliver pointed. It was Haldane who carried their sack now and Oliver who led the way.

"Ah," red-haired Noll said with relief. "We'll seek our shelter there." He coughed too deeply and spat to clear his throat. He had been coughing steadily since they crossed the ford, even after he had given over the bag. "Another night in the open will be the finish of me. Be Giles now, and let me speak for us. If you must speak, speak Nestorian."

Haldane made no answer. His head ached fiercely and his mind wambled. He was very tired.

He could not read this man's face as he could read Oliver's. He did know this Noll did not have Oliver's sharpness of wit and tongue. He would answer questions only if they were repeated. He ventured nothing. It was as though the spell had struck deeper than appearance. There were moments when Haldane could doubt that it was Oliver at all who walked beside him and wonder why he kept company with this strange peasant man.

It made Haldane mull over the changes that might have been wrought in him that he could not see. He kept testing himself to see if he was really Haldane. He thought he was. But how could he be sure? His hands were not Haldane's. He might be a peasant dreaming he was a Get.

He followed Oliver as he led the way into the clearing, content to trail behind and watch Oliver do things that the Oliver he knew would not do. Stacks of seasoning wood made short walls everywhere. A small boy peeped abruptly from behind one like an archer behind a palisade, then ducked away.

The hut they had seen from the road stood in the center of the clearing. It was clinker-built, the lapping shakes brown under the hanging thatch, weathered to silver where they lacked protection. Over the door of the simple house was its one touch of color, the many-armed wheel of Silvan in red and yellow. A simple god for simple folk. The colors disturbed Haldane. They made him agitated and he did not know why. They matched the colors of Lothor's traveling carriage, but he could not quite remember that.

Silvan's beast, a little white nanny-goat, was tethered to a stake beyond the house under the trees. Scrawny chickens scratched for their lives in the dirt before the door and around the woodpiles, too busy to notice them approaching. A lean shaggy dog lying in a heap did take note. It leaped up, lowered its ears, and advanced growling. It was no little yapper like Lothor's toy. It showed yellow teeth and barked as though it meant them harm.

Haldane stayed safely behind red-haired Noll. He could not cope with growling dogs tonight.

A ragged untrimmed girling appeared in the doorway then and piped of their coming to those within. She was set aside by a man who filled the door. He stepped into the yard followed by a boy who resembled him nearly. The boy was older than Haldane appeared, but younger than Haldane's true age.

The falling sun lit the thatch with evening red. Gentle smoke lifted lazily from the chimney and Haldane thought he could smell dinner simmering over a fire. His head buzzed with hunger and weariness. He ached within and without. At the best of times he was not used to walk like this.

He wanted to stop walking. He wanted food and sleep. He wanted to mend.

He wanted to cry.

The man lifted a hand. His words were courteous, but he was an unyielding wall after his many walls of logs. He said, "Well met. What do you seek, strangers?"

In his other hand he carried an axe and he did not look friendly. Haldane wondered how you could order such a man if you were not a Get. He could lie to one like Aella, but he did not know what to say to a peasant with an axe.

"Well met," Oliver said. "My grandson and I are lost sailors out of Pellardy making our way home overland."

"Lost you are," the man said. "I have never seen a sailor here before."

The dog continued to growl and glower.

"We are not used to walking and we have come

far today," Oliver said. He coughed his racking, hacking cough. "My name is Noll. My grandson Giles. We seek shelter and food."

"What are sailors doing so far from the sea?"

The strange man who pretended to be Oliver pretending to be a sailor said, "Put away your dog and I will tell you the tale."

The woodcutter called the dog away. It ran behind the peasants barking proudly of its courage.

"I'll hear your story."

"Is it worth dinner to you?"

"Would you bargain with me, then?"

"Would you turn away a sick old man?" And Oliver coughed again. "My own tale is rich but it is nothing to the other stories I know. I can tell you of the secret beasts of the sea and how they play. I can tell you of strange lands and their treasures."

The woodcutter scratched his head as though in argument with himself. Then he said, "Oh, aye, stay for the meal. Come away in to the house. Cob, run inside and say that there are two more to eat with us."

"There's little enough for us as it is," said the son. "You know what Mother said."

"Have you not heard that manners are better than meat? There will just be a little less for everyone," the woodcutter said. "I want to hear about the sea and these secret beasts."

Oliver was not content to have won him. He must shake his red head and say, "Ah, where is the old hospitality? Is Pellardy the only duchy that still keeps the true Nestor?"

"Pellardy is the only duchy not ruled by the Gets," the woodcutter said. "They leave us little in

Bary to spend in hospitality. These are not the old
days of Nestor."

He led the way toward the house. They were
trailed by the little boy who had spied them first
from behind the woodpile. He stayed a safe distance behind in company with the dog, burying his
face in the dog's fur when Haldane looked at him.

Haldane said in a whisper to Oliver, "Is a story
all?" A story seemed too small a reason for the
peasant to share his food. Noll didn't answer but
only gave his head so small a shake that Haldane
could not be sure if he had shaken his head at all.

Oliver spoke loudly then. "It is my brother who
did this to us. We own a boat in common but since
he is older he thinks it is his. We quarreled in
Eduna. He sent us ashore on an errand and while
we were gone, he sailed off to Grelland. He left us
with only a single small coin, and that is long
spent." He coughed again until he caught himself
against the doorway and leaned there rattling for
breath.

"That is a hard tale," the woodcutter said. "It is
a long walk from Vilicea. You must be weary."

"We did not make it in a day," said Sailor Noll.
"A longer walk to Pellardy before us, too. But every step I think of my brother's face when he sees
us waiting on the quay."

He told what he would do to his brother when he
found him and winked his shy eye. The peasant
nodded and laughed with him, happy that sailor
and woodcutter could think so much alike.

"Aye, hear that," the peasant said, turning of a
sudden to the small boy with the dog. "Did you
hear? Mark what it is to be quarreling with your

brother. Take a lesson from that." To Oliver he said, "It is all I can do to keep them from fighting long enough to eat and sleep."

"My brother and me exactly," said Oliver. "Listen to what your father tells you."

Haldane did not know from what source of strength this changed Oliver drew his strange lies. Haldane wanted nothing more than to set his bag down and put his face against it.

The hut was dimmer than the evening shadows of the forest and warmer than the evening cool. It seemed like a sanctuary to Haldane, a place to stop at last. Cob stood beside a shapeless peasant woman stirring her kettle over the fire. There were besides a gammer snoozing in the corner with a cat on her lap, and a girl suckling a baby at her breast. She seemed no older than Marthe, the Princess of Chastain who was sought by the treacher Gets. Children that Haldane was too tired to count were in and out the doorway.

The woman turned from the kettle, spoon in hand. "And who is this you've brought to eat my children's food?"

"This is Noll, a sailor, and his grandson Giles," said the woodcutter. "Noll is going to tell us stories of the sea."

"I care nothing for that," she said and swung her spoon at them. "There are too many of you in here. You are in my way. Take your stories of the sea back outside."

The woodcutter did not try to argue. "Call on us when dinner is ready."

The woodcutter picked up a stool from beside the table and grasped Oliver's arm, turning him about. "Hey, come all ye who wish to hear tales."

Tales from a sailing stranger were a treat, and everybody but the dozing grandmother and the cat in her lap leaped to follow the two men outside. A small boy, near a twin for the one with the dog but a touch smaller, gave Haldane a wary look and then scuttled past him out the door. Haldane didn't follow. He had no wish to hear Oliver's grandfather stories. He just wanted to stay here in this warm dimness and smell the rich simmer. He cuddled the bag, put his back against the near wall and slowly sagged to the floor.

Young Cob took the girl with the baby by the hand. Was he a man with a wife of his own? The woman at the kettle reached out with her spoon and rapped him on the shoulder before he could get out the door.

"Bring me my wood in before you settle down, Cob."

"You have wood," Cob said. "You don't need any more. The woodbox is full."

"That's rainy day wood. Bring me in wood now, and no argument." The ragged girling who had first called their arrival almost slipped out the door, but the peasant woman stopped her with a look and a wave of her spoon. "And where are you off to, Magga?"

"I want to hear the stories, too," the girl wailed, anticipating that she couldn't.

"I need you to stir the pot."

"You always say that."

"It's stir the pot or milk Nanny."

"Why is it always me?"

Haldane paid the squabble no mind, even when

the girl burst into hot burning tears. He put his
cheek against the cool canvas of the bag, yawning,
yawning. He was so tired and his head ached like a
beaten drum. He felt wonderful and wretched as he
tried to snatch sleep.

He felt the warmth of pleasure at the memory of
his cleverness in fooling Aella of Long Barrow at
the ford. He had taken the simple stupidity of the
peasants he had met mucking in the water that day
at New Bridge and made of it a polished shield to
catch the sun and blind the eyes of traitor Gets.
And who else but he would ever have thought of
that? But he felt the warmth of embarrassment at
the thought of mud on his hands, even to fool one
like Aella.

All his mind was like that, as lost in strange seas
as the brother of Sailor Noll. His sword had tasted
blood and he had taken wounds. But his sword was
buried and his wounds were lost in this disguise.
He had fought bravely and given no ground. He
had slain Heregar the Headstrong, who was a man
of reputation. But what was that when Morca was
dead?

If he believed Oliver. If he believed the man who
pretended to be Oliver.

He did not remember killing Heregar. If he had
killed Heregar, he would remember it, wouldn't
he? He didn't. He had only Oliver's word for it. He
had only Oliver's word for many things.

Yes. How could Morca be dead? How do you set
down a mountain? You cannot do that. But that
was part of what Oliver had said. Only one of
many implausibilities. If Oliver were to be believed.

But Oliver, whom he knew, had changed before

his eyes into a stranger. It came into Haldane's head to doubt Oliver.

It was the only thing he could do.

The world was not right. The world was past caring whether it was right or not, and it was up to Haldane to see it put back right again.

To do that, he must think as carefully as he could, in spite of the distractions thrown into his mind to keep him from grasping two consecutive thoughts. They would not let his brain sit still. It must keep moving. But he would fox them, Oliver and those in league with him.

He was stubborn. He was known for being stubborn. In spite of these distractions, he would remember.

They had him locked out of the dun in this nightmare, this unending rush of awfulness, confusion and implausibility. That was first.

What was second?

Oh, yes. Second. This strange darkness of warmth and unfamiliar odors was a distraction. As long as it continued, he could not find his way home again to his bed where he belonged. But it was not real, this place. He knew that now.

Some while after, he thought about third.

Third? What had third been? In the search for third, he almost lost his grasp on the thoughts that came first and second, but by an effort of will—for Haldane was stubborn above anything—he held on to them, and brought third safe into his breast.

Third, knowing that he was caught in a snare, he knew the secret. If he could shut this place out of his mind, if he could concentrate long enough and hard enough, the nightmare would be over. It would be over now. He would wake to find himself home again in the bed he had been born in.

That was all.

Haldane skwunched his eyes, and knew the sensation as one more snare to trap him in this unreal world of never-ending shape change. He concentrated. He concentrated. He blotted out everything. But . . . but . . . but.

He could not blot out the insistent sound of crying. No matter what he did, he could not make it go away. It had him trapped here in the nightmare. He could not shake it from his eyes—his ears saw too much.

Resigned—for it meant that he was not ready yet, less than fully ripe for rebirth, and not that he had forgotten his hard-won truth—he opened his eyes.

He saw the most likely implausibility they could conjure to match the sound he had heard. The woman was gone out into the evening somewhere. The little girl—they had called her Magga, hadn't they?—was stirring the hanging pot. She was barely tall enough. She stirred and stirred. And she bawled in open-hearted loss. Almost he could believe that what he saw was real. Almost—it was that much familiar and that much strange.

The grandmother in the corner came suddenly erect in her small chair, as though she had been given leave to begin now that his eyes were open. The movement disturbed the sleeping cat in her lap and it stood tall on tiptoes and stretched itself in an abrupt and unlikely manner, front legs, back legs, before settling down again in a new and more comfortable position as though it had not moved at all.

But he remembered.

"What's the matter, child?" the old woman asked. "Did the world end while I was asleep and I nodding through it all?"

The little girl turned her way, never ceasing her sobs nor her stirring.

"There's a foreign man telling stories in the yard and everybody gets to hear but me. Mother says I have to stir the pot, and it isn't fair. I always miss out. I'm always left to stir the pot while everyone else goes off."

"Ah, it isn't fair," the old lady said. "They don't know what they are missing. I can tell better stories than any foreign man. I know the best and truest stories in the world. And they . . . oh, what do they know? Mind the kettle, Magga, and I will tell you a story."

She was a very plausible implausibility. She was like the Nestorian nurses he had had when he was small. When he was tiny. Like one—the salty one who said strange things. Not the other, the stupid one they had sent away. The one they kept, they who controlled the dream.

What was he trying to remember?

Rebirth.

The girl said, "But you don't know stories about the strange beasts of the sea."

Haldane had an image in his mind of a sea beast, black and warmly sleek, being born, *pl-l-l-op,* into the sea.

"Hush, now," the old woman said. "Are you as old as I to know what I know? Are you as wise as the strange black eyewhisker of Tiddly Thomas, my old cat? I know every story there ever was, I know it better, and what is more, I knew its mother before it was born. You don't need to listen to a cock-eyed sailing man when you can listen to me. Now which is it—his story from my mouth, told better than he could ever tell it, or a new story that no one else has heard from the day the world was hatched until now?"

The little girl gave off crying, but not stirring, though the stirring was an effort. She said, "As good as the story of the bad brother and the good brother and the wonderful bird?"

"Ah, that. Better. A story with a meaning like the nut hid in a walnut fruit. Stir. Stir. And we'll find the nut together and crack it."

The little girl stirred on. "Cob says a story is only a story," the little girl said. "Cob says that stories don't mean anything."

"Are you trying to stir me, girl, or the pot?" said her old grandmother. "Every story has some meaning, even one about strange beasts of the sea. Stories mean more than their tellers know. There was a time I knew no better than you or Cob, but I've learned enough now not to stub my toe on a dark night. Any fool can tell you a story, but it is a rare fool who knows what his story means. I'll tell you the story of the Prince Jehannes and the Goddess. If you'll stir. If you'll stir. The stirring makes the making."

"I'm not ready," the poor little girl said. But she never ceased to stir. "I'm not ready! I'm afraid. I've never stirred so long. I've never stirred so long. I can't stir much longer."

"You can do it," the grandmother said. "You can stir until the story is made."

The little girl screamed then, but she continued to stir. Round and round the pot she swept the spoon.

Haldane pulled himself out. He had almost let himself believe that the world was as he was finding it. But he did know better. The old lady had been asleep. How could she know of the cock-eyed sailor? Wood! Cob had been told to bring wood and he had not come. The peasant woman had gone out to milk the goat, but she had not come back. If this were real, she would have come back with milk to believe.

It was the mention of the Goddess that had told him—reminded him. That was where things had gone awry. He was asleep in his bed the night before Morca's return if only he could find his way back there again. That was where the world had changed. That was where the nightmare had started, there in the woods with the witch Jael.

Oh, they thought they could fool him. They thought they could make him forget, but he was stubborn and he would remember no matter what they did. He would. They should not have talked of the Goddess in front of him. He had caught them unawares again.

He tried to shut the distraction away as he had tried before, now that he knew more than he had before. But again he failed. Always when he had shut it all away, there was one last likely sound that drew him back into the nightmare. One something. One last likely. . .

There was a sudden intrusion on his foot, as

though someone had stepped on it very loudly and
followed it with a splash of sudden warm wetness
along his leg.

Was he born again? He opened his eyes to see
and they had him again.

The peasant woman said, "Oh, I didn't see you
there." She set her pail of milk down. "Magga,
leave off that stirring and light a tallow dip."

Magga said, "You left me there to stir so *lo-ong*.
You were coming right back."

"Ha!" said the peasant woman. "I got to listening to the sailor man's story and I forgot myself."

Behind the woman, crowding into the house out
of the night as though to impress Haldane with the
troop, were Sailor Noll and all the other phantasms of Haldane's dream. The woodcutter. Cob
and his wife and baby. Four children, one after the
other, the two little boys at the tail shoving at each
other.

Haldane stole a quick look at the old gammer in
the corner. She was fast asleep, her mouth hanging
wide, as though she had never been awake. But
where was the cat? He had misplaced the cat.

He looked around wildly for it, and there it was
at his elbow. It was larger than he had thought and
orange. And over its left eye was a black whisker,
a single whisker standing amidst the lighter
whiskers.

The cat pressed its head against Haldane's shoulder and shoved. Then it looked up at him with all-
knowing eyes and said, *"Mrr-ee-ow?"*

11

Haldane was placed at the end of the table by Oliver's left elbow when they sat down to eat. He did not resist. The little girl Magga was seated opposite him. He stared straight ahead at her without seeing her clearly while the peasant woman filled bowls from her well-stirred kettle all round the table.

Then the woodcutter blessed the food in the name of Silvan. Noll added words in the name of Porton, the sailor's god.

Magga said, "And Libera." And was overheard.

"What was that?" her father asked. "What did you say?"

"I said, 'And Libera, too,'" she answered in a small voice.

The woodcutter looked from his small daughter to her grandmother asleep unaware in her small chair in the corner. "Has that old woman been filling your head with the Goddess again? It is bad enough to see a wurox running in the woods without having the name of dangerous gods used in my house. I want none of it. We live by Silvan here." He turned to his wife and said, "I thought I told you there was to be no more of that?"

"What have I to do with it?" said the peasant

woman. "Don't tell me. Tell my mother if you dare."

"How can I? She is always asleep when I try and she will not hear me. You women are in this together. All of you."

"Not I," said his son's wife, seated at his right. "I know nothing of Libera."

"That's true, said the woodcutter, ruffling her hair. "You are a good girl."

He seemed ready to round on his daughter again when Sailor Noll said, "What matter? Thrice-blessed food tastes best."

"What was that?"

"It is a saying we have in Pellardy." Noll coughed, shaking his head with the effort, then dipped his spoon deep. "And this tastes good. The best we have had since we left home port."

The moment was saved and all turned to dipping their spoons and sopping their bread before the food grew cold. The woodcutter and his son took turn about in plying Sailor Noll with questions. Between coughing and spoons of food, he answered them all with patient invention.

Haldane did not even listen to what they asked, even when a question was addressed to him. They were noughts, these peasants that had been placed here in the woods for him to meet and be further confused by. They were empty phantasms. If he could not shut them out of his mind to end the dream when he wanted it to end, he would ignore them.

He dipped his own spoon in his own small bowl. He did not know what the dreamfood was. There were vegetables and little light bits of twisted meat in a gravy broth. Though he did not know what it was, he ate it. This was his compromise with the dream.

Noll apologized for Haldane's silence. "Do not expect much of poor Giles. I do his thinking for him. He is a poor simple dumbstruck boy. Do you mark his stony stare? My grandson was fetched a great clout by a swinging boom when he was small and it knocked all the sense out of him."

Haldane continued to eat as Noll spoke, making no sign that he understood the words. This was not cleverness. It was continued disbelief. He was caught in this evil dream and the dream continued. He wanted desperately to find his way safe home again, and did not know how to do it. Well, he could wait. He would wait if he must.

Cob stared at him across the table. "I see it," he said. "His eye is fixed. It's very like that staring agate the man once showed us at market."

"Very like," his father agreed.

"But what is a boom?" Cob asked.

Haldane listened to Noll's voice as he answered, letting his words slip away. He cared nothing for the words. He wished to know if Noll was a nothing like these peasants, one more shade used by the unknown dream master to fool and fuddle him, or was he a more active tool, able to choose for himself what he said and did? Haldane could not tell.

And the dream gave him no quarter. While Noll spoke, there came a knock on the door, a signal. There was a triple rap followed by a double tap. Noll fell silent. The knock was repeated.

In the silence Cob said, "It's Uncle Jed. It must

be." He leaped up to take down the bar that was
fixed across the door of the hut to keep strangers
out. Outside the dog was barking.

"But what would Jed be doing here?" asked the
woodcutter. He pointed at the woman. "If he's in
trouble, it's you and your mother who must see to
the mending of it. I'll have no more of it."

"Is that the thanks he gets for the food he brings
you?" the woman asked.

Out of the night came a great large peasant man,
red as an apple and excited as a jaybird. His breathing was labored. Cob kicked the dog in the nose
with one foot and barred the door again behind his
uncle.

"Sit here. Sit here," said the woodcutter, waving
to his son's seat. "What is the excitement? Why are
you so far from home this night?"

The peasant man motioned him silent. He
cleared a space in the air with his hands. He took a
deep breath and swallowed hard.

There was something familiar about him, but
Haldane could not say what it was. He must have
seen him about the village when he was awake. The
dream was economical to bring him to these distant woods.

"It is great news! The world is turned upside
down. Black Morca is dead! They say the Gets are
at war amongst themselves. They have killed
Morca and stuck his head on a pole over the gate
of his own dun."

"Why would the Gets kill their own king? How
would you know of it?" asked the woodcutter.
"When did you ever see Morca's dun?"

"Never. But why wouldn't I know? They say the

pole is there to be seen by anyone who passes. The news is all through the village. And the Gets are out in troops around the country seeking Morca's son to do the same again for him."

" 'They say.' 'They say.' " the woodcutter repeated, shaking his head. "How could Black Morca be dead? Who is there that could kill him? You've been drinking bad brew again."

"You won't believe him because Morca was your favorite," said the peasant woman. "You likcd him too well."

The woodcutter shook his head.

"It's true," the peasant man said. "He's dead. I know it's true. Four Gets stopped me as I was coming here and asked me if I had seen the boy Haldane." He had his breath back now and hc played the teller. "I thought on it long and then I told them that I had." The peasant assumed a vacant slack-jawed look for a moment. He nodded his head earnestly, and then he laughed. "They were happy until I told them that it was a week past."

Haldane knew him then. This was the great lout who had been fishing in the mud at New Bridge, the one who had asked after the fallen bridge just as Haldane had asked Aella this very day. And in the same manner. Haldane's heart tumbled as he realized that he had been made fool of.

The peasant woman shook her head "You'll buy yourself more trouble than you have any use for if you go on playing games with Gets, Jed. You always were a silly boy. They will kill you someday."

But she picked up an empty wooden bowl from

the sideboard and began to fill it for him from the
kettle hanging over the coals of the banked fire.

Poor Haldane. He hated these peasants for what
they said and he hated the dream for stupidly continuing when it had already squeezed him dry.
Enough! Enough! He had learned all the nightmare could teach him, hadn't he? And yet it went
on. Why couldn't it stop? He had not been able to
force it out of his head. He had not been able to
ignore it by sitting numbly. He felt called upon to
act, urged to act, compelled to act.

Noll said, "Yea, I think what he says must be
true. We were stopped by three Gets on the road
today and they asked after this Haldane and others. And they showed their teeth when they did."

"Gets are always showing their teeth," said the
peasant woman.

"Who is this stranger?" asked Jed.

"It is a sailing man with great stories to tell and
his idiot grandson. They are staying with us this
night," said the woodcutter. "If Morca is truly
dead, what are we to do?"

"Keep the door barred until there is a new
king," said his wife.

"Not I," said Jed. "This is the time to act while
the Gets are all at odds. I'm off to carry the word
to Duke Girard. We will throw the Gets out of
Bary now and make life as it used to be."

"Me, too," said Cob. "I will go with you. I want
to be an outlaw, too."

Haldane's head was wild. He stood slowly. No
one paid him heed but Noll, who put a restraining
hand on his arm. Haldane shook it off. He looked
from one peasant to another. He was suddenly

aware of something looming over his head and he ducked away before he saw that it was only cheeses hanging from the rafters.

"You shan't go," said Cob's young wife.

"Wake your mother, Jed, and ask her," said the woodcutter. "She is old and strange, but she has seen much and I trust her advice."

Jed crossed the room and went to his knee in front of his mother's chair. Before he could shake her, she came erect, spilling the cat from her lap, and fended him off.

"I'm awake," she said. "I'm awake. Hear my word, Jed." She spoke prophetically. "If you join Duke Girard, you will starve and die in the forest, fight and die in the forest, die in the forest. The time will come when the Goddess sends help to Nestor and all the West and a new and peaceful Golden Age will dawn. But this is not yet that day. That will be another spring. For now, go on home and keep the door barred until the Gets have chosen their new king."

"See," said Cob's young wife.

Jed rose, shaking his head. He pointed his finger at his mother. "*That* is why I sent you away. *That* is why I sent you away. You are always saying me no. Well, I won't listen to you. I will join Duke Girard whatever you say."

"Shh," said his sister, the peasant woman. She held out the well-filled bowl. "Here, now. You must be hungry. Have some of the good clams that you brought to us."

Clams?

Clams? Was that what the dreamfood was?

It was all too much for Haldane. His stomach

turned a somerset inside him.

He looked wildly round the room. He must do something. He must break his way out.

As Jed turned toward his sister, Haldane lunged between him and the steaming bowl of food. With a sweep of his hand, he knocked the bowl away, the food spilling, bowl flying. Then he swung around and with his fist he struck Jed square in the nose.

There!

There indeed! But the nightmare continued. The peasants unbarred the door and hustled Sailor Noll and his idiot grandson out into the darkness. And they threw their bag after them. The door slammed.

12

Oliver was sick from his spell that night and could not sleep. As proof that wizards are as silly as any mortal man and twice as silly as some, he blamed Haldane for that, as though Haldane would not have preferred that he had left his spell uncast. The hard forest ground was an insult to Oliver's aching body, striking him small coward blows every time he coughed. His face burned. His soft palate was raw and clotted. His chest was filled with sick syrup that no cough could clear. He lay, wrapped in his night cloak and his resentment, listening to Haldane's even breathing.

At last he picked himself up and set his back against a tree. He arranged his cloak around him as a cover against the clear probing coolness of the night so that he was as comfortable as he could manage. Sitting, his chest bothered him less, and the tree bole was more of a friend to his back than the ground had been.

In the normal way of things, he thought much and he made many plans, but he did not think or plan now. He let his mind drift with the night. He heard the forest move around them. He let his fevered face be washed by the breeze as though it were a damp cloth in the gentle hands of good mother night. He turned his face up to welcome it, dreaming that he was a boy again at home in Palsance with all his life's adventure yet before him.

He watched as a bright star slowly rose above tree shudder and sway. He was no country man, nor a sea man neither in spite of his stories, to be keeping track of the course of wandering stars. He was only a wizard whose spells of occasion failed— though never when it was truly of moment that they succeed—and he spent his nights in bed in the comfort of his cell, not gazing at the skies.

But though he had not followed the progress of this planet in many long years, he knew it at first sight for the seat of Gradis. He knew many more things than he could remember learning and his eyes, which needed aid when he pored over his book, were otherwise keener than other men's when he chose to employ them. Other men might not always see the pale white corby Con, Gradis's faint companion who brought messages winging from Jan and Libera and the other gods. When Oliver was a boy, he spied it often when others might not be sure they did, and he could see it now even with his old eyes.

If Oliver had a god, which he did not, it might have been Gradis as well as any. Many noblemen in Palsance held by Gradis. But when Oliver was a grown man, the craft master Vidal of Grelland had made for him his reading spectacles, and while he waited for them to be done, Vidal had offered him a look at Gradis and Con through a long glass that brought them nearer the eye. There were those, Vidal said, who were afraid to look. Not Oliver. He had lost faith in all gods when he was young. The gods had left him to his own devices and he had prospered best when he did the same for them. So he looked. And he saw that Con was no corby, no winged messenger. Con was a moon, like Jana, and only one moon among three. Vidal said there were four, but that one was hid behind Gradis. Oliver was neither afraid nor surprised by this new knowledge. He was rather delighted to know one more thing that other men did not.

Oliver was a man of hard sense. He believed only in things certain and exact—like his book of spells and himself. Like new knowledge.

He never failed when success mattered. That was why his failure in the Chaining of Wild Lightning, his great failure, had shaken him to his marrow. He thought he believed in nothing uncertain. To learn of belief's uncertainty only in that moment when belief fails is overtoppling. He had lost his faith for the second time, and this time the jolt was greater, for his unknowing faith had been in himself.

And here he was, lost in the forest, cast out into the night with a boy as bewildered as himself. And needing the boy to live. These were hard days.

The gentle curve of root and trunk made him a cradle to lie in. He lay back and watched the progress of Gradis as it climbed in the night sky. He coughed sometimes. In time, he dozed a little.

He was wakened suddenly by Haldane. The boy sat bolt upright and screamed wordlessly so loud that his voice cracked and went soundless. Haldane leapt to his feet and struck out at invisible enemies with wild scything arms. He was crazed with fear.

Haldane cried out: "Ayeee! Libera let me alone!

I will not go with you!"

What was most strange to Oliver was that Haldane's cry was not in Gettish, but in country Nestorian. Oliver could not explain that. He did not know that it was Haldane's breast language.

Oliver was frightened, too. He cast his cloak aside and struggled to his feet. He was desperate.

"Be quiet," he said. "They will hear us." And he made to interfere with Haldane's striking arms.

He was muddled himself. His first waking fear was of a forest filled with enemies listening to hear them and ready to sweep down with naked swords. He wanted most for Haldane to cease to bellow his cries.

Haldane was not properly awake. He was in a blind fighting trance and he kept Oliver at a distance with the wildness of his undirected blows.

"Nay! Nay! Stay away from me!"

Then Haldane tangled his feet in his night cloak and fell heavily. Oliver was on him instantly, pinning him to the ground.

"Quiet, boy! Quiet, Haldane! For our lives, quiet!"

But Haldane writhed and struggled under Oliver's hands. He made lost and frightened sounds like a strange whining tune.

It was all the wizard could do to keep his seat and contain the boy, and he felt his sickness overwhelming him. He used his greater weight to hold Haldane down and used his hands to wind the boy's cloak around him and inhibit his wildness. One desperation was pitted against another.

Haldane cried. "The wurox! I am being taken! Gets assist me!" He cried now in Gettish.

"There is no wurox here!" Oliver cried in return. "There is no wurox here!"

To silence Haldane's cries, he took the last corner of the cloak and stuffed the wad into Haldane's mouth until the boy gagged.

Oliver fell away, struggling to cough, coughing in order to breathe, unable to breathe for his coughing. He was old. His head rang in circles. He coughed, spat and choked. He coughed until his lungs were raw and he was near to vomiting and he took no note of Haldane who was coughing and choking himself as he fought against the cloak.

When Oliver looked up, he could make out Haldane panting as he was panting, struggling to rise as he was struggling to rise.

Haldane said, "Where . . . What is this place? Who are you?" He was speaking Gettish still, and what was better, he seemed aware of his words.

"It is me, Oliver," the wizard said, fighting a battle for every word. "This is the forest. You had a nightmare."

"Oh, no! Nay. You are not Oliver. That is not Oliver's voice."

"I am Oliver. Come to yourself! I cast a spell to guise our appearance until we win through to Little Nail. Remember! Remember!"

"But that was the dream!" Haldane said, and his voice was wilder again. He pointed a finger at Oliver in the cool night dimness and pushed away like a broken crab on one hand. "You brought me back into the dream! I was home safe in my bed and you dragged me back to this again."

"Nay, nay. Stop," said Oliver. "I am Oliver and you are Haldane. If you were home safe in your bed, that was the dream. If this forest be a dream, it is the dream that can be ended only by death. It is the dream in which you will gain your vengeance."

Haldane halted his progress, fetched against a sapling that would not break. "Where . . . Where is Morca?"

"Morca is dead. Don't you remember? The peasant Jed said that his head now sits on a pole before the dun."

Haldane stroked his cheeks with his fingers as though to test them. He said slowly, wonderingly, "But Morca was alive. I was asleep in my bed. I was sleeping there and I dreamed. I dreamed—oh, many strange and awful things. I dreamed of a battle. Morca brought a Western princess and I was to marry her only there was a battle instead. Then . . . then I don't remember, but there were peasants. They were not real. I knew they were a dream. I struck one because he was a dream and I wanted him to know it, too. But the dream did not end. They cast us into the forest. And then the wurox came to me and spoke."

"Nay," said Oliver. He waved his hand to silence Haldane. He hawked to clear his chest. "All that you thought was a dream was true. All but this wurox that you dreamed."

Haldane must not have seen the waving hand in the darkness for he answered in an angry voice as though he cared not to be disbelieved: "There was a wurox! It came and it tried to carry me away with it. I would not go. I struggled. I fought free and ran. I ran and ran and I hid, but it found me. I ran again. I hid in the small deep darkness and it found me. It was about to take me then, but I struck it down. But it rose up again and took me and I cried for help. And then I woke. But I was not in my bed. I was here in the dream again!"

And he cried in fear and desperation. He rocked back and forth as he cried.

Oliver sighed deep. How like a Get this all was, to dream of gods and to strike them with his hands. Things like this did not happen to him. Simple reality was enough of a trial.

He said, "You have seen your own bed for the last time until you and your grandfather Arngrim raise an army and retake Morca's Hill. And move Morca's head off the pole where it sits. This is no dream. You were asleep here all the time you thought yourself in your bed. And you will be here when you wake in the morning."

"But the wurox . . ."

Oliver picked up Haldane's night cloak and threw it at him. "Listen to me!" he said in exasperation. "This is no dream and there is no wurox here. There never was. You have been wounded and you are confused. You slept little last night, Haldane, and you walked far today. If we are to reach your grandfather, you have far to walk tomorrow. So please, go to sleep again, and let me do the same!"

"But how can I trust you?" Haldane asked. "Oh, my senses are deceived! What can I believe?"

Oliver said in a wearied voice, "Believe this. You must trust me. You have no one else to trust. If we are to live, we must trust each other. Go to sleep now. When you wake in the morning, you will wake here. I will keep you from all wuroxes."

Fine brave words. Falsely spoken. For all his years among the Gets, Oliver still saw them with the cool eye of a stranger. He did not truly trust Haldane and would not. Even unfuddled, the boy was a raw and reckless Get who required careful watch. Oliver bore Haldane because he needed him.

Oliver turned away. Pretending to ignore the boy, he found his own cloak by the base of the tree where he had left it. He wrapped it close about him once more, cleared his chest of phlegm, and with great show lay down, his back to Haldane, and left him behind.

That was the last he remembered until morning came to them in the woods. It was a cool and misty morning, and Oliver woke damp, aching and grouchy. Still he had slept. Haldane was frisky as a colt. He made no reference to his behavior with the peasants or to his nightmare. He was quick to fold away the night cloaks and to bring out the very last of Oliver's dried beef. Oliver suffered him in surly silence except for occasional reproachful coughs.

As he ate, he thought. If his map and his calculation were correct and he could force himself to continue, they were no more than two days from Little Nail and Arngrim and a safe place in this chaos of Nestor. He thought he could go so far with Haldane's help and Haldane's vouch to open the gate for him. Oliver's strength was not great, but his endurance was to be reckoned with.

When they finished the last crumbs of beef, Haldane made to shoulder Oliver's bag again, but Oliver pulled the bag away.

"No!" he said.

He swung it up onto his own back and they left
their broken bedding place in the small greens of
the forest floor. They set off again to find the road,
the Pellardy Road for these two Pellardy sailors,
the road that ran under the eye of Little Nail, where
they would leave it.

But as they departed the glade, Oliver saw something strange. Coughing, weaving a bit as he found
his stride under the weight of the bag, he found
himself looking at the track of an animal in the soft
floor of the forest. It arced around their bedding
place as though the animal had circled round them
while it thought its own thoughts. But most unsettling was that the tracks were the great split hoof
marks of kine. And great, indeed! If the track were
a true index of the animal, this boss was twice the
size of any mortal cow that Oliver had ever seen.

As long as he had been in Morca's dun, as long
as he had been a wizard, Oliver had made it his
business to hear and weigh all mention of strange
happenings. He was as well aware of the talk of
wuroxen in the woods current these past weeks as
he was of Haldane's dream this past night. And he
knew whose beast the wurox was.

Oliver may have lost his faith in the gods, but he
had not cast off belief. The tracks there in the forest round about their camp bothered him more
than he could like. He was ready to argue that they
meant nothing, but he was readier to pretend that
he had never seen them and readiest of all to leave
them behind and forget them entire. He wanted no
part of Libera.

He said sharply, "Stop dragging. Either you set
a pace, boy, or I will."

He made no light talk of dreams or the tracks of wuroxen. If Haldane saw the circle there in the forest, he said nothing either, and Oliver was content to have it that way.

13

Like a gosling trailed by a goose in reverse of all the common order of the world, Haldane led the pack-burdened old man along the turns of the Pellardy Road. He pretended to be blithe, but his lightness was a lie. He felt eyes on his back.

Haldane knew Noll for a liar and his enemy, this cock-eyed shade who claimed to be Oliver and was not. He aimed to fool him and be free. Around his neck, and lost in the illusion of a Nestorian sprout-ling that he still smothered under, was his good string. Hanging from the string was his horn and his knife. When Haldane had brought out their crumbs of breakfast from Noll's deep blue bag, he had slipped out all his possessions and secreted them on his person. Now that he had his own things about him once more, he was unbound, free to run in the first moment when Noll's back was turned. He was free to be free.

But he was also afraid. He had meant to carry the pack and Noll had seized it from him. Did he know what Haldane had taken? Would he notice?

As Haldane walked, he paused long enough to pluck a heavy blade of bog grass from a seep by the wayside. To still his heart, he stretched it tight be-tween the tips and the balls of his thumbs. Then

with deliberation he blew into the gap where his
thumbs met, just as he was used to do when he was
small. The reed fluttered, shrieked and honked like
an abused women until the hills were filled to overflowing with the secrets of his heart. Haldane
laughed.

"Why are you doing that?" Noll cried from behind, looking up in pretended distress from under
the weight of his sack. Oh, the liar!

Haldane mistrusted him in everything. It was
Sailor Noll who had kept him so spun about with
new fancies that he was too dizzy to be sure of any
truth. It was Noll who had lied to him about the
wurox. Haldane had seen the tracks this morning
round about their camp. But he knew Noll now.

"Hey, now, it's a beautiful day and my spirit is
singing," said Haldane. He blew another frightful
blast to prove his words, and smiled cunningly.

It was a beautiful day only for those who love
dampness. The high-shouldered hills were covered
with muted spring shades of green, red, purple,
white and yellow, a textured surface of dull running color. It set Haldane in mind of a tapestry that
Morca had carried home through the Great Slough
of Vilicea and hung in his hall in spite of its ruin-
ation because he liked the strange unsettling thing
it had become. And because others did not. The
skies that capped the narrow valley where the road
sought its lean way south were as cool and wild and
grey as old ice.

"That noise will only succeed in bringing enemies upon us. Or rain," said Noll. "We can do
without both."

What need of new enemies? The one at hand was

enough for Haldane. He blew another screeching
trumpet call on his grass horn.

"Enough!"

Haldane grinned and threw the rush away.
"Mayhap it will be our enemies who are rained
upon," he said. "Let us wish them wetness and
shelter for ourselves."

His mind was working clearly now, or so he was
given to think. In truth, he was only in part recovered, like a muddied stream half-settled.

His strength was greater today than yesterday.
His head ached less. If there were confused places
in his memory even yet, he could remember clearly
enough what had happened to him yesterday and
last night. He did not know the truth yet of what
might be trusted and believed. There was much in
his mind to be made sense of. But since the wurox
had tried to steal him away, there was one thing of
which he was sure. He wanted most to fly free of
the Goddess and her tool, the ugly red man with
whom he was forced to keep company.

If he was not as blithe as he pretended to be, he
was happier in his anticipation of escape than he
had been at any other time in this prisoning dream.
And he waited like an archer with a hard target,
seeking the right moment of wind and light to pull
and loose his arrow. He the archer, he the bow, he
the arrow, all in one.

His gnarly shadow lagged and wilted. Noll was
even slower today than he had been yesterday.
Haldane did not know whether it was one more
trick to throw him off guard, or whether Noll the
Tool truly failed. He listened to him choke and
cough and he made the pace harder, hoping that he

might outwalk the old man and leave him far behind.

But when he was thirty paces ahead, Noll called
for him to slow. "Not so fast. Not so fast. I am not
able to keep up with you."

Did he play with Haldane?

"I thought you wished for me not to drag?"
Haldane said in all false innocence. "I but do my
best to please you."

"Aye, Haldane. Giles. I must remember to call
you that always until we are safe. And you, to call
me Noll."

"Be content," Haldane said. He tapped his head.
"You are Noll in my mind even now. I have you."

"Good. Remember that when it matters. When
we set out this morning, I did not know how tired
I was. My bones are water. I cannot march like a
soldier."

"What kind of soldier marches?" asked
Haldane. "Any soldier worth the name rides."

Like the best of bad servants, he teased and
joked and laughed to prove his constancy. But
soon enough again, he was twenty paces ahead of
Noll and the old man was wilting under the weight
of the pack.

"Stop," he said. "I must catch my breath."

So they halted and when they rose again, Noll
gave the pack over. But Haldane still led the way,
setting the pace with his lighter feet. The pack was
nothing to him.

This was not yet the time for escape. The hills
were too close and steep and set about with tangles
of trees and brush. Haldane did not mean to run
away into wilderness and lose himself.

The second time they rested was no better. Haldane contented himself to set too brisk a march, not quite enough to earn complaint, but stiff enough to weary this wander-eyed untrustable man, and make him unwary. When they came upon the proper place, Haldane would know it and call the halt himself.

And in time they came upon a jamble of high grey rocks, the Pellardy Road passing by on one side, a trail angling past on the other to find its own way south into the hills.

And the place said to Haldane, "Here I am. Make use of me." For facing the road there was a natural shelter tucked under the rocks that many men had used for a camp since the world was new. They came upon it as the wind began to speckle them again with finger flicks of wetness. Wind and rain said to him, "Haldane, we are with you, too." Haldane heard them and rejoiced in spite of all fear and apprehension.

He did not ask Noll if he was ready to rest again. He did not trust himself to speak. He simply led the way off the road without a word, and the man who dogged his heels followed ten paces behind, saying, "Hey, it's Leaning Rock. It is marked on my map. I remember it."

Did Noll pretend? Did Noll suspect? What would he do when he found Haldane gone? Would he wait until Haldane was ready to flee and then reveal himself? Haldane's stomach was clenched so tightly that he could hardly breathe.

Noll hurried his pace so that by the time Haldane was under the great rock loom where the ground was dry and out of wind and weather, the old man was beside him. And when Haldane had swung his bag down from his shoulder and seated himself, Noll was there before him, heaving great breaths like a blown horse.

Haldane felt like Wisolf the Cunning outside the tent of his enemy. This was the moment.

He forced a smile and said, "Here we are. Shelter for us, rain for the rest of the world. Just as we said."

Sailor Noll said, "We must not rest here too long and spend our day on nothing. Only a minute. Unless the rain becomes too hard, Giles."

But he sounded as though he wished the rain to grow hard. He leaned back with a sigh, putting his head on his bag, which he shifted and plumped until it was comfortable, moving one small hard lump until it ceased to annoy.

Haldane held his tongue in check while he counted ten. He would not be too swift with his words.

"We'll wait and see if it does," he said. "Now is the time for our enemies to suffer while we have good shelter over our heads." Then he said with what he hoped was easiness, "Hey, I'll tell you—let me step forth and test the wind. I need to piss anyway. I'll judge the weather."

He had not relieved his bladder all the morning long to make this excuse water-tight when his moment came. He hardly dared to look at Noll. He rose from the ground without use of his hands. They were his danger. He wanted to touch his body and be sure that all that he had hung about him was still safely there. The things that mattered. Knife, horn, string. The things that made Haldane.

His fingers itched for his boar's tooth.

He shot one look at Noll because he could not help himself. Noll's eyes seemed to be closed.

Haldane stepped outside into the light sprinkle that was spatting the earth. He put his hands to work. He held them out under the rain and cocked his head as though considering what they told him, then turned left out of sight around the rocks.

Before him lay the trail into the hills. Haldane wanted to run, but he did not immediately take to his heels. He needed to piss too badly.

He outdid the rain in wetting the base of a tree. All the while he kept an eye turned over his shoulder, looking for Noll. His heart fluttered and he looked of a sudden to the other side of the rocks expecting to see the old man standing over there, watching him, smiling at his simplicity in believing he could escape.

The wind and rain blew harder, shoving at him to be gone, but he could not go. He pushed at the piss until his penis hurt. He stood there for an agonizingly long time, his head switching from one side of the rocks to the other. But Noll did not show himself.

And then he was empty. Then he was free to run. He took the path, panting with relief, feeling surer and happier than he had at any time since he could bring himself to remember.

That was only two days. It seemed half his lifetime.

He ran, and every step said he was not Giles. He was Haldane. He was free. He was free. He was Haldane. He was himself. He was Haldane. Haldane, Haldane, Haldane.

Rain, wind, earth, rocks, trees, broken path. Haldane at one with them. Never Giles. He pushed Giles out of his mind.

He ran until the tumbled rock pile beside the Pellardy Road was far behind him. He pounded up the hillside trail until the breath was harsh in his throat and there were needles in his chest. He ran, half-afraid, half-convinced that he would turn a corner in the angling rock-fractured path and find Sailor Noll waiting for him, laughing at him, playing with him. That was Libera's way in all of this—to toy with him like a Get carl loose among the playthings of the West.

At the best of times, Haldane was more used to ride than to run. First his calves began to bind and then his lungs failed him and at last he fell to a walk. The slope of the path before him increased and he pushed at his thighs with his hands, whoofing and panting. At last he caught at a rock and leaned against it for a moment, eyes closed, before pressing on.

From then on there was neither looking back nor fearing what was ahead. There was only walking. And as time passed and Haldane walked higher into the hills, his heart lightened. He began to believe that he was free. There was only himself all alone in this rain-sodden world. This was the end of the evil spell that had gripped him for so long. They might do what they wished with him, play with him, lie to him, beat and harry him, but he was Haldane Hardhead, Haldane the Stubborn, and he knew his own power. He had proved it.

He laughed. Oh, they should have known better

than to test their wiles on the son of Black Morca! They would know now.

It continued to rain. He wiped his forehead with his fingers. He was wet clear through his own clothes beneath the illusion and in some moments he could feel them binding and chafing. But he did not mind the rain. It had been a good friend to him this day.

Or so he told himself. But when he turned a corner in the trail and saw the first tumbled house of the village, his thoughts were immediately of shelter. He found he did mind the rain when there was promise of something better.

Then in the second moment he turned around and around, caught in a dance of wonder, marveling at what he saw about him. This distant village was dead, an empty silent unpeopled shell.

Nowhere within it did four walls stand together. Haldane saw fallen roofs. He saw stones thrown down. He saw charred beams glistening blackly in the rain. And he saw trees springing up again amongst the ruins, as though log walls, shattered and scattered, had in dying given birth to new strong children.

The destruction was complete. It was good Gettish work. Since Haldane had never raided into the West, it was the best he had ever seen.

He knew this place for what it was, though he had never seen one before, but only heard stories. It was a Wild Village.

Long, long ago, in Garulf's time, the Gets had not ruled in the duchies of Nestor. They had been but guests, content to live in Nestor and accept its tribute, as they did even today in Pellardy in the south. And that had been well. Then, in the dark days after Stone Heath, when the Gets seemed weak and unable to help themselves, the nobles of Nestor had risen up and rebelled and refused to pay their lawful tribute. It was after that, when the dukes were dead or were fled into the West, that the Gets had learned to rule in Nestor. They had gathered all the people of the land close under their hands so that they might be better ruled. But there were some peasants who resisted and ran away into the hills and made new villages there. These were the Wild Villages.

All were in ruins now, burned, torn down and broken long ago. Haldane thought it strange of fate that such a place should give him shelter now. He sat himself down on the dry side of a wall, comfortably out of the rain, which now, so late, was waning, to rest, think and plan.

There was much in his mind to be put in place. There was much to be decided. But at least he was himself again, no longer Giles the Nestorian, no longer the plaything of the Goddess.

While he leaned his back against the logs and thought, he plucked a stalk of field grass and absently stripped it apart. When he had only a straw left, a bit longer than his finger, he picked up a tiny spider with it. He watched it closely as it ran back and forth from one end to the other as he tipped the straw. Back and forth. Back and forth. He smiled to see it scramble.

As he was absorbed in this pursuit, there came a sudden startling hard hand on Haldane's shoulder,

shaking him. He looked up to see the great looming bearded face of a wild man. The man was
dressed in skins, his wet hair stood out in spikes,
and he carried an ax in his hand. Haldane jumped
to his feet in terror, dropping straw and spider.

He had never seen anyone like this before. It was
a strange and frightening sight, a high-smelling
bogey appeared out of the stories his nurses had
told him when he was small. Was he so soon back
in the hands of the spirits he thought he had escaped?

"What are you doing here, boy?" the apparition
said in Nestorian. "Who are you?"

Haldane drew himself up and faced the bogey.
He would not deny himself. Not again.

He said, "I am Haldane, the son of Black
Morca!"

The apparition laughed.

14

In late afternoon, the clouds that had been dooming the day broke at last into great floes and sailed apart. That was while Oliver was following the hill path that led down into the glen where Duke Girard lay encamped. On his heels were the two boy outlaws who had come upon him in his great confusion after he awoke alone at Leaning Rock. These boys still wore clothes sewn by their mothers, though oversewn with patches of experience. The day continued cool in cloud and tree shadow, but in other moments bright. Grasses shivered then in sunlight and Oliver must narrow his eyes.

Oliver appeared the knobby sailor, Old Noll, he of the pendulous earlobes and the hairy nostrils, he of the red hair and the eye cocked on another world. At this moment, Oliver did not just wear Sailor Noll as a mask. He did his best to be Sailor Noll, to be no more than Sailor Noll, a man of no consequence. He had not done any of those simple things Oliver knew that would win him free of these outlaws minor. He did not wish to win free. He had welcomed their arrival.

Oliver sought the comfort of a fire, a fair portion, a place for his head, and time to regain his mind's balance. In return he might offer the news of the day as it had come to a land-bound sailor walking the long road home from Eduna to Jedburke. Sailor Noll had said what was necessary to persuade these two damp lads to leave off their patrol and bring him and his news back to the warm and dry of camp. They had welcomed the persuasion.

This winter camp, tucked away in the range of hills that rose like a hedgerow between Morca and Arngrim, was the center of Duke Girard's power. Girard was he who would have been ruler of Bary if the Gets had never come. He had been raised in exile in Palsance and was now returned to live at the edges of Gettish vision in his home hills of Bary, where he commanded fifty men among whom were more boys than just these two. They named themselves soldiers of the duke.

They had no more than reached the edge of camp, Sailor Noll and the two young soldiers, passed through by the watch, when they were set upon by a lank man whose many more patches were token of his greater authority. Camp was a well-used clearing, and there were more than fifty, men and women both, in camp today. They wore rude and simple clothes, and some even wore the skins of animals. So much Oliver could see at this distance.

The lank man was angry. He swore at the boys and said, "I will see you whipped. Will none of you follow orders? I put you wood-lice on the Pellardy Road until dark! Is this darkness?"

"Be you calm, Rab," the smaller boy said pertly. "We bring news for the duke."

Rab was not calm, nor ready to be told to be. Oliver paid the noise no mind, waiting for it to cease. He looked away. A dozen women, as many old as young, played camp wife around the smoky fires. Men sat, worked or played there in the glen in the glowing blue and orange of the cool late after-rain.

He was not much of an Oliver, that powerful man of magic, this fugitive Oliver. He was no man of whom Gets must be wary. He was a man of no consequence. He was content to be mere Sailor Noll and go where mere Sailor Noll would go. He ached to sit.

The world of his mind was as strange now as Haldane's. From the time that he was a boy, Oliver had been acquaint with his failings. He was self-bound to narrow practice. He was indolent. He was timorous. He excused himself from much.

Nonetheless, he would not be stayed from walking at large in the world. He had countered his failings with his strengths. Agility was his chief strength, and he had forced his agility to carry him where diligence and courage and breadth alone would have failed him. Agility had made Oliver into Morca's wizard and adviser, the one man of magic amongst the Gets. Naught else but agility could have done so much.

And once he had found his balance there among the Gets, that was a safe and easy time, the years with Morca, the first that Oliver had known since he was young. He had let himself forget that he had bade goodby to safety and ease when he left home. He had let himself forget that narrow practice was his failing and practiced narrowly. He had lost himself in study, lost himself in thought and question, paused for a moment in dream while he wondered where his youth had flown and wither he was bound. To what end had he been born? And while he was occupied so in reverie, he had lost his balance.

Oliver had tricked Oliver and received a blow from Oliver that had set Oliver down. Where was order? His world was broken. His mind ran on its own heels in subtle circles.

He knew not what to trust, or what to believe, or what to do. Small things were disturbing—like Haldane's dream and the trail of the wurox. He knew not what they meant. He did not know what was important and what was not—and in this event, how could he make up his mind to anything?

Oh, if instead of practicing narrowly in his cell, Oliver had truly studied to know the meaning of small signs, like the presence of kings and witches, then Morca might be alive. The world might be whole. And Oliver might still be safe and happy practicing narrowly in his cell. What of that?

But when this Rab, this lank sergeant of outlaws, loomed over Oliver and said, "What is your news, old man? I will be the judge of it," Oliver was not so lost that he could not wither him with one squint of his odd eye. If this Rab could be defied by two wee boy outlaws, he was not a man meant to be Sailor Noll's master.

"None of yours to know," said Oliver. "My news is for the duke."

And as they made their progress through the camp, Oliver gained confidence in this small game he was playing in the guise of Sailor Noll. This was

a camp hungry for news if not for meat. Men called
to ask what was afoot as they walked, and when
the two boy outlaws said it was news, they hurried
to swell the progress. Sailor Noll with his news was
a safe and simple size to be.

"Is it Mainard returned?" some asked.

And others, the rougher men in skins, said: "Is
there to be drink at last?"

The Duke Girard, rightful heir to Bary in the
eyes of some, stood separate from other men, his
back to a great standing stone, an ancient raised
tongue of rock placed alone there where they
camped. Nearby him were several leaders of outlaws, commoner men, come here to confer, and to
eat and drink with Girard. Beyond Girard's shoulders, close by the rock, stood a strange Man of
the Woods, one of those who were the first people
of Nestor, one of different breed than all the others
here. His hair was fine and black, and his robes
were brown. And so they all gathered: the party
with news and those they had attracted, the outlaw
leaders standing together, the strange Man of the
Woods standing apart, and Girard alone in their
midst.

Girard was a pretty and well-made youth with
the air of a dream-walker lost in some dream other.
Among these men, Girard was singular in fashion
and dress. He wore his hair long after the style of
the Western courts and his clothes were Western
clothes of Palsance that had not survived the winter whole. His singularity was one of the proofs by
which Girard commanded his fifty loyal men.

Thus it was that as the sun set, Oliver stood
before young Girard and divers other outlaws. The

price of a night's hospitality was on his tongue and
his true self was invisible, and he was content to
have it so.

If Oliver had been fully Oliver, he might have
worried over the meaning of the raised rock. This
place was an old place, and old places are not the
same as new places. Oliver might have worried
over the rock and its seeming guardian man in his
robes of brown.

Sailor Noll only managed to take in Duke
Girard, his back to a stone that stood taller than
he. But he was enough Oliver to know before a
word was spoken that Sailor Noll could take in
Duke Girard indeed. He could see it in Duke
Girard's bearing.

"Lord, here is one who claims news for you,"
said lank Rab. "I think he is a vagrom who would
lie to have the advantage of your table."

One of the two young soliders of the duke suddenly declined responsibility for Sailor Noll. He
leaned toward those around him to seem one of
them. But the other young outlaw saw in Duke
Girard something of what Oliver saw. He smiled
and stood tall behind queer-looking Sailor Noll.

"We share with all who visit us, Rab. My table is
open to all of Bary. I am duke."

"Yes, lord," said Rab.

"Nay, I do mean it, Rab."

"Yes, lord."

"Is it news of the train to Palsance?" asked
Girard. He smiled. "We all shall be less cross when
the ambock has arrived. And my wardrobe."

"Lord, he has not said what his news is, if news
he has," said Rab.

"I should not have guessed," said Girard. "Who are you, strange old man, and with what news have you been sent to me?"

Oliver said, "My name is Noll and I am an old sailor walking the road from Eduna to Jedburke. My lord."

"If you must be a sailor, I will accept that," said Girard. "Or is that part of the message?"

It suddenly became evident to Oliver that this dreamy-eyed young boy saw him as a portent. Girard saw through Sailor Noll, not to Oliver behind, but to words of import clothed in strange human form. And with a sudden surge of heart, Oliver realized that Girard saw truly. Sailor Noll, with his news, was a portent in this camp.

Sailor Noll became a portent. He swung his sack down to the ground. On the instant, he changed his bearing. Without being any less Sailor Noll, he took on stature. He expanded his will. And all present but the Man of the Woods and Girard himself fell back a pace from the sight of ugly shy-eyed Sailor Noll. The Man of the Woods cocked his head on his shoulder and watched Noll steadfastly. It seemed the life of these outlaws was not his life, and great news for them was not great news for him, a man of other kind. As for Girard, he bravely held his ground before momentous words.

Oliver signed the sign that commands silence and grave attention from all men. His arm outstretched, his hand raised, thumb a-cock, forefinger pointing high.

He said: "Once there was a king, a barbarian tyrant. Because his skin was black as a frog, they called him the Black King."

And he told the story of Morca and Morca's banquet and Morca's head as though it had happened in another land many years ago. He made a place for Duke Girard in the story.

And when he finished, the outlaws asked each other, "What does this mean?" They did not know of what Oliver spoke because the names had not been Nestor and the Gets and Lothor of Chastain and Black Morca. They looked into each other's faces to see the meaning of what they heard. Some thought it was an aimless story. Some thought it was a riddle. Some thought it was news of strange foreign politics.

As the outlaws looked to each other, Girard put his face in both hands against the force of the words of power this gnarly messenger had borne to him. He believed that he understood the story and who it was who came after the black usurper king. He put his face in his hands to think, but he did not cover his eyes. The words he had heard were weightier than any he had invited to hear.

He dropped his hands and asked his portent: "Is it Black Morca who is dead?"

The wildest of the hill outlaws, not a leader of anyone, but one who stood by himself, said, "What is this news? Does he say that my old enemy, the Hammer of Gradis, is dead?"

"If this be true, then our day's planning is spent for nothing," said one of the leader men.

"Black Morca is dead," said Oliver.

Girard, in strange mind, spread his hands. His hands trembled and his face rolled. His soldiers knew that this was the sign he made before he spoke the words by which they were guided.

Strangers to the camp, who knew Duke Girard best by repute, watched in wonder.

He said in a clear and even voice: "If the barbarian king is Morca, then I am the boy Jehan. I am the new Jehannes!" And his face lit with an inner light. "I wish Mainard were here so that I might tell him."

He said: "Listen to me, my men. Black Morca is dead and his head sits on a pole like a cabbage! The Gets have fallen on each other with the fury of their own battle pigs. Now is the moment for us to strike them as we may. I am the heir of Jehannes. I will rule Bary. I will rule the world. Have faith and follow me."

And the men stirred at that. And then they continued to stir. Someone was arrived, and a cry went up! "Mainard! It is Mainard!" The outlaws fell away and in the still half-light another young man, of cut similar to Girard but wearing a new coat, came running in, stopped, panted once lightly for effect, and threw his arms wide to show himself off for inspection. Then he and Girard made the noises made when good friends meet again, and fell to hugging each other.

Girard said, "I am the new Jehannes. I'm going to lead us to strike against the Gets wherever we may find them."

Mainard said, "I was so hoping I would find you crowding the fires before dinner so that you might truly admire the clothes that I wear. Not in this murk."

"No, my good friend Mainard. Hear me: Black Morca is dead. He has been struck down by his fellows and the Gets now rip each other recklessly.

We have been given a moment and we must act on the moment we have been given."

Mainard fell back. He said: "This explains much. The country is aswarm with Gets. We had to dig a cache and leave the greater part behind us. I could not bring you your wardrobe. You will have to look at me and dream. Why do we stand here? We could be eating."

"Only to gather strength," said Girard.

"That I will do," said Mainard.

"Did you bring nothing with you from Palsance?" the outlaw men asked.

"Nothing but the ambock," said Mainard.

And the men all cried hurray and turned for supper. And there the kegs of dark brew were. Oliver followed behind, his moment as a portent complete, his meal, his beer and his place as close by the fire as he liked all earned. He remembered ambock from other days and he could taste it now.

Jana, the moon, showed half her face in the sky overhead, but her eyes were unveiled. She watched all in silence.

15

Sailor Noll sat without company at the farthest glimmer of the fire circle. His bag was by his leg where he could be sure of it. He had a well-filled plate on his lap, with a thick slice of good meat. A jack of dark beer sat on the ground before him. He was alone because there was no man nor woman in this company that did not feel that he was best left by himself. That was a safe space in which Sailor Noll could eat his meat as though it were the world-in-all and drink his good dark beer. Oliver attended to the camp only with his ears.

The air at his back was cool and only lightly stirring. He got but hints from the fire, but was content. The night was close behind his ears. The meat was as good as Morca's meat. Oliver was well-content to sit and fill himself. He did not look up even when he sipped and savored his beer. He did listen.

This was a restless camp. There was much moving to and fro, voices were quick and intense. He could hear much drinking and the rowdy games born of much drinking. Women laughed. The wild men proved their wildness. There were many arrivals.

He heard Girard speak to his friend Mainard of being the new Jehannes as it was prophesied. And he heard Mainard answer as though he was but biding his own moment to talk.

He heard a women shriek and then laugh. And then he heard a man protest and many laugh.

He did not hear the Man of the Woods. Almost he looked to find him.

He heard the wild outlaw who had spoken of Morca as the Hammer of Gradis boast of the Gets he would kill.

A woman came to him and asked him if he would have more beer. Without looking at her, he held his cup to be filled.

He heard great tumult, laughter and hooting as many chased one around the campfire and threw him down and beat him. And then there was a turnabout.

He heard many wild outlaws boast of the beer they would drink.

There was a serious fight and one was hurt.

He heard Girard speak to his friend Mainard of his clothes from Palsance that were left behind in the cache and other things. And he heard Mainard say, to avoid answer: "With so many Gets about, we may find one or two to kill, if we be careful."

Duke Girard said then: "Mainard, my friend, be serious. With Morca dead, I am certain that this must be the moment to strike at the Gets. But now I am asking you of what is being worn at Richard's court and who is being talked about and what is being said of my poems."

But after that, Oliver opened his eyes and came to his feet. He left his place of silent attention behind. For suddenly, as Duke Girard spoke, there was one more arrival in the great fire circle. And there was a voice that said, "I am Haldane, the son of Black Morca! I will kill all you dream creatures!"

The voice was not the voice of Haldane. The voice was the voice of Giles, the strange grandson of old Sailor Noll.

Oliver opened his eyes to see Giles the peasant boy, Giles the fool, the young simpleton in his smock. He was gripped by a great wild outlaw dressed in animal skins. This one threw Giles to the ground before Duke Girard.

"He says that he is the son of Black Morca. When I spoke of you, he wished to fight, Haldane against Girard, so I brought him here to you."

"I am the son of Black Morca. I am Haldane. Had I my sword, I would have slain you, wild man."

Drunken men cheered at the audacity of this silly boy's words. As Oliver stood, he saw the Man of the Woods rise to the boy's assistance. The man of strange feature and fine black hair knelt to brush the dirt away. But though he beat at the smock of the Nestorian boy, Oliver's spell held true.

Girard looked down at the boy sprawled before the fire. "You say you are the son of the King of the Gets."

"Do you not believe he is, my lord?" asked Oliver. He was become potent again. His plate was cast aside. His jack was upset. He recked for nothing. "You have been warned, but warned for nought. Now, listen whilst you are warned again. This is a Nestorian boy, a simple lad. But this boy is inhabited by the voice of Haldane, the son of Black Morca. What he says, Haldane would say.

Harken to him. Contest with him if you would be heir of Jehannes."

The man in brown, the Man of the Woods, withdrew attention from himself then. He became nobody and was not in sight. And so also the wild outlaw. Haldane stood and looked to Duke Girard. And then to Oliver. He raged around and pointed in a circle to all the standing men.

"I will kill all here," said Haldane.

In front of the man of portent, he said, "I know you. I know you, Sailor Noll. I will kill you first, devious one. Are you master of the dream?"

Duke Girard stepped forth then, casting off Mainard's restraining hand. He had his look of lostness with him again, as though he saw in leagues but not in lesser distances.

"Do you dream, too?" asked Girard.

"Who are you?" asked Haldane.

"I dream I am Girard. It is very strange to be Girard. What do you dream?"

"I dream . . . I dream . . . I do not know what I dream. I think I dream that . . . No. I do not know what I dream, but I know that I dream."

"But you are Haldane?"

"I am Haldane! Yes. I am Haldane."

Girard smiled then, a slow sweet smile. He stepped boldly. His men cheered him. Some threw ale and wounding words at the boy who spoke for Haldane. Even the wild men watched Girard with new respect, thinking they might become soldiers rather than outlaws.

For Girard said, "In my dream, Morca is dead and his beribboned head sits on a sharpened stake."

And Haldane screamed and shook his head and
fell to his knees. He struck at the ground with the
flat of his hands.

Men cried at him: "We will kill Haldane and all
Gets," and "We will throw you to the ground as
your father threw your mother," and "The Gets
eat dogs."

This last must hurt Haldane because the Gets
would not eat dog and did not like those who did.

Girard said, "In my dream, Haldane must hide
from all other Gets who will kill him. But Girard
leads his soldiers against the Gets and sweeps them
away in the name of the Goddess, and all holy in-
spiration. I am the Prince of Bary, the heir of
Jehannes who came of Bary. You are no prince.
You are not even a baron. If I knew where you
were in truth, and not just in word, I would kill you
as I would a beetle, with the heel of my shoe."

Haldane said, "I am a baron. I am a baron." But
then the stupid peasant boy face he wore broke
into pieces in the most comical way. "But my army
is dead."

And the outlaws all laughed at him in his
bewilderment and grief.

Haldane looked at Sailor Noll, who stood silently watching. He scrambled toward him over the
ground like a piglet in panic.

Haldane said to Sailor Noll: "If you are the
dream master, will you not make the whirling stop?
I cannot hold on to anything and I am confused."

Gay young Girard called, "If you are the dream
master, my sailor, then let the dream play on. I
know now who I really am, and I thank you. I am
grateful." He laughed.

All Duke Girard's soldiers cried for him and longed for Gets to kill. They would become an army, a state, more than a state.

Mainard called in joy, "I am your good right hand, Girard. I am your good right hand."

Girard said, "You doubted me."

"I do not doubt you now."

"Then shred your coat," said Girard.

But such was the force of passion here that Mainard ripped the new court coat from his back in the instant of Girard's words. He had a knife out and he laid the coat to the ground in strips and pieces.

Girard stood over Haldane, who lay at the feet of Sailor Noll. Girard said, "You cannot face me in my glory. I have bound myself to Libera and I will rule the world and write poems to her. Do you not see?" And he pointed to the fine court coat of Palsance that was now rags as it were proof. "I am Libera's Liege. I am the heir of Jehannes."

Haldane the fool, Haldane the double fool, Haldane the fool of the fool of the world; Haldane, in the guise of the Nestorian boy, Giles—he who had been struck by a swinging boom when he was small, he whose eye was like a staring agate: Haldane gazed at Dule Girard, Libera's Liege, the heir of Jehannes, and at crooked Sailor Noll, the portent, the master of the dream, as these two stood above him, and knew that he was helpless.

It was wrong. It was not right. He said, "But she told me I was Libera's Liege. I understand nothing. I understand nothing."

Then he cried, "Libera, free me!" in a voice that was all his agony.

He fainted then. After a moment, he relaxed as he lay and betrayed himself, wetting his smock before the whole camp of outlaws.

Girard looked down at the incontinent Nestorian peasant boy who lay as dead. Then he turned to his friend Mainard, standing on the rags of his court coat.

"You saw it all," young Girard said. "Am I the heir of Jehannes, or am I not?"

Mainard nodded.

Duke Girard turned to Sailor Noll: "I am, am I not?"

Sailor Noll nodded.

The soldiers of the duke all cried their passions. They cheered Girard for his dream, and they drank to him. They drank into the night, and some of them came to kick Haldane. Haldane did not protest. He lay on the ground and moaned, and sometimes his limbs twitched.

When Haldane woke, it was some other time. He lay on the hard cold ground. The camp was as silent as a winter grave. All the outlaws did not move, nor could Haldane hear them breathe. They slept as the dead sleep under their warm snow blankets, without turning.

The moon was set, her eyes no longer witness. Only the Get Fathers watched from above, their distant stare brilliant and crystalline. They had never reached Haldane when he had striven to call upon them. Perhaps they had never tried to come. Perhaps he had never called aright.

The wind died suddenly.

The fire embers, red a moment before, ceased to glow.

Haldane's heart stilled in anticipation. All his

life, it seemed to him, had been a mystery. He understood none of it. All that had seemed secure, seemed secure no longer, as though it had become past mystery antecedent to present mystery. And this moment was the sum of all those that had come before it. This moment he was in the presence of total mystery. He knew nothing. He was nothing. He was helpless, and he sat up, spread his arms, hands upward, and opened his mouth in gaping helplessness.

He was surrendered.

And in that instant, his heart was struck like so much ice on the anvil of a smith. And he was become Haldane again—Haldane the whirly-headed, who reserved from surrender.

For as he sat helpless, of a sudden a light but powerful grip seized his chin from behind and a finger skated over his teeth like single foot on winter ice.

"In truth, I do believe that you are marked as Mine, though I had doubted it," said a voice. It was the rich firm voice of a woman of command, like a Nestorian nurse when he was small or his mother.

In cold fear, Haldane turned to see who it was treating him so. The hair on his neck prickled. He saw a giant woman's body but One who was not a woman. He saw warts and growths and thought of the horrid snow monkeys of which Oliver had told him, and of nightmare pigs. But She was more whelming than either. She was more than he could bear.

"Are you Libera?" he asked. "Are you the one I dread?"

The Thing-Woman gobbled hideously. Haldane

looked about him, but no one roused at the sound.
All continued to lie silent and still.

If this was Libera, then this light by which he
could see Her more clearly than night should allow
was Libera's light, and this time in which all slept
but Haldane was Libera's time. The face of the
creature altered before Haldane's sight and became
such that Haldane must look away, then back, then
away again. His limbs were boneless before Her
and he disgraced himself again, bright and hot on
his leg.

"You are as artless as the flimsy cantrip you hide
under," She said. "Poor wee warrior." She laughed
or cried again, and Her various growths shook like
colored caterpillars in the wind. "You should be
abed. It is late. Come ride My horse until you sleep
and I will judge you. I will see whether you are
Mine, or whether you are yours, or whether you
are Someone Else's. Come horsie, come, give in-
fant Giles a lullaby ride."

Haldane could not even say, "I am not Giles! I
am Haldane!" His mouth would not work.

He cowered before Her. His eyes were lowered
to the ground because he could not bear the sight
of Her. He heard the sound of Her steed as it
picked its way through the camp and he feared to
look upon the beast. Its sound was clopping, seeming aimless, slowly wandering. Then it ceased. She
—Libera?—made the noise She made once again
then, as though that were the call by which She
fetched Her horse. Closer it ambled. It stopped.
Was it here? Where was it?

When Haldane could not bear waiting longer, he
looked up at Her. And when he looked at Her, She,

the great Thing-Woman, gestured to Her night-horse. She gobbled again, Her face bright blue and red in the darkness that surrounded him. But there was not the sound of hooves again. Instead, at that moment, there was hot moist breath on Haldane's neck.

He started hugely and scrambled about. Libera's horsie was limned as brightly as milk in twilight. Her steed was the great wurox cow, head lowered. It was larger than any natural animal. Libera and Her beast made Haldane feel smaller than small again, as he had when the world was huge. The wurox gazed at Haldane and looked as though she might speak. She opened her mouth and lowed. He could not bear the sound.

Libera seized him suddenly in a grip that took no account of his dignity or manliness. She whirled him through the air and set him down on the broad felt back of Her white cow. The cow shook her head. There was no purchase and Haldane felt that he was about to fall from a great height, and was frantic. He was aswim. He scrambled to help himself, but could find no help.

"You must ride around my old standing stone like thread around a spool," said Libera, She of hideous aspect. And She gestured at the rock which Haldane could suddenly see, standing like a brother by the camp.

"You must ride around it three times, and if you fall off, I will eat you alive," said She. "I would you held on tight." And She put Her face close to Haldane, showed Her white teeth in their dark red gums and made Her lures to jump and jiggle.

The cow began to step, and Haldane cried in desperation, "I cannot even ride so far," tears starting from his eyes. He was tossed like a die in a shaken cup, like a mouse by a cat, like a snowflake on the wind.

"You must ride so far," She said, "if you would be my Lover."

It was ferocious logic and Haldane could not withstand its force. He could not hold on for there was nothing to hold onto. He must be thrown. He would be devoured. He chose to be devoured, and found that when he did not strive to hold on, he did not slip. He was tossed lightly on the broad back of the white wurox as though he were a feather juggled on a coverlet. The wurox halted when they reached Libera's standing stone. But he would *not* be Libera's Lover.

Libera then said to Haldane: "You are Mine. You would have fallen and I would have ground your bones in My teeth if you were not Mine. You will love and serve Me. You were marked rightly as My child."

She touched Haldane's brow by his right eye most tenderly then, and the touch was like a wasp walking with burning feet.

"But you are not yet ripe," She said. "Now is not yet the time for you to ride alone around my standing stone. You are not yet the man to ride alone around my standing stone. But still you shall ride. I will ride with you."

She leaped onto the back of the wurox behind Haldane. And the wurox ran as no cow could run, faster than the swiftest horse, faster than a sky-catcher, faster than thought, around the tongue of stone. At this speed, Haldane could have been no feather juggled. He must have fallen. But the grip on him that held him secure and steady was no more than a fingertouch. Haldane felt Her great presence behind him as they sped so fast he could not see over distances he could not reckon.

His heart surged within him and She said, "You will not be My Lover until you deny the Gets."

They crossed great leaps. Time was forgotten.

He expanded and She said, "You will not be ripe until you deny Morca."

He was warm. He rocked.

In fullness, She said, "You will not be Giles until you deny Haldane."

Sleepily, he said, "But you know I cannot do that, Mother. I am Haldane."

The last thing he remembered was that Libera said: "When next we meet, it will be in other light." But also She gobbled once and it almost made him wake.

When Haldane did wake, it was morning, just before dawn. The air was cool and clear, and so was he himself. Birds were singing. He was sitting on a height, his back resting against a firm support, and his neck and head, too. From this comfortable seat, fields and forests were to be seen stretching below like a tapestry with a pattern, and as he saw the pattern in a burst of revelation—recognized the fact of interrelationships deliberately made—the first light of the sun swung from the heavens and made his eyes water.

Haldane was gripped by sudden awe. He didn't move. He didn't stir. As though it had been a farewell gift from the Goddess, he was able to see shape and pattern in the bones and tissues of the land, to feel power coursing like blood, where before he had only seen random trees and hills and streams. From this sudden new perspective, with this sudden new perspective, he saw design everywhere.

It was no passing idle. He could not doubt the truth of what he perceived, even though he could not comprehend it. Like an ant overcome by the majesty, design, and rectitude of his anthill, Haldane suddenly perceived that which was larger than himself.

He felt this place where he sat as a place of power. The landscape all around was molded and sculpted and channeled and directed to focus the power of the land upon this height. The power made his skin prickle. He could not doubt what he felt.

At a sound, Haldane turned to see Oliver sitting beside him, his back also against the wood of a stockade fence. Oliver—Oliver himself! short, plump, white-bearded, winter-thicketed—wore magenta satinet with many rents. He was calmly striking a light with his firepump and applying it to his clay pipe, which he puffed until it was lit as he would have it. Then he nodded to Haldane and commenced to smoke.

In that moment, Haldane realized that he was Haldane. Oliver was Oliver, and not Sailor Noll. And Haldane was not the Nestorian moonling, Giles, but himself once more as he had been before Oliver's spell.

He scrambled to his feet. He touched his head where he had been wounded and felt a great rough scab under his fingers. He looked out at the land spreading away and his heart rose and fell.

Haldane said, "I *know* that tapestry."

He unstrung the horn from around his neck.

He said, "I know this place from my dreams."

Haldane pointed to the gate against which Oliver sat, still smoking his pipe as though half-bemused. Haldane swept his arm wide and pointed to the country 'round.

"This is my grandfather Arngrim's dun!" he said. "This is Little Nail, and we are here!"

Oliver came to his feet, pipe in hand. And Haldane, the son of Black Morca, blew the horn that had been given to him by Arngrim, his mother's father, outside Arngrim's gate, announcing his presence. He blew the horn and blew it again, his heart overflowing.

And in time the gate was unbarred. It swung open, revealing the hospitality waiting within. Standing together before them were Arngrim, who was once most trusted by Garmund, and Ivor Fish-eye, that dagger man.

And Haldane knew in that moment that all that was old and familiar and true was now scattered and wasted and could not be regathered. Morca was dead, his head on a pole. Arngrim, Haldane's grandfather, was in league with Morca's enemies. And there was no haven in the world of the Gets for Haldane, Morca's son.

PART III: ENGAGEMENT

16

On a morning that was bright, cool and still as a clear teardrop of dew hanging from a spider's eye. On a hill that was higher and safer than Morca's.

Below, the pattern of land was as deliberately made as writing on the page of a book. But the pattern was visible only to one who could sense the power that the pattern gathered. Otherwise, it was invisible, unsuspect, unimaginable. And still, the power gathered in the land, as palpable as fear and hate, as imminent as catastrophe, awaiting direction, awaiting discharge.

Four men stood in a tableau vivant, two within the open gate of a dun, and two without. Even the wind did not blow, honoring the moment.

Haldane, dressed in bridegroom finery, stood poised with his horn, which was his from Arngrim's own hand. Oliver held his pipe, as though by and by to knock it against his palm, but not for now. Arngrim—who was like a silvered sword, or a falcon, or an ugly tall monkey with a large nose and eyes deep set in circles within circles —displayed no expression. Ivor, a fixed half-smile on his face, peeped around the corner of his grave-yard eye.

When this frozen moment ended, things were

not the same as they had been before. Time itself was shattered, never again to be reassembled as it was.

What outwardly happened was suddenly begun, suddenly over, and of no import in itself. That is, Ivor spoke. Haldane passed his horn from his left hand to his right, drew Marthe's black dagger, then rushed at Ivor to kill him. Arngrim, that tall powerful private old man who seemed to understand all there was to be understood, struck Haldane a terrible efficient blow that knocked him to the ground just within the gates of the dun. Then he spoke words to Haldane, and all went within to breakfast.

Outwardly, nothing was changed. Nothing was different. But after this moment all was changed in Haldane's mind. He was not the same Get he had always been, but one step along the path toward being something else, something there was no name for that he would yet accept. The Get world had no place for him. Very well, he had a glimpse of a larger and older order.

Here is the outside and inside of it:

Ivor Fish-eye unfroze his smile and spoke with the relish of a starving man watching a suckling lamb at play. He said, "Now—so soon—we begin. It is no matter now when Romund arrives with the pig."

Oliver thoughtfully tapped his pipe out on his palm. He coughed rackingly—the expectable outcome of the weight of spells he had carried so far. The cough seemed dry and forced, and more racking therefore.

For one blazing moment, Haldane hated Ivor

fiercely as he who had broken the old warm secure world, the island fortress in the Sea of Nestor, the safe near horizon. This was the last moment that Haldane still thought as a Get. In his anger and rage, he felt that the dun of Black Morca had been a glowing gem, precious and enclosing, now shattered by men like Ivor Fish-eye who had no concept of its value.

He unsheathed the thin knife with the fine black handle and rushed at Ivor with determination to kill him. While Haldane was striving to rise from the ground, Arngrim picked up the fallen knife, cleansed it of spring dirt with a finger, and made of it something to keep.

Then he said to Haldane, "By the horn you hold, and have, it seems, learned to sound, I take you to be my daughter Freda's son. If this be your main method, you will soon be dead."

It was when he heard these words that Haldane changed. He nodded his head once in assent, for it was then that he realized that he must be different than he had been.

The old world was truly shattered. The jewel could not be mended.

He was at sea, and he was bound to swim for his life in this shocking and promising universe, so vast and incredible—this universe in which everything was always new.

Later, after they had eaten, but before they had fled the dun on Little Nail, Haldane said to Oliver, to indicate what he now knew: "It is exciting and fearsome, both, to be out here where everything is always changing."

Oliver tested his cough and then said, "That's

what life is like. One thing after another. It is something you can forget when you are near a man like Morca who wraps the world around himself and holds it still."

But in that moment before breakfast, when Haldane was on his knees before Angrim, his head still ringing from Arngrim's blow, it was within this moment that Haldane woke up. In an instant of splendid clarity, for the first time since the death of Morca, Haldane knew where he was.

He was at home in the unknown.

He was no longer lost in the unknown.

It was a great difference, as different as up and down. As different as being a Get and not being a Get.

Arngrim said, "Breakfast waits. You must surely be hungry after your long journey."

It was a strange feeling. All that Haldane had ever known, all that had sustained him and given him being and definition, all this lay thrown down and broken. But he was not thrown down and broken. Through a miracle, he still continued, independent of the world that had given him birth.

As they went in for breakfast, Haldane's heart turned over at the very thought of not being a Get any more. Strange to feel joy in the midst of danger and uncertainty, so frightening and exciting. But the day was still clear and cool and sustaining, by itself giving him being. And when he shot one last look through the open gate at the message writ for him on the land, the design in the tapestry was still there like a key.

A Gettish woman, wholly unlike the Nestorian serving-women Haldane was used to, served their meal. He was taken with her braids. He allowed himself to look at her twice when to do so meant glancing away from Arngrim and Ivor. But he felt reckless and powerful.

That recklessness was still with him when he and Oliver were alone. That was in the moment before Ivor burst upon them to kill them for his own reasons.

"How is that cough of yours, Oliver?" Haldane challenged. "How are your pains?"

"I am . . . not so ill as I might be. Ill, though, mind you. What demands would you make on me?"

"We must be gone from here," Haldane said. "They are certain to kill us if we stay. There is no one in Nestor to trust, so we must leave Nestor."

"And where are we to go?" Oliver asked.

"Let us go to Palsance as you proposed before."

"Palsance . . ." said Oliver, and sighed deeply for what might await him there. Then he raised his head and said, "Let it be Palsance, then. But how are we to leave? We are in the grip of hosts, and their hospitality is strong."

Haldane nodded. With cunning certainty he said, "We must use your magic." If he was no Get, he did not mind magic.

Oliver attempted to protest, waving him away, breaking down into coughs. "How can you ask that? I can only bear so much."

"A small spell only. You once instructed me in such a spell—the Pall of Darkness. I don't ask that you magick us to Palsance. But cast a net of invisibility over us, and let us leave this place."

Haldane was strangely sure of his words. He was delighted to be in the new universe where the stuff of education—like spells—might be applied to make more newness.

But Oliver protested. He said, "No, my young friend," and patted his chest. "Lend me a hand with your strength. You cast the spell. Remember your studies with me and cast the Pall of Darkness for us."

Haldane shook his head. "It is for you to do. I cannot. I would an I could, but since I was granted justice by my father, I cannot . . ." and he gestured to show that memory and voice must fail him whenever he approached the spell.

"You cannot remember at all?" asked Oliver in amazement.

Haldane shook his head again. The passage surrounding Morca's death was still a blank to him. If this were not so, he might not have been so blithesome and so certain. He might have had questions to ask of Oliver. As it was, his very lack of memory permitted him to act, and to demand of Oliver that Oliver act.

"You must suffer another spell for us," Haldane said. "I will supply our strength and see you safe to Palsance."

"Do you swear that?" asked Oliver.

"I swear it," said Haldane, who was still Get enough to make oaths and to keep them.

That was when Ivor burst upon them.

Throughout the meal, Ivor had played them with his eye, enjoying his power. He had talked of the art of tracking with pigs, of which he was evident master. Arngrim had not interrupted him, but let him speak. Haldane and Oliver had made no comment.

Ivor talked of great hunting boars that killed redly.

Ivor talked of pigs set to hunt their masters.

Ivor talked of hunting.

Ivor talked of the minds and tricks of those who trailed and those who were trailed.

Ivor talked of his great ability to kill.

Then Haldane looked from the door closing behind the woman who had served them, and said to Ivor: "But I do not recall that you killed the wurox for which you hunted so long. Perhaps the quarry must be large enough for you to see."

"The wurox does not exist," said Ivor. "That I may tell you. It is but a peasant jest. If it had existed, your father would have eaten it for his last meal."

"You have overstepped yourself," said Arngrim.

"Your pardon, Lord Arngrim. I was in error. I will talk of hunting."

"Some other subject yet, Baron."

"I be confused," said Ivor, and hid behind his eye. When he came out, he said, "Let us talk of the meal. This is very good. Do you smoke your own meat, my lord?"

"Yes."

"When my friend Romund arrives, I'll have a small pig for your butcher. I'll return in the fall for a taste of the bacon."

And he smiled as though he had, at great risk and daring, won through to a prize. Ivor was a triumphant man.

As Ivor entered that brown room where they were with its well-carved furniture stolen before Arngrim was born, Haldane was swearing to lend his strength to Oliver. Ivor had his sword drawn.

Ivor paused but a brief moment to let them know who he was and why he had come. Then he proposed to kill them swiftly. He crossed the small dais.

Haldane did what he had never done before. He struck a new blow, made of nothing he had ever learned, filled with power, while Ivor was stumbling over Oliver's bag. The bag was suddenly there as Ivor stepped on a stair. And Haldane as suddenly struck Ivor a blow much crueler than that which Haldane had had from Arngrim. The sword clattered on stone. Ivor went wandering in night realms.

Oliver could only look on in surprise at this swift passage. Violence had always held the potential of surprise for him.

Haldane turned with the sword recovered in his hand and saw Ivor helpless.

"He would not have killed you," said Arngrim from the doorway, "for you are my daughter's son, and I would not have let him. But neither will I let you kill him, for you are the son of Black Morca and good men have seen him rightly dead, as I have report. I will not let you be killed here, but I will not let you stay here. Therefore, you must be gone. And with you, this foul wizard of Morca's. If Morca had not bargained for advantage with witches in the forest and given refuge to this man, then he might still be alive at this moment. I would have let my voice be heard. But I do not like magic. And you, my daughter's son, smell of magic. You are like your father. You are not Gettish."

Arngrim stood waiting, sword in hand. Haldane

did not look up at him, but rather at Ivor.

He said, "I must kill this man."

Arngrim said, "Bind him. He will not be found immediately. I've seen that your bellies are full. I will see you out the gate of the dun and three hours on your road. You must run for your lives."

So Haldane bound Ivor. He used the cord that he had from Rolf on the night of his betrothal. It occurred to Haldane to wonder how Princess Marthe fared in this universe where everything was new. He used the rawhide thong from his horn to bind Ivor's knees together. He gagged Ivor's mouth with a dried fish from the breakfast table that he had brought away to chew on.

"Leave the sword," said Arngrim. "You must rely on your magic, since you stand to die for it."

"I will leave the sword and I will rely on my magic," said Haldane. He stood before Arngrim who was still two steps above him on the dais. "I am not a Get, as you say. But you are my grandfather and I would lay eyes on you again. Take this from my hands."

He held out the horn which Arngrim had given him so long ago when his mother was alive and they had come here to Little Nail. At the sight, Arngrim looked downward at his feet.

"Your rebuke is sharp," he said. "I do what I must, not always what I would like."

"It is no rebuke," Haldane said, and laughed strangely. "Or take it as a rebuke if you want, Grandfather."

He was not the same person any more. He was not like Arngrim. He could do what he liked. He did not know what that was exactly. He did what he did and said what he said, and surprised himself.

Haldane said, "But no, I say, take this horn from my hands and keep it close until I return here. Someday, perhaps, when you have forgotten me, I will pay you a visit."

Arngrim could only think Haldane's words to be boyish bravado, spoken by one who did not fully appreciate his situation. The old man shrugged his shoulders and shook his head, as though his life was drowned in the bitter tide of iron fate, and he was resigned. He took back the horn he had once given to his only grandson, the last of his line, whom he had condemned to die.

"Do you know the sound of this horn?" he asked. "Do you know its voice?"

"Yes," Haldane said. "I do know the sound of that horn."

Arngrim said, "When your chief hunter is unbound, he will blow his hunting calls on this horn. I will place it in his hands. And when you are dead, I will see that this horn is buried with you."

Arngrim's world and Haldane's world might once have been the same, but they were the same no longer. Haldane heard Arngrim speak and did not lose his strange new certainty. He answered the old man in plain words, straightly spoken.

"That would be honor if I were still a Get," said Haldane. "But I am not a Get now. When I am gone away and your huntsman returns your horn to you, keep it close until I come again. I will see you by and by."

How strange and foolish of Haldane not to know that he was dead! Arngrim would not feed this folly further.

"I will escort you to the gate," said Arngrim.

"There is no need," said Haldane. "We will find our own exits with our magic power."

"No magic here!" Arngrim said. "I will not allow it."

But Haldane made signal to Oliver to draw the Pall of Darkness over them. That was not a necessary act, since Arngrim would have seen them out, but Haldane wanted to demonstrate his otherness to his grandfather.

And Oliver obeyed him. It may have been because Haldane had sworn to lead him to Palsance. Perhaps it was because he had been unsettled by the sudden violence and wanted to match its surprise and power with surprise and power of his own. But Oliver did obey.

He cast his spell. Haldane and Oliver became invisible before Arngrim and stole out of the dun on Little Nail unseen.

The trail down from Little Nail to the Pellardy Road was tortuous and difficult. Before they reached the bottom of the hill, they encountered a man on horseback riding up.

Mortal eyes might not see them, so Haldane and Oliver did not hide. They but stood to the side to let the rider pass.

He was one they recognized. His name was Coughing Romund and he was a baron who had not liked Morca, for he was chief among the Farthing and could not like he who was chief among the Deldring. His face was narrow and he had cheekbones sharp as axes. A gaunt man, but his lean limbs were powerful. He wore shellacked leather armor.

His horse climbed at a steady pace. As it climbed, Romund coughed insistently.

Before Romund on the saddle was a black pig. Haldane knew it. It was Slut, that he was used to hunt with. As the rider passed, the little black pig raised its nose and sniffed the air urgently. Then it squealed and wriggled to be free.

Romund held it in place, but to do that he must pull his horse to a halt. Haldane and Oliver ran down the trail, for they knew that the pig smelled their presence.

At first bend, Haldane turned to cast a last look behind.

He slipped then, and landed on his behind. But he looked back to see Romund setting the pig down. It squealed and looked about uncertainly, and then Haldane was down the trail in a new surprise of rock. And Slut was left somewhere behind them.

17

They did not hear the horn that day.

They ran along the Pellardy Road until the Pall of Darkness failed. Then they were themselves.

Oliver was an old wizard, sadly out of breath. He carried his sack. Things from it had been left behind and the sack was lighter than it had been at other times. Oliver wore magenta satinet and could be seen at a distance. He felt himself conspicuous.

Haldane had only his bridegroom clothes, which had once been new and fine Gettish clothes, but were not new anymore. He had no weapons. His pockets were empty. All that he had which was especially his was a boar's tooth with Deldring markings that Morca had encouraged him to wear to remember the boar, and Deldring, and other things.

"We cannot stay here on the road," said Oliver. "We will be seen. But if we hide, they will find us. They will put that little pig on our trail. You heard what Ivor said of trails and hunts. What are we to do?"

Haldane said, "We will go inside the country. We will not follow the roads, but we will go by other ways."

"What other ways?" asked Oliver.

"The ways in the country."

"I do not know what you mean."

"There," said Haldane, and pointed to nothing in the land. "Don't you see the path?"

"No," said Oliver. "But we cannot stay here on the road. If you see a path, lead us on it."

Haldane led the way. They left the road, brushed through brown grass and then were on a way that Haldane could see and Oliver could not. Oliver followed where Haldane walked, and he did not suffer as much as he had anticipated from his spell compounded, his Pall of Darkness.

There were some signs by which Oliver could see that a way did exist. At times they walked in forest galleries, places that only now seemed made. Sometimes they walked in lanes between fields. Three times they passed by standing stones like that in the camp of Duke Girard. Once they came to a ring of stones.

But Oliver did not know how the way was found. He could not see how Haldane knew when to walk here and when to walk there, nor how he found the confidence that the way would be here when he walked here and there when he walked there.

They stopped to rest at the ring of stones.

"I wonder if three hours have passed?" said Oliver. "No matter. There are Gets all over this countryside, everywhere between here and the Trenoth. So Mainard, the friend of Duke Girard, said. We are in grave straits."

Oliver coughed, a dry cough. He forced it again.

"Did you see that I forbore to cough when Romund coughed? Not even a clearing of my throat. I think that was well-done. If we had not been invisible, we might have met Coughing Romund and been killed."

But after a minute, Haldane said, "If we had not been invisible, we might not have met Coughing Romund."

A bird sang intensely nearby. The sun was pleasantly warm on them.

"Everything is always so new!" Haldane said, marveling. "Do you sense what it is like . . . *now.*" He pounced on the moment and missed, and smiled at the fun in his folly.

Then Haldane said, "What was that that I said?"

"I don't know," said Oliver. "What did you say?"

"It seems to me now that it was important," said Haldane.

Oliver felt obliged to say something important then. "I will tell you this," he said. "We may be better off going this way than by the roads, but unless we change these clothes we wear, we will not be safe. If anyone sees us, we will have no chance to lie about ourselves."

"No. That was not the important thing I thought I said."

Soon Haldane led the way again. The country spoke to him and he listened to it. The way was open to him.

It was as though it was this way:

Once upon a time, men had taken a large landscape and remade it into a mirror.

Or, once men had made the western world into an engine, aligning the land so that power was gathered and loosed.

Or, once men had taken mountains and moved

them, had put land in place and taken it away, so that a country that in a later day would make an empire was but a map of a greater world, copied in miniature. Alterations so immense that the play of children might destroy villages and let bridges tumble but never disturb the great meaningful permanence.

The land of Nestor—and who knew how much more?—was a pattern, a written book. It was a fabrication beyond the mind of a Get to admit possible, even to notice.

Haldane did not know the meaning of the writing. But he knew that it existed and he could follow it with his feet. Inside the land. Not the roads and the places where men now gathered.

He laughed. He said, "Children. It's all so large. I hadn't thought it would be so large."

But he could not explain what he sensed to Oliver. It was as sealed as the spell he had once known and could not now utter. He didn't know the words. He could only lead the way across the countryside by routes that were not the routes of Gets or peasants or outlaws.

For instance, he said, "Was Little Nail made? Were all the hills made?" And Oliver could only shrug, gesture and cough. There were no answers in Oliver.

But Haldane did not doubt that he could now see madeness everywhere in the land. He could see his way markers and the path was not hard.

Haldane led the way by paths along water, through marks in distant vantages, in forest cathedrals. The day was timeless and golden. They met no one. They saw wildlife, and groups of birds flew overhead. Twice they heard voices calling or crying, but they saw no one and hurried on. They were in a country unknown to any but them. To Haldane it was constant surprise, the constant revelation of existence.

Oliver said, "They will have put your small pig on our trail. They must now be after us."

"Can you keep the pace?" asked Haldane.

". . .Yes," Oliver said in wonder. "I know not the source of my strength, but I can keep this pace. I do not yet feel the full weight of the Pall of Darkness."

And in the course of the day, these two walked farther together than they ever had any other day. It was a fine day for walking. Everything was large and old and part of itself here where they walked and neither Haldane, nor Oliver for all his travels, had been inside the country before. They had lived on high made places, and ridden in long made places, and swum in soft made places, and eaten their picnics in the shade of hard made places—but they had not been inside the country before.

Oliver followed Haldane blindly. His feet stepped where Haldane's feet stepped, and found a safe and easy way. But Oliver felt conspicuous. He was sure that he could be seen. His magenta satinet was an unnatural display in this wilderness they walked, and would surely be perceived.

He fretted. He had worn red wool in Morca's Dun, and on great occasions magenta, but when he had fled from Palsance to find Morca, he had worn gray so that he might not call attention to himself.

Haldane was calmer, striding along as though he were still invisible, stepping with the unconscious sure foot of a sleepwalker. Almost as though bound in a trance. As though he led them safely and surely by constant concentration that withheld the outside world.

They stopped at dusk. In late evenglow they shared a dried fish like the one that Haldane had left for Ivor to chew on.

Haldane's state of mind changed then. He began to think and even to remember a little that he had forgotten. As he did, without his quite noticing, some of his inner sense of certainty slipped away from him.

"There is something that we need to do," said Oliver.

"What is that?"

"We must disguise ourselves. I cannot chance another spell. We must buy, take or make simple clothes for ourselves. We must be Nestorians without the aid of spells. We must lie and pass for peasants."

Haldane shook his head. "I don't like it. I don't think we should turn aside, but make straight away for Palsance."

Oliver said, "Do you remember the manner of our arrival at Arngrim's Dun?"

"Yes," said Haldane. It was not something that he would forget lightly. Though he did not quite remember how Oliver had arrived.

"As we labored the slope in the last of night, we were passed on the trail by a greasy Nestorian abroad on some bad business or other. He saw in us two like himself and gave us the go by."

"Yes," said Haldane, though he did not remember things quite this way.

"If we had been dressed then as we are now, he

would not have. Nay, he would have killed us, or sold us. Dressed as we are, we must be victims to anyone we meet. Dressed as we are, how can we win through to Palsance? And when we do arrive in Palsance, how can we appear thus? We must surely pass for peasants then."

"All right," said Haldane. "If we see a place along our way where we may disguise ourselves, we will stop."

"Good," said Oliver. "Before we halted for the night, I saw smoke rising against the late green of the southern sky like ink in water. Let us pass that way when we rise."

"I don't think the way we follow leads south," Haldane said.

"It is not far. It is but over the next hill or so. It will not take us long. We will go to that place in the morning and steal clothes to disguise ourselves. Then we can pass on to Palsance."

"I would rather press on directly," said Haldane. "I don't want to stop. I don't want to turn."

Oliver said, "If there is one thing I know, it is that haste ends many men's lives. I have seen it to happen. We will rest easier and travel faster when we have assurance that we will not be recognized from afar by anyone who spies us. We have no weapons. We have no power. We must make the best of our chances."

"No," said Haldane.

"You said you would give me aid. You swore to see me safe to Palsance," said Oliver. He coughed awfully to show Haldane's responsibility for him. "Does your oath mean nothing? Give me the aid you promised."

In that late evening mood that had seized him,

Haldane was still Haldane enough to be vulnerable to this questioning of his oath.

"All right," he said. "Enough. I will aid you. We will steal simple clothes in the morning, if we can. Now let us sleep."

He lay back in the nest of cool grass he had made for himself.

Sometime later, Haldane said, "What was that?"

Oliver stirred. "What?"

"Just as the gloom finally darkened, I thought I heard a horn sound."

Oliver said, "I did not hear it."

18

When they awoke in the morning, the day was uncertain, neither one thing or another. The skies were thin and gray. The trees around them huddled close.

Oliver said, "We must go over this intervening hill. I think we will see the source of smoke then."

They left the path and struck out overland against the grain of the country. The climbing was not difficult, but it was a constant strain. They must lean, or they must bend, or they must clamber. Oliver was feeling wearied before they reached the top of the hill, and his cough was more fluid and less forced, but not less severe.

At the crest of the hill, they stopped. There was a higher crest, hidden from below, still looming above them. And they could see where they had started down on the path.

"Let us climb on," said Oliver.

"When you have caught your breath."

"Let us not wait that long."

This hill was more steep. To climb it took thought and time. When they reached the top of this hill, there was brush and they must push through it.

When they came into the clear, they could see that though the day had worn on, it was not different. It played at smiling and frowning, Jan, the sun, peeping through distantly. There was no source of smoke, no house or cabin.

"Oh, I think I see," said Oliver. "From the direction we came last night, the place we seek would be beyond this lower hill before us, not here. We must go on."

But his cough was much graver. He shook off Haldane's hand and strode down the hillside. "You see. The slope is easier here."

In time they came beyond the farther lower hill. As they looked over into a little glen, Jan shone brightly so that all was clear in the narrow valley. And they saw there a small house in the woods, a Nestorian house something like the one where they had eaten clams. It stood alone in the silent morning, caught in the spear of the sun.

They were not in sunlight where they watched.

Oliver suddenly sat down. "You must go," he said. "I now feel very ill. I will wait here for you."

"What if I do not find what I seek? What do I say to gain aid? What do I use for payment?"

"Approach the house naked. Approach silently. See what opportunities there are to steal clothes. If you are seen, ask them to clothe you, because you are naked."

"I will do it," said Haldane.

Haldane stripped his clothes off his back. He took off his boots so that he was barefoot. All that he wore was his boar's tooth.

Then he set off to find the hut they had seen. His bare feet were cold and he had to watch carefully where he stepped. He made his way cautiously so as to approach the little house unseen and unheard.

With so much care, he spent a long time reaching a place from which he could see all.

He looked up at the hillside, which was now in sun, then not. He could not see Oliver hid there.

There was no sun here in the little valley. The day was drear again.

The house sat silent the throw of a stone distant. It was a square little house. Its roof was shake instead of thatch. It had windows of glass like eyes, and it seemed to brood and watch Haldane as he crouched.

Behind the house, a frayed rope was stretched between two trees. Thrown over the line, as though forgot, were two gray smocks.

Haldane had not thought to hope for such a thing. His heart was seized at the sight of the two smocks drying in the wind.

He cast a look at the house, but he could see nobody. He crawled on hands and knees over the cold spring ground. He sheltered by the chimney of the little house and then he ran to the line and took the smocks. In a brief fit of nonsense, he matched the smocks and took the longer and put it on. It fit as well as most smocks on most peasants. But it was clean, and in the undecided weather of a late morning he stood and smelled the freshness of the cloth while his hair was teased by the ruffling hand of the wind.

He could not stand not to know, so he ran with the other smock trailing behind him from his hand and looked through the window of the house. He could see no one inside.

Haldane rubbed at the window and looked to see better. The house was empty. But Haldane could

tell by the angle of the light that came through the
farther windows and made a sharp splash on the
floor that it was summer within the house. The
light he saw said that it was very hot and that the
house was a pleasant refuge from the sun. Haldane
saw dust motes swimming in the bright sun. On a
table within the house, there was an earthenware
pitcher and beside it there were two jacks. The
pitcher was somehow so cold that it sweated.

Haldane felt thirsty from the brilliance of the
sun, the heat that had dried his throat. He looked
from the window to find a door so that he might
drink from the pitcher. But when he looked, it was
Bud-Month again. It was cool and windy, and Jan
played rare tricks with the great clouds. There was
no sun now.

He ran from the house, feeling its windows like
eyes on his back. He did not want to linger here.
He feared the return of the unknown owner of this
place. His throat was still dry, but he no longer
craved to drink from the pitcher.

He scrambled up the slope, the second gray
smock over his shoulder. His bare feet slipped and
scrabbled in the leaves and loose brown mold. He
hurt the outside edge of his left foot stepping on a
weathering branch stub hidden among the leaves
so that there was small blood and he was limping
when he came to Oliver.

He threw the gray smock down. "There is your
smock," he said. "You may be a peasant now."

Oliver was sick. When he did not cough, he was
aswim in nausea and weakness. It seemed that the
climb they had made had brought on sevenfold the

effects of the spell that Oliver had ignored as they walked yesterday.

"You have done well," Oliver said at last. He slowly took off his magenta satinet, sweating and shivering in the coolness of the day. "How did you deal with those at the house?"

Haldane sat to put his boots on once again. "No," said Oliver. "If we are to be peasants, we must be peasants. We must go barefoot."

And lay wracked with the sick swirl of his innards.

Haldane said, "The house was empty."

He looked at the cut on his foot, small, bloody and dirty.

"You must bear the pain as though you were a Get," said Oliver. For Gets do have virtues—they bear pain bravely.

The gray smock did not fit Oliver well, but it did fit him as it might fit a Nestorian.

"Do I make a peasant?" Oliver asked.

They were slow in ascending the slope that had seemed easy when they had come down it. Haldane had to aid Oliver when his sickness was upon him.

"It was as well that we stole these clothes," said Oliver. "The longer we are in Nestor, the more need we have of disguise. As I am feeling now, we will be a long time in Nestor."

They had to push through the brush again, and only at last came to the farther side of the great hill.

"The path is just below," said Haldane. "It is but two courses down the hillside."

But Oliver was not encouraged by these words. He stopped to rest and be sick. He vomited there in the leaves. It was conspicuous, but less conspicuous than magenta satinet.

"I will go spy our way," said Haldane.

He made his way down the slope. Before him was the last smaller hill hiding the path. As he came to its crest and a view of the way they had come yesterday, there was sudden wringle-jingle in the forest. He fell to the ground and peeped to see the riders.

First he saw a small black pig. It scented briskly and then trotted eagerly the last distance to where they had made their camp.

Behind the pig came three riders riding. The first of these was Ivor Fish-eye, casting close behind the pig, alert for the dodges of those who would flee him. Behind Ivor was Coughing Romund. He leaned on his saddle and cleared his throat. And third was another rider like a spear. When the pig found the camp, this one lifted a horn to his lips and blew.

He blew, *They were here, they were here*. It was the call of a hunter of man, not of game.

The call was none that Haldane had ever blown. And it was not Haldane who blew this horn. But he knew the tone of this horn as his fingers knew the texture of his graven boar's tooth. It was the horn that had been his, now in the hands of his hunters.

Slut whuffled and peered dimly.

Haldane slipped back out of sight of the camp and the path. He tumbled over his feet as the horn sounded again, out of sight behind his shoulder.

Then he climbed the hill faster than before. He did not mind what happened to his feet, hurt them, and ignored the hurt.

He came upon Oliver standing and gazing urgently down the hill. Oliver's disguise was successful. He was the very image of a sick and unhappy peasant.

Oliver said, "Did you see who blew the horn?"

"I did see. I saw that and more. There was the pig, Slut. And behind the pig there were three riders. There was Ivor Fish-eye, and there was Coughing Romund, and sounding the horn as they came was Iron Arngrim."

"Where did you see them? How close do they press us?"

"They are not far. They dismount now in our camp of last night. We cannot return to our path. We must go otherwise."

Oliver said, "Let us go along the hill here. You shall confuse our trail as we go to slow pursuit. Then, when we can, we may find your easier path."

This was bravery for Oliver to offer. Here he was, sick and continuing sick. The country that lay before them to the west was cross-grained and difficult. Yet one of Oliver's virtues was perseverance, his dogged ability to continue. So they worked west and south, and west and north, and west and east and west, running when they could, sometimes crawling or climbing. They turned on their trail. They walked in water. They went where a horse might not go. They went where a pig might go only with great difficulty and left the trail there where a pig could not.

They did not hear the horn blow. They labored in fear of its sound. And though Haldane saw many signs that the country here was made, he saw no way inside the country.

Oliver lay in a hollow of grass. His legs were pulled tight and he rocked and nursed his side. Haldane came dashing in to earth beside him like a field rabbit to its hole.

Haldane said, "I emptied your yellow smoking mixture on the false trail. I pity the pig that finds it."

He tumbled over to take heaving breaths. He watched the clouds blow by in wisps and clots. The world he saw as he looked to the sky was silent. The air was so very quiet. One could stay still and nothing would be new but the changing clouds and the brooding and flighting of his heart.

"How do you fare?" he asked Oliver.

"I can . . . continue."

"Let us continue then," Haldane said. "For if I am right, then I see a way before us into the country."

Oliver ran, holding his side. Haldane ran, carrying Oliver's bag.

"Here is the path. Follow me."

They ran down the path. The earth was cool and soothing to their burning, broken, bleeding feet.

But it was dark on the path. The clouds gathered close overhead, and the sun ceased to show itself.

"What was that?" said Haldane, as they two suddenly stopped.

"I think it was a man by that standing stone."

"Nay, I meant that which I heard behind us."

"I did not hear anything."

"Then listen." With peeps from hiding at the man before them by the standing stone in their way, they looked away again at nothing and listened, hardly daring to pant.

"I do hear," said Oliver. "It is the horn. But that was not where we were."

"No," said Haldane. "It is on the path behind us."

"I cannot go farther," Oliver said. "You must leave me here to die from this one who waits or from Arngrim and Ivor."

"Nay, I swore I would help you and I must be honest. Who is this one ahead whom we must pass?"

"I make it to be a Get."

Haldane studied for what he could see through the trees that intervened. It was a Get standing like a bear with a bow and an arrow set to his string.

"It is a Get, but I do not know him."

"What are we to do?"

Haldane said, "I will go forward and let him see me and I will see what he will say. It may be that I can open our way."

Oliver rested his head against a tree there where he sat. He could not seem to catch his breath. It was unpleasant to see him labor.

He said, "What if we are separated? I do not know the way."

Haldane said, "If we are separated, follow the path straight to the great hill."

"What hill is this?"

"We saw its rough presence to the west where we rested last."

"I cannot follow your path," Oliver said.

"But it is the straightest way."

"I cannot see it to follow. Let me have my map."

The horn sounded: *On the trail, on the trail.*

Oliver said, "It is here. Barrow Hill. It stands

alone. I will follow my map and meet you there if
we are parted."

So Haldane walked forward along the path to
the standing stone. As he came close, the Get
stepped forward to meet him.

"Where are you from, young boy? Where are
you going?"

"I am returning from a visit to my mother who
is ill."

Haldane was dressed after the manner of a
simple peasant. There was nothing about him that
was not simple, for all he wore was a gray smock.
His feet were bare. He had nothing in his pockets.
He had no pockets. He spoke with humility, as no
Get might speak. He had nothing to fear.

The Get, who looked like a bear, said, "Come
with me. I need your strength."

So Haldane followed behind him to the large
standing stone. There the Get set his bow down
and motioned Haldane to go before him.

"Add your weight to mine," he said. "I wish to
overset this rock."

So Haldane joined him and together they put
their shoulders to the rock and pushed against its
hardness. They heaved and strained and only at
last they paused for breath.

The Get said, "This land is mine and I will clear
it as I like. This boulder must go. Push again."

Again, they pushed as though they were oxen,
dumbly as oxen. But the rock resisted them
without effort and remained as it was.

"If you but knew how to make the lift, we could
have this rock up and out of the ground. You are
not trying. All you peasants are alike. No, do not

hide your laugh. Heave again with all your strength."

So Haldane bent himself to the cool rock, wondering how easily it had been set in place. Straining and red, he was a parody of the Get, as the Get was a parody of him. He could see his own sweat mirrored on the Get's brow.

"We aren't even holding our own," cried the Get. "Give it a turn."

And then suddenly, for one brief moment before it surprised them and then fell back, the tall boulder came alive in their hands and strained free of the ground. It was like touching the great beast of the sea in its questing aliveness.

But then the rock was seated as firmly as it had ever been, and no two men could dream to move it. The Get turned to Haldane and before he could make protest, the bear man fingered the thong around his neck.

"Let me see what you wear. Let me know whose dog you are."

But Haldane pulled away. He would not have the Get see his tooth with the Deldring markings. He did not know any Get to trust with his final secrets.

Haldane seized the thong and pulled free. He ran into the forest. An arrow was loosed behind him and struck in a tree very near.

Haldane ran away into the forest. The Get ran after him, and thereby the way was made clear for Oliver to follow his map along the second straightest route to the solitary hill. For they were now separated and they must meet as they had agreed.

Haldane dodged as he could. He pulled the rawhide thong from around his neck. On the thong was a carved boar's tooth with the markings of Deldring, a clan that did not now exist.

Here is how it was for Haldane:

When he was safe with Morca, he had known who he was. He was Haldane, the Son of Black Morca. He was a Get. And in his heart he believed that he was special among Gets because he was Haldane, the One Son of Black Morca.

He had lived as these things when it was easy to live as these things—held safe by Morca, straining against Morca's horizons but not defying them. When at last he did defy these limits, the world had changed and become always new.

Was he, Haldane, responsible for the Night of Slaughter? Or were there other wills at work, too? Was he to blame for Morca's death?

He and Oliver had fled into a strange world where it was pain and confusion to be what he had been: Haldane the Get, Haldane the Son of Black Morca. The tighter that he held to these things, the worse the whirl, until at last he had lost himself at the feet of Duke Girard the Outlaw and Sailor Noll.

The Goddess in his dream had told him that he need no longer be a Get, and set him down on Little Nail. She had shown him the key in the land. And after Haldane had seen Arngrim and Ivor together there was that strange moment when he had ceased to be a Get.

Since that time, he had not acted like a Get. He had been different than any Get.

The world had continued strange, both wonderful and frightening. He fit it better—he was not so fuddled—but not yet was he fully at home here— no matter what he had first leaped to think after he saw the key in the landscape.

He had ceased to be a Get, but he had not yet surrendered Haldane, the Son of Black Morca. He had continued to wear the boar's tooth. It did not mean Deldring to him. It meant Black Morca, me, us, my father, the father, the king, the tyrant, the rider, the mother-killer, the thief, the liar, the emperor, the sun, the universe, himself.

As he ran, Haldane swung the thong with the boar's tooth, and as he dodged away, he wrapped the thong with a neat throw around a tree limb above the eyes of those who might pass. And he ran into the forest, between trees, across a clear place.

The Get came into the clear place, lumbering straight, arrow nocked on string. He called Haldane to hold.

And Haldane, who knew somewhat of the skill of Get bowmen, held. The Get approached close and backed Haldane step by step to a tree. He fingered at Haldane's neck and found nothing there, then pulled the smock down to bare Haldane's shoulder.

The clouds gathered close overhead began to rumble.

"What is your name?" the Get asked.

"Giles," said Haldane.

"I don't believe that you are returning from a visit to your mother, Giles. I think you are a runaway. Since you wear no brand now, you shall wear my mark, Giles. How like you that, Giles?"

19

It began to rain in the late afternoon which was premature night. The back of the pen, this close-barred wooden cage, was less wet, so the three waiting to be branded crouched there in the dimness and waited.

There was a lost man, a warty-faced babe of middle years. He would say nothing but, "I am lost. Where am I? I am lost. If someone would explain, I would try to understand. But I am so lost."

There was a boy younger than Haldane. He said, "There is true freedom in being a serf. That is why I sought so long and skillfully to wear Lyulf's mark."

And there was Haldane.

It hardly seemed possible to Haldane that this was yet that same day. Since Oliver and he had set out this morning up the hill, this day had seemed like many days. As yesterday had also been many days.

It was long ago that he had given the horn back to Arngrim. Then he was not a Get. But he was still Black Morca's son. He had thought then that though he was not a Get, he would still overspread the West and seize it all, from South Cape to the Hook, from Orkay to Grelland. Chastain, Palsance and Vilicea. From Lake Lamorne to the sea. He would show them who he was. He would show them all who had been hurt!

One day he would meet Arngrim when he, Morca's son, had men at his back who followed him for choice. On that day, he would give Arngrim, who was the best of all the Gets there were, the choice of becoming other than a Get, or dying than rather. That is why it seemed right that Arngrim should carry the horn and blow it rather than waiting for the empty-handed huntsman to bring the horn back to him.

For Haldane had no doubt that the son of Black Morca could pass safely into Palsance. He could grow great in strength there and return again to Nestor. He could build a maelstrom. He knew that he had the power.

He might not have run from the Get. He might not have thrown the boar's tooth away. He might have said, "Haldane, son of Black Morca," to the Get instead of "Giles." If he had been fearless.

If he had been the son of Black Morca.

But he had not been fearless in the name of Morca.

Who was he? Whose dog was he? Whose name was he fearless in?

The Get came to the cage then and took the lost man away. While he was gone, the boy said, "I only wish I knew beforehand what it is like to be branded."

Haldane did not want to be branded. He hated the thought. What Get could be branded and live? Arngrim, perhaps. But Black Morca, who was more than Arngrim, could not be branded and be

Morca. And Haldane could not be branded and be the son of Black Morca. No man with a brand on his shoulder, and so marred, could be followed from choice by a maelstrom.

Haldane thought that he might escape when the Get should bring the lost man back and take away the boy. If he could but remember the spell that once he had learned from Oliver, the Pall of Darkness that Oliver had cast over them at Arngrim's. Then when the door was open, he might slip away unseen to find Oliver on Barrow Hill. He still might have his whirlwind and his empire.

It was his if he could think of the spell. And that should be possible. Sometimes as he had hunted in the afternoon, when he was drowsy, the words would come back to him and he would almost be invisible. He should be able to recall now when it was of moment to remember.

But the spell would not reveal itself to him no matter how he strove to approach it. It hid from him. He coaxed. He laid in wait for it. He mumbled to it of Oliver and the way he used to teach. But the spell would not let itself be caught. The rain continued.

The door of the pen opened. The man was returned, and the boy taken.

"Are you ready for my private mark?" Lyulf asked. "Boy, you are so young."

"I am ready to prove myself! Is your iron hot?"

Then the pen was closed after them. The lost man sat, his smock pulled tight over his brand, as though he would not let Haldane see the mark. He did not speak, he did not babble as before. But he

stared directly at Haldane with knowing eyes. He
had a secret in his mind and he held it close and
looked at Haldane. Haldane could not tell why.
Did the man hold the secret so that Haldane might
not have it? Or did he wish to tell the secret—if
only Haldane could read faces as he could read this
great arrangement of country that most men only
knew as lice know kings, with intimate ignorance.

This place, this very place, he knew, was an old
place, older than Haldane, or Morca, or the Gets,
or the Empire of Nestria, or the long-ago Prince
Jehannes who came of Bary. It was older than
story.

Just so had it been here: A house. A stable and
smithy. Even this pen. That had been here too.
Waiting for Haldane forever so that this moment
might be. Haldane felt certain of that from signs.

But the man said nothing to Haldane, and
flickered his eyes away when Haldane opened his
mouth to speak, so that Haldane must say nothing.
Then the man who had been lost stared at him
again with his secret until the door opened.

It was the boy, unconscious. Haldane helped to
carry him into the pen. But the Get then pulled
Haldane away by the shoulder, jostling him, not
allowing his feet firm purchase.

"Come along, Giles. You have hung back long
enough. I must see what you are made of."

The rain dripped on Haldane's neck as they entered the stable. It was warm there from the heat of
the animals. The air was pleasant with the smell of
manure.

The building glowed with the light from the
smithy fire. Shadows flickered on the wall.

Haldane could hear the sound the animals made as they shifted place. He could hear the hiss of late afternoon rain in the thatch. He could hear the separate sound of the drizzle of the rain in the yard. And he could hear the drip drip from the eaves before the door.

This moment was immediate. All the world was gathered here in this little building, expressing presence in the feel of the air, and the smell of the air, and the taste of the air, and the various sounds. The sag of two posts, one this way, one that. The mustiness of straw. That it was late afternoon was token that all rightness should be gathered in dark late afternoon.

Even the smell of burnt flesh that lingered was late afternoon, and now, and very much of this thisness.

The Get took Haldane into the smithy. Against the wall was a framework of wood and leather.

"Kneel down on that," said the Get. "Place yourself in yon mother's arms."

Haldane took his place on the frame. It held him comfortable but helpless, his arms around the wooden bar, his cheek laid against leather that was surprisingly cool. It made him think of the pitcher that sweated in the summer house.

The Get moved to his fire and Haldane could hear the sound of bellows working, the clank of metal, and at last the hiss of an iron being tested in water.

The Get came back to Haldane and without warning pulled his smock down so that his shoulder was naked to the air. Then he touched Haldane with cold wet fingers. Haldane waited for the sizzle of flesh, but it hardly hurt.

"It is a great test you are facing," the Get said to Haldane. "Have you strength to face it, boy? Or should I knock you insensible as I did the last one?"

"I know not," Haldane said. Into the leather he said, "I would flee you and not be branded." He spoke in Nestorian.

"But, Giles, you must be branded," said the Get in Gettish, and rumpled Haldane's hair fondly. "Hold your chief strength in mind, and leap with it when the iron strikes. Only then will you live."

Haldane could hear the even pace of a horse walking in the yard beyond the sounds of rain. The Get ceased to rattle his ironware. He walked to the door. There was silence then.

Haldane lay helpless in the arms of the kneeler. He might struggle to his feet. He might strive to break the machine with the strength of his arms. Or he might lie as he was and be branded.

Then Haldane heard the sound of a cough, deep, rough and gaunt. Was it asking a question?

The Get said, "Is your nose stopped? Branding serfs."

The cough again.

"And why should I answer the questions of one like you, Romund, who was never a friend of my clan?"

The cough, scratched and hoarse, said: "Because Black Morca is dead and you Deldrings have no friends, Lyulf."

"Is Morca dead, then? And who could kill a man who was as much as Morca? Tell me that."

"Many men might have killed Morca, but it was

I, and Egil Two-Fist, and Ivor Fish-eye, and others!"

There was the sound of force against force, the panting of breath, and then a rattle and thump.

Romund said, "I will stand inside. I have been in the saddle from one Libera's Day to the next, and from that one to this. I have been eight days on the trail of the cub of dead Morca to see him dead, too, much of that in rain. I will stand where it is dry until it is time for me to leave. Shall I kill you, Lyulf?"

"Carry your quarrels elsewhere than me," the Get said.

"But you are a Deldring, and you are loyal to your Deldring master—Morca, sprung of Deldring Garmund."

"Who says this is cause to fight?"

"I say it. I, Romund, who am Farthing. What say you, Deldring?"

"I say, yes, that I am a Deldring. And if the son of Black Morca should come to me, then I would aid him as I could against you and all Farthings. But I have not seen him. So ride on, Romund." There was the clank of iron. "Ride on, unless you would fight."

"Nay," said Romund. "I will not try to kill you now. I would not wear your brand by accident, Lyulf. Men would not understand. When you are armed with other weapons, we will meet again. Mayhap we will meet at the Storthing."

There was the sound of one moving sideways in the straw.

"Who is this?" Romund asked, and touched

Haldane's bare shoulder with a hand like dry nettles or snakebite.

"It is a serf I brand as my own. Do not stand between us or you may wear his mark."

"No, I will not. I will go back to my divided trail. I will hunt Morca's Get until that boy is dead. I will hold night and day to his trail in my slow steadiness and the son of Morca will be as nothing as your old dreams of Morca who was, and now is not."

There was silence. Haldane could not hear the Get Lyulf. There was rain. There was dancing shadowplay. There were the warm animals in the darkness of the stable.

Then he heard the horse move slowly on through the yard. At last gone. At last only the sound of rain again.

Haldane lay cradled in the arms of the kneeler, trying to recall his chief strength.

Lyulf worked at his fire.

Haldane smelled hot metal.

Fingers fumbled at his neck and his heart was suspended. His shoulder was gripped. And then something so cold that it penetrated his entire being, bowled his heart over like a swollen stream after the early melt of winter, the opposite of expectation, the pain of pains that cracked him apart, the great cold burning of flesh, *that* touched Haldane.

He must ride the kneeler as helpless as the great white back of the wurox. He floated in that which passed his understanding.

He was now no son of Black Morca. Who would

believe that he was? Morca's Son could not wear the private mark of a Get burnt in his flesh. The choice had been his. When Lyulf had approached with his iron, he might still have announced himself Haldane, the son of Black Morca. And if he had, the maelstrom and the empire would have been his. But he had passed that binding and loosing by.

He could not live Morca's dream. He was a branded man, and the one who would live Morca's dreams would not wear the private mark of anyone burnt in his flesh.

He was someone else.

20

Haldane sat in the darkness of the pen. The rain had stopped and the early night was fresh-made. The air was cold. The clouds were broken. Haldane's shoulder throbbed as though it were a warm heart at labor. Haldane's shoulder throbbed as he thought.

He thought on his chief strength:

He could suck a teat, and crawl. These were strengths. He could hold his shit like a man. He could walk. He could run. He could ride. He could read. He knew all there was to raiding save for a raid, which was a small difference. He could lead men. He could lead men thus far only to death. But there were other things that he could do, too. Many things. Many strengths were his.

But, since yestermorn, he could see keys in the very shape of the land, and ways within the country. Next to this his other strengths were all as nothing. This was a great gift to him that he did not deserve, a gratuity, a lifting of the Veil of the Most Precious. He could not say why it should have happened. He could only feel small before that for which the land was made—that unknown. And that by which the land was made—that unknown. These unknown things were much greater than the

Gets or Morca or any strength he had from them.

It seemed to Haldane that if this cage he was in was the cage of a Get, the close prison of one who was a Deldring who followed Morca, that it should have no strength that was greater than his strength. For the unknowns that were the source of his strength were much greater than the Gets or Morca and any strength that they might have.

So Haldane looked about him in the cage, and he saw there the door that was the way out. As Haldane had known even before, this place was an old place. There was a door in the pen. There had always been a door in the pen for those who could move in other ways as long as there had been a pen.

Before he was branded, Haldane had not seen the door. He had seen only those things that said that this place was an old place. It was as though the country were a book that none but he knew of, and in it he could read the letter "a". Before he was branded, Haldane had seen sign of the book, but nowhere a letter "a". So he was helpless.

Now he could see the door that left the cage through other ways. One more sign of the book was clear to him, if not all.

And so he left the pen.

He stood alone. Jana, the moon, was rising, full and fat. The night was new. Haldane stood, bare feet spread, naked but for his smock, one who was stripped to nothing but his essential self, and tasted of the night's chill clarity.

Haldane thought then that he would make his way inside the land to Barrow Hill and there he would find Oliver, and together they would walk to Palsance. He would do this not because he was still the son of Black Morca, one who had need of a wizard, but because he had promised to help Oliver with his strength and it would wound his strength to break his promise.

And so he set out along the path, for there was a way into the land immediately thereby behind a bush. Feeling at one with himself, he followed this easy way, for it had been easier than he had ever expected to leave the place of the Get.

It was enough to make him laugh.

It was sprightly gay.

For he had shed great weight when he left Black Morca behind him. He had been paralyzed by Morca, and for that he had been branded. If it was not so, why was the way not open to him before he was branded? If not for Morca, could he not have thought of the Pall of Darkness, and left the cage?

His feet were light. Barefoot he sprang because of all that he no longer was.

It was to race beneath the moonlight, under the skying clouds.

It was to leap.

It was to merry springtime, ha-ha.

Hu-yah.

So it was that the boy went along the way to Barrow Hill through bright and flighty night, through calm chill under flying skies. All around him was infinitely alive, infinitely sensitive.

He had survived, and he had not thought he would. After all that had happened, he was still himself, and he rejoiced.

And then he began to notice the strangeness of the night.

The clouds ran wild across the sky, but the night

was windless. The night air was cool, but it *was,* it did not stir about. He looked more and more to the skies as he walked.

Because his attention was in his eyes, he did not know when first the leaves in the trees about him began to shake and shiver. Now and then, the whispering rattle. The talk of leaves in wind.

But there was no wind. The night air was clear, and, but for the leaves, it was silent. It was so lucid that he could hear the throb of his shoulder in the silence.

He began to walk faster then, to leave the sound behind him.

The silent clouds hurtled overhead, and cast large shadows over the land.

The leaves clattered in the windlessness.

Was it before he began to run that the wind began to howl? Or did it first howl and the trees to lash about as he began to run?

But where he ran it was windless. The winds of the earth were loosed all about him and he could see their great force, and he could hear them like screaming birds, and waterfalls, and winter, but naught of it touched him.

The stormwind battered the land. It flung trees. It made his ears to ring as though great gongs had sounded but a moment before. But nothing of the wind touched the boy. He ran within the calm and silence of the night.

He ran toward Barrow Hill, which he saw before him, bald and alone.

As he came through the hills to the plain, light and shadow reeled beneath the moon.

Power circled around Haldane. It lashed at his heels.

He ran into the plain that lay before Barrow Hill. When he left the hills and set foot on the plain, clouds coasted over the face of the moon and all grew dark. In that darkness, the wind became silent and all was still. There was no howl. There was no clash of leaves. The clouds lay unmoving before the face of the moon.

In the middle of the plain, the boy came upon a standing stone. He was winded from running, so he paused to lean against the stone in the silence and in the darkness. He felt it a familiar thing, almost a place of safety.

He listened to the pulse in his shoulder, the pulse of his heart, the pulse of his breath, the pulse of the universe in his ears. And as he rested there against the stone, the moon suddenly shone again in its fullness, as though a hand had swept the clouds away. Then, before him, he saw the rough place, Barrow Hill, like a boulder alone in a wide field.

Then he turned and there saw three riders. One was in link that shimmered in the light. One was in lacquer that threw the moon back to the moon again. The third wore no armor but carried a golden horn and blew at the sight of Haldane.

And before the riders came a monstrous black pig. Lather from its jaws snowed the ground. Its breath was so hot as to alter the coolness of the night. Moonlight reflected from its tushes would wound sharply.

The snort of the pig was like the sucking out of his bones. The cries of the three riders were night-fears given tongue. The calling horn struck him like the cold wind at last.

It cried: *Here is the quarry. Gather for the kill. Here he is. Gather quickly. Kill. Kill.*

It was the wind he had not felt before, cutting lightly through his simple smock, cutting away skin, flesh and bone, flaying open the heart.

He ran and did not know why he was pursued. These men sought the Son of Black Morca and he was not that anymore. He had no army anymore to match against Ivor Fish-eye. He was small and never would be large. He would never play Deldring to Romund's Farthing. What were Farthing and Deldring to one like him who wished only to melt into the land? He would never return with men at his back to make Arngrim no more a Get. He would swear to it.

He was nobody. And yet they pursued him through the night. They blew the horn after him. Why would they seek to kill him so hard, these three inexorables? Why was he the quarry? Why was he to be killed?

They came after him across the plain. The pig snorted and they cried halloa. *Ta-ta,* the horn, *ta-ta.*

All the Gets who hunted for Haldane through all the Gettish ways of Nestor were called to gather here as he, their victim, was brought to bay. They would dismember him and silver his red blood with moonlight. They would throw the pieces of his body into the abyss and turn their backs on it.

And the monster pig harried after him to have its own desire. It meant to drag his body away from the huntsmen and devour it in greedy secret as a sow sometimes consumes her own farrow. And it would befoul his carrion bones with dirt and filth as it fed.

He reached the base of Barrow Hill and began to climb. Up the rocks and through the scrub. And then he clambered. All among the boulders, around and over, up the hill he went in his bare feet.

He climbed without looking since there was nothing that he might do but climb. He lost himself in climbing, climbing to climb. Where they were behind him, he knew not. Who they were, how many they had now become—he did not look to know.

He knew they followed him. He knew there was no hope for him. He climbed because he could still climb.

He would show them who he was, what little was left of him. They must climb this hill his way and his way would be the hard way. Then only might they have him.

All the while as the boy climbed, he could hear the great black creature-pig slavering behind him. It touched his heel hotly and he wore its spume on his smock.

He came at last to a place where there was no more to climb. Only one final great block of stone overhead. When he was there, that would be the place they would tear him down and kill him.

The pig was close, and then he left the pig behind well below at the base of the rock to find its own way to the top. As he climbed his chimney, the fetid black animal trotted back and forth looking for another route.

At the top of the rock there were several small trees and lichen growing on the rock face like a small landscape. The boy sat on the countries of lichen as though they were a carpet and looked at the many men scrambling up the rock hillside to be part of his death. He felt sorrow and infinite pity for them because they were only Gets when there were larger things to be than that.

The evil black pig squealed madly. It looked at him and knew him. It agonized at the rock.

In that instant, Haldane remembered the Pall of Darkness. It seemed to him that of course he must know it.

The one who could not remember the Pall of Darkness was the one who was son to Morca. He was not that one any more. He was not the son of Black Morca. Therefore, he could know the Pall of Darkness. Of course. Of course.

He knew the spell then. He remembered the words as though they were the Lineage of Wisolf. The gestures of hand were as familiar as those in training horses. It was all open to him.

Also open to him was the memory of the Night of Slaughter, the night of his betrothal, the night of Morca's death. He remembered the Chaining of Wild Lightning, and Oliver's failure. He remembered all: fighting, death, sickness and blood, and he remembered the Pall of Darkness. Now much was clear to him.

And here he was now on Barrow Hill with the Pall of Darkness again on his lips. And where was Oliver?

He stood and called, "Oliver! Oliver! I am here. Where are you? Oliver!"

But Oliver did not answer Haldane.

The eager creature-pig squealed in triumph as it found its own way up the rock.

The horn blew just below. It said: *The game is up. The game is up.*

But it was not, for Haldane could still pull the Pall of Darkness down around his shoulders and steal away down Barrow Hill. No mortal eyes could see him. He could go away and continue to live as he was. He could be safe.

But for the pig! But for the black pig!

Haldane turned and looked away from the rock and over the moonlit country at his alternative. And before him, curving away, there was a stone bridge. It was clearly limned. Below it there was mist and voidness. The bridge was without foundation. Where the bridge led was lost to sight in the mist. He who fell from that bridge would be forever forgot.

Bridges may fall down, as all who know Nestor know.

The pig was upon him then, and he fell onto his knees before its power. It struck him with its heavy body and then it was past him. Haldane looked up and the pig grunted and trotted out onto the bridge as though it were substantial and might easily bear great weight. Haldane watched to see what the pig would do. It had lost all interest in him and it walked out farther and farther on the bridge that had no support. Haldane wanted to call to it.

He thought once more of the Pall of Darkness and looked out to see Arngrim, and Romund and Ivor. But he could not see them anywhere. Where had they gone? Where were the other Gets who had come from all Nestor? He could not see them around the base of the rock.

The mist circled the base of the rock now. Beneath it, there was great nothing. Haldane stood on the rock in the Void that supported the bridge over the Void. There was bright moonlight and there was mist clear as cloth.

Haldane looked to see the black pig. As he looked, the animal became a white wurox and disappeared into the mist.

21

Haldane stepped cautiously onto the bridge. The Winds of the Void that had surged about him through the night now whistled like hollow desolation and waited below in the emptiness for him. Haldane tested the stone, but it bore his weight without wag or sag.

How strange, how very strange this all was. Since Morca's Banquet, all was always strange. It was a mystery and a delight and an awfulness how strange things had been. Those things that had befallen him were like nothing that had ever befallen him before.

What was this place? What was this bridge?

It was a causeway over the Abyss, resting on nothing, passing over the Void. How could such a bridge, hanging giddily, hang? It wound slightly, sometimes curving as though following the slope of emptiness. Everything that Haldane knew—his senses, his fears, his desire to survive—all these told him that the bridge was not to be trusted, even though the wurox might walk upon it.

But his chief strength, which was his new ability to find his way within the inner mysteries of the land, insisted that he walk forward boldly, that this was the true way.

And so he paused, torn between nightmare and dream.

He knew only this: that he was afoot in a universe that always changed. He was not in Morca's old world where all was safe and still until the world broke. He was in a universe that always moved and never broke.

The old unmoving world had broken that he might not break. But now, he might break, but he knew this new ever-changing world would not.

Was this nightmare? Was this a place he did not fit and could not fit? Was it always to be endless whirling confusion? Was it Libera, the hideous caterpillar creature, She Who lured, promised and lied, toying with him still as though he were a little spider made to run madly on a green grass stem?

Or was this the place that he dreamed of? That place where he was at home, even though all was always strange, because he was one with that great mysterious power which inhabited this country.

Before him, the wurox returned to stare silently out of the fartherness of the mist. Then it became vanished again in the white folds of gauze. Haldane followed where it had disappeared, stepping out onto the bridge.

The clouds were gone now from the sky. The moon shone clear. The night air was still and cold. Mist hung about the bridge in ribbon curtains.

Haldane walked firmly, one foot after another, each set down squarely on the supporting stone. In the Abyss, there were moans. Something awful lurked below. It was lonely and alone. It was that which was hacked to pieces and forgotten. It was that which was fouled in mud and devoured by the sow. It was that which was dead. It howled and seethed to have Haldane. It tested itself against the bridge, pushing and scrabbling to tear it away.

Could this be the dream where he was more at home than with Morca because he was one with that which always changed? How could he be safe and not be broken and cast down? How could he be one with this? Morca's name was not enough that he should cease to fear. In whose name was he fearless, that he might live?

All that existed was himself, Haldane, alone, afraid. There was no wurox. There was himself and the causeway and the moon and the mist and the Thing waiting below. It was like Libera in its hideousness.

The Thing reached for him. It tore away small stones from the bridge and hurled them into the roiling turbulent nothing. It cried like oily black water in the Void. It meant to swallow him whole that he should be absorbed into it and be one with its awful, lonely, solitary power.

He had thought when he escaped from the Get that he was safe. He might be branded. Morca's Son might be no more. But there was still Himself, Haldane, who was free and would survive as he had always been. Haldane was that which was really real, which might find refuge for its self in some safe place in Palsance and there never be troubled again.

This Haldane was no Get who might not don other clothes and live. This Haldane was not Morca's Son, with his dreams of maelstrom, who might not be marked with another's private mark and live. This Haldane was that Haldane that was sure it would be Haldane in any clothes, in any condition of body, in any body, at any age, always. That which continued. That which cried.

Haldane cried in pain and hopelessness.

Haldane cried in fear his one last inadequate name of power.

Haldane cried, "Haldane!"

And the Void echoed "Haldane!" eagerly, as though now that it knew his true name it was hungrier than before to devour him. It would rip the meat from the name. It would gorge itself on his flesh, lick its lips, and leave him isolate and nameless on the place of lonely bones.

Before him, the bridge suddenly came to an end. It hung there unfinished, as though he had been brought so very far, through worlds on worlds, to this ultimate brink. As though this end had been made for Haldane.

This world—so always new! So nightmarish, but always hovering on the edge of dream.

There was a great echoing crash then as though thunder boulders dropped clashing into the Well of the Worlds. And then again. The stone bridge was collapsing section by section. Before the echo of one collapse had fairly rung, another section would fall, pulled after it into empty forever falling by the Thing of the drowning Void. The bridge fell away, and the mist swept after, so that the last remaining sections of the bridge stood alone under the moon, hanging in nothing. Their fallacy, curtained by the mist, was now clearly revealed and they could no longer hang unsupported, but must fall.

Again: a rumble like the hungry stomach of time, and the stone curve was gone—echo, echo,

echo. There were but two sections of stone now remaining.

Haldane stood on the final coursings that the mason had set in place. Behind him, one more section of the bridge gave way. So little was left—no more than the stones he stood upon. The black waters of infinite loneliness and separation awaited him below.

He closed his eyes. In the darkness, he thought of one great security amid fear. A Name came to him. With the Name, he stepped forward, off the rock, into the Abyss, as the last stones of the bridge fell into the storm.

He was unsupported by himself or by anything that he had ever known. He stood on nothing. But he stood!

His eyes tight closed, he stepped and stepped again. And there, where he could not see, there was always something beneath his feet. Again, and again.

He did not fall. The winds of the Abyss cried in self-pity that he did not fall.

One step at a time he proceeded. Each step was different than the last. It might be hard and sure. It might be soft and uncertain. It might yield and sway. It might not even be there—so that he stepped and caught himself, heart swooping, on a stair below. But as he fell he did remember the Name, and lo, a stair was there beneath his foot.

That which was below his feet might be like rock, or like a bog, or like a grassy hillside, or like a tree trunk bobbing in water to tip and spin. It was this, it was that.

And then again, it was nothing! But always he

remembered the Name. With the power of the Name he pulled his foot free from the bog that sucked at him. And a stair was there instead of the Abyss, which cried for him.

Then there was another stair, stair upon stair. Eyes tight closed, teeth set, he stepped away into uncertainty as though he walked Morca's Stair by night and was confident. And again and again, the next step was there, waiting or created, for his reaching foot.

Then a Voice suddenly said: "What do you do on My Staircase?"

His heart leaped and he ceased to step. His eyes were still tight shut.

He said, "This is my Stair. I found it, and I may follow it down."

"But these Steps that you have found are My Steps and not your Steps. There are Rules for those who walk My Steps. If ye would walk the Steps, ye must mind the Three Rules of the Stair."

"What be the Three Rules of the Stair?"

There was a sudden tug at his smock that threatened to overbalance him, so that he cried aloud.

The Voice said: "None may walk my Staircase who is not naked to himself. Are you naked?"

"I am not naked," he said. "The night is cold. All that I have in this world to keep my bones warm is this smock."

"Rule the First broken," the Voice said. "Smocks are expressly forbidden on My Staircase. No one may wear a smock here. You must leap from the Stair."

"Must I?" he asked. "I did not know the Rule. May I not take off the smock and cast it from me?"

There was a long silence. Then the Voice said, "Just this once, I will bend My Rule. You may take off the smock and cast it from you."

Eyes still shut, he pulled the smock over his head. He held it in one hand and threw it into the teeth of the Abyss. The mad Thing snatched at the tidbit, swallowed it whole, and whined for more. Cold air beat around his shanks.

"Rule the Second," said the Voice. "No one may close his eyes and walk My Steps. Are your eyes closed?"

"They are closed," he said. "If I ever opened my eyes, I would surely fall."

"Rule the Second, broken," the Voice said. "That cannot be. Now you must jump from the Stair. You cannot stay." The Thing howled at these words.

"What if I should open my eyes. May I stay on your Staircase then?"

"Bend another Rule?" the Voice asked. "Very well. I have bent one Rule. I will bend a second. But no more. You may open your eyes."

He opened his eyes then. He saw nothing before him. But he did not look at his feet. And his feet continued to stand on the stair that was in nothingness.

"Rule the Third," said the Voice. "All those that walk My Steps must have my special let-pass. Do you have my special let-pass?"

"Is a chipped tooth a let-pass?" he asked.

"No," said the Voice. "A chipped tooth a let-pass? Never such a thing."

"Then I have no special let-pass."

"No special let-pass? Then Rule the Third is bro-

ken. And this one cannot be bent. And so we are at
an end. At last. You cannot walk My Staircase.
You must hurl yourself into That Which Waits."

That Which Waits swirled about and moaned to
itself.

There was no help for him now. He was naked
and alone. He was without power. He was helpless.
He was nothing.

He was nothing but the Name in his heart. He
stood on the stairstep over nothing. He breathed
one last time, and then cried the Name aloud as he
hurled himself into the Void. He was nothing. The
Void was nothing.

All that was was the Name. The Name was all
that was.

And the Name held him safe in Its arms.

The Voice, which was the Voice of Infinite Gen-
tleness and Love, The Voice of Truth, said: "Who
am I?"

He said, "Thou art that for which the country
was made."

And the Voice asked again: "Who am I?"

He said, "Thou are that by which the country
was made."

And yet again: "Who am I?"

"Thou art Thou. Thou art Libera."

And the Voice said: "Open your eyes."

His eyes were open for he had opened them on
the stair.

He said, "But, Mother. My eyes are open."

"Open your eyes," She said.

And he opened his eyes. Before him there was
radiance, which was light flooding the mind to
fullness and overflowing.

The Voice said: "Thou art my Lover, Giles."

He who had been Haldane, but was now Giles—which was the name of the Lover of Libera—lost himself in Love of the Goddess. She was that One Who united All that was Lost and Scattered. Who was the Path. Who was the Home and the Dream. Who was the Always New. Who was the Pig. Who was the Wurox. Who was the Abyss, and Who was That which lies beyond the Abyss.

He Loved Her for a moment that was eternity. And She cradled him like mistress, like mother.

When it was time for him to leave Her and return to the world, She said: "There is yet More. There is always More."

He, Giles, said: "I would know More. I will know More."

She said:"If you would know More, then you must discover these answers: Why were you born? And for what purpose did I make this country? Study the questions well. When you bring these answers back to Me, then ye shall surely know More."

"I will," Giles said. "I will return."

"In time," the Voice said. There was a note of—was it compassion? Was it pity? "You will learn that it takes time. Go now with My Love and Blessing and meet your trial, for ye have trials to meet. Remember My Name."

22

On Stone Heath, the menhirs, the great standing stones, stretch in rows across the moor that rises above the western bank of the Trenoth River, away from the river, eleven rows of stones in all. And at their heart, a tump, a hillock raised by men, with a stone circle at the top. Like so many giants, they stand imprisoned, sunk to their knees, rank on rank, for a league—fully three miles. They are rough-hewn misshapen things, crudely made, with no art in them. Some are as tall as a tall man, some the height of a tree. All are beyond the power of any ten men to lift with simple strength of arm and leg. They stand by the thousand, testament to the great will of those who hacked them from the mother mountain, brought them here from so far away, and put them in regularity for purpose forgotten out of time.

Those who put them into place were not like us. They did not think like us. They were neither artist nor artisan who made these rocks. If these menhirs be giants, some of these giants have their pointed heads buried, their gross legs high and kicking, as though they managed a poor head-stand only with aid. This is a strange and careless way to place a

rock. And within the great regularity that marks
the whole, the rows are disorderly. But yet, to any
man who lives with these rocks, it must in time become evident that these rocks are shaped as they
are shaped, placed as they arc placed, precisely as
they were meant to be shaped, precisely as they
were meant to be placed. There is power and
purpose here beyond our power and purpose.

Such things are frightening. Few men live with
the rocks.

Men do not dwell on Stone Heath, even far from
the menhirs in their alignment. Stone Heath is a
wasteland. Men come here to fight. Many men
have fought in the shadow of the rocks. Single
men. Armies. There are bones here, and armor.
Cattle graze among the rocks. When Palsance was
fiercer, men would sometimes say that blood made
the children's milk richer. It is not a thing that a
modern man would say, not with the Gets for
neighbors in Nestor, but some cattle still graze on
Stone Heath, amidst the rocks, amidst the bones.

The face of the full moon shone on Stone Heath.
It was a chill night, and the rock legions were
locked in mist, Libera's Coverlet.

Naked the boy stood, alone among the towering
rocks, lost in the mist that glowed from moonlight
like the heart of a pearl. Neither mother nor father
had he. He had no nation. There was no thing in all
the world that was his. All that was his was a Name
that was graven on his heart, and the Name was
Libera.

He had no name of his own. He wore the name
of Giles, which to him meant the Lover of Libera.

For a moment, he was cold. He did not know

where he was. This was not the Stone Heath of his dreams. It was a far greater and stranger place than that, and he did not know it at first. All that he knew was the night, the moon and the mist, the cold, and these great presences that might suddenly topple and crush him. And then he remembered the Name and all was well.

He wrapped the mist around him like a blanket. And he walked among the rocks as though they were his own domain. He did not need to know the name Stone Heath when he knew the name Libera. In the name of Libera he could see beyond the mist, see with the mist. It was as though the mist was his own senses, and anywhere there amongst the rock lines he might let his senses roam over the bones and armor.

Very nearby, he suddenly sensed Oliver. He was sure in his heart of hearts, without knowing how he knew, that Oliver was close. The knowledge leapt into his mind.

He called to him: "Oliver! It is me . . . Giles!"

And he was both not surprised and surprised, because Oliver called, in a voice that revealed much: "Here. Here." His voice was close and urgent, relieved and terrified, constricted.

They met between, nearer Oliver, for Haldane moved more surely and with less fear. The pearl mist glowed about them with moonfire.

Oliver said, "You are naked."

Giles said, "I've met no one to ask if he would clothe a naked man."

"But it has been so long," said Oliver. "I counted you . . . I counted myself . . . You did not come to Barrow Hill."

"I did come to Barrow Hill," Giles said, "but by

then you were not there. How many days has it been?"

"It has been four days since I saw you pursued by the hairy Get into the forest. Then I followed my map to Barrow Hill. After I got to Barrow Hill and was spying over a boulder there, I lost my map. A breeze took it from my hand like a swallow taking a fly. I do not know what happened to our pursuit while I followed my map, but then after two days in which I waited for you, Ivor and Arngrim were there together. I escaped them barely. I went in all directions until I lost my bearings. I did not know my right hand from my left. But Ivor and Arngrim followed me. I ran, and still they followed me. I ran from the pig and the horn wherever the flow of the countryside took me. Always I stayed before. Always they stayed behind. The sun was ever hidden and I did not know whether I ran through the heart of Nestor and beyond into the vastness of the Great Plains or whether I spun around and around in circles like a finger-top. But then I came to the Trenoth River and there was a boatman there. I could hear the horn behind me. I bargained with the boatman. I had naught else to give, so I gave him my magic book and my reading glasses to ferry me over the water. I kept only this cloak of all that I had. Then I followed the path that leads from the river to the bluff above and I found myself here. This could be Stone Heath. It must be Stone Heath. How came you to be here before me?"

"I did not know that I was before you," Giles said. "In this mist can you tell before from behind?"

"No."

"I was taken by the Get. He laid his mark upon me. Then I escaped. I went to Barrow Hill. Then . . . Then I came here."

"You were branded?" And there in mistglow, Oliver did turn Giles around and examine the mark on his shoulder. He said, "Yes, I see. It is a strange red mark. It is a great letter—an L."

Giles was struck by silence for a moment while his heart leapt to remember and wonder at the mystery. Libera. Libera. Then he said, "The name of the Get who captured me was Lyulf."

And then, like some reminder that they were not alone in the mist and the night, came the golden sound of Arngrim's Horn. Oliver started and kicked a helmet of some war against one of the great stones that was an inverted giant. It was a rattle in the night and Oliver looked about in apprehension.

He said, "Arngrim and Ivor and the pig are still behind me. We must run."

"No," said Giles. "There is armor here. And weapons, if we seek them. Look, here is an old knife."

This knife that he found with the aid of his senses, the mist, was a wide-blade knife of iron, much rusted, with the handle broken. He held it out.

"That is no weapon for me," said Oliver.

"We will find you a better," Giles said, throwing it away. "But if it be you and me against Arngrim and Ivor and the pig Slut, then remember that Arngrim is old and Ivor has but one eye. You are fat and I am young. And the pig is a pig. I have

chucked it under the chin. It may still love me. So
let us turn and fight."

Oliver was silent for a long time, and it seemed
to Giles that he might set his cloak under his arm
and flee again West down the line of stones.

But then Oliver looked at Haldane, as he
thought him, but Giles as it now was, and said: "I
will fight with you. I have not ever fought with a
sword before and I will be no aid to you. But I will
fight beside you even if they kill me."

And so they cast about them. Oliver found a
helmet that he thought befit him but did not. Giles
found a short sword for Oliver, in the mist between
the rocks.

Oliver tried it on the night, waving the old sword
straight-armed, holding his cloak which he carried
in his left hand as though he had meant to drop it
but then forgot. Giles leaned back from the cut of
that poor sword in the hand of this one who was
not a swordsman. Then he turned to look for a better weapon for himself.

He could not find one. The mist did not tell him
of swords. It told him of one running upon them.

Giles looked up. It was Ivor Fish-eye, doing
again as he had done at Arngrim's Dun. He was
rushing upon Giles, that defenseless boy, his cutting sword in his hand, intent to kill him.

Oliver threw his cloak at Ivor with his left hand,
a toss to break his charge, like a slap on the nose to
a bear. And it did that. It blinded Ivor's one eye,
hanging and clinging to head and shoulder.

Ivor snatched it away, turning on Oliver. He
said, "Once again as at Little Nail. I do not like

you, wizard man. I do not believe in wuroxes and I do not believe in you. I saw you wave your arms high and chant while I surrounded Morca, but while my back was turned to you, I killed Morca and you ran away. I wanted to kill you then. I will kill you now."

Oliver tried to interpose his sword, but Ivor beat it aside with the ease of one who sets aside a kitten's batting paw. Then he killed Oliver. He struck him a blow to the helmet that undid him and then casually but viciously struck him a great hacking blow that no man could survive. It was a backhanded blow with great power. And then Ivor struck him once again another blow as great as that. Oliver fell dead.

"Now we shall finally match armies," Ivor said, turning upon Giles.

But Giles had a sword. "Libera," he said, and came forward to meet Ivor.

Ivor wore a link shirt. He laughed at the boy's rusted weapon. It was no match for his sound and well-loved piece. The boy's nakedness was no proof against his great bloody long sword.

He said, "When I came upon you to kill you at Little Nail, the wizard tripped me with his bag and I knocked my head against a post. I will not knock my head against a post here. This wizard will trip no one again. He is dead, and so are you, Haldane of Morca."

Giles swung his rusty weapon as though it were new. Ivor blocked the blow and flinders of rusted iron flew.

Ivor laughed.

Giles swung as before, and again Ivor blocked the swing and the sword came more to pieces.

"And once again," said Ivor, and laughed a second time.

Giles did strike one more blow. The sword dissolved to nothing on Ivor's blade and he was left with naught but the handle which was bits in his hand.

Ivor laughed a third time. And Ivor died.

He fell down dead. A sliver of rusted iron had passed through his link shirt to pierce his heart. The first of Haldane's enemies was dead at the hand of Giles, now that it was no longer of moment to Haldane. But that is always the way of life.

Giles knelt by both men and both were dead. Ivor was dead and Oliver was dead. He took Ivor's sword and rose again.

With his senses, he searched between the stones for Arngrim. He cast about to find him, his horn and his pig. It was like being in an outhouse on the night of the new moon and still knowing where everything was in the darkness—but the reverse of that. It was the full moon, not the new. There was a flood of light. And Giles was not an intruder in a place known, but was himself the place Stone Heath knowing an intruder.

And he sensed one in the mist, between his rocks, and he knew the place. There was a regularity in the ranks of rocks, and the one who moved among them was irregular.

Giles walked to meet Arngrim. When the one who tracked through the mist moved between the rocks, Giles matched him, so that ever more surely they two must meet. The place was there awaiting them.

Stone Heath was alive with power on this night. The mist glowed with it. The rocks surged with it.

And the men who walked the lines were men with claim to power.

Their sources would be matched, one who was a Get against one who was not. He whose purposes were less would surely die.

So Giles moved lightly, naked young man, sword held before him, to meet the one who trailed and trailed. He knew that he was only the distance of the mist away. That close. Beyond the nearest rocks hid, there was the man.

And from that place, Giles heard a gaunt cough. Romund and he came together in the grass between the rock rows. The grass was cool and damp beneath his bare feet.

Coughing Romund coughed again. It seemed hollow in this moonfire mist.

He said: "Deldring, I am Farthing, come to kill you."

"I am not Deldring," Giles said. "I am not Haldane. I am not of the Gets. I am Giles. I am only of Libera."

"You are Haldane, and you will die for it," said Romund.

"I would not die for that. If you should kill me, I will have died for Libera. If you kill me, then I will know that Libera has willed it so."

"I will kill you," said Romund hoarsely.

Romund was a powerful man for one so gaunt and thin. He was a swordsman by whom swordsmen were measured. Giles fought well, but to Romund he was as Oliver to Ivor. He was but newly a man. Romund was a master.

Giles only managed to parry three blows from Romund. His arm was benumbed by the great force of Romund's blows. Romund coughed, and still coughing delivered another blow that Giles raised Ivor's iron sword to meet. Romund's sword skipped away and the flat struck Giles in the head and knocked him down, sword flying wildly from his hand.

Coughing Romund stared at Giles as he fell face downward and rolled away. He demanded: "What is that disgrace you bear on your naked shoulder?"

"It is a brand. It is the great letter L."

"You spoke truly. You are not of the Gets. Deldrings are not fit to be reckoned of our kind. I know you now. I know your back, which I have touched. That Lyulf should lie to me with my very hand touching you. That he would try to save you by branding you as a serf. And that you would agree. Even Morca would be ashamed of behavior such as yours, for if he was a Deldring, he was proud."

Coughing Romund prodded at Giles with his sword, backing him step by step. "When you strove to save your coward life, you spoke true. You are no Get. You are not Morca's son. And you are no threat to me, for no Get would follow such a one as you. But I would not have you save your coward life by such means as these. It is not right that such a one as you, without shame or propriety, should live. You are without manhood. Your father died killing many men. They and he would not rest if such a one as you remained alive. I foul my sword to kill you."

Giles was without help as he was forced to retreat. He was naked. He had no power against the sword in Romund's hand.

He called on Libera in his heart. He thought of her and not of himself.

And suddenly he thought of the stone that he and the Get Lyulf had lifted in the forest. It was a stone as large as some of these, and they two had lifted that rock, which no two men might do. And the rock had surged in their hands with its vital power. There were many rocks here like that rock. And he reached with that sense that he had here on Stone Heath this night and he saw that all these rocks were gravid with power.

Romund raised his sword to lay renegade-Haldane down. Giles placed his hands behind him, palms against the towering menhir, and Romund danced like a puppet and then was dead, over-filled with the force of the living rock. Giles' palms were left as hot as though they had touched a stove, and pulled away on the instant.

"Is this your magic?" a stern voice asked.

It was Arngrim there, coming out of the mists. By his knee was the black pig, Slut. In his hands he held the Horn of Life and Death. He wore a sword but did not touch it.

"Yes," said Giles. For only now did he realize that the powers that he had—the power to see, the power to walk, the power to direct—these new powers were magic powers.

"I heard what Romund said. Show me your brand. I must see how you are marked."

Giles turned and let his grandfather see his shoulder.

"It is true. I see that you are not a Get. Let us try swords together."

"You wish to fight me with swords?"

"Would you kill me with your sly magic? I would not have such a coward for a grandson. Seize a sword, and we will fight and I will kill you cleanly."

Giles took Ivor's sword, and Arngrim, that old man, drew his own sword. But then Giles suddenly thought that he should not do this. To fight with the sword was the Gettish way, and he was not a Get. No longer a Get. Even for his grandfather, there was no reason to behave as a Get would behave.

"Libera," he said within his heart, and cast the sword from him.

Arngrim said, "I had not thought to see this. Must I kill you defenseless?"

Giles said, "Would you do that?"

"I will kill you." And Arngrim stepped forward.

Giles backed then against the great menhir. "If you strive to kill me with your sword, I will place my hands on the rock and strike you as I struck Romund. This is a place of magic beyond all the wizards of the West."

The eagle old man put down his sword. "Would you kill me with your magic? I cannot believe that such a thing is possible. If you would employ such a means as this magic, then it is better that I should be dead."

Giles said, "I would not kill you defenseless." And he stepped away from the rock.

Arngrim raised his sword then and walked towards Giles, the pig Slut pressing close to his leg. "Take sword or die."

Giles stood back to the rock a second time. Arngrim put his sword down once more. "Kill me then with your magic."

Giles stood away again from the stone. Arngrim again raised his sword and advanced. "Fight me, coward, or die."

Giles stepped back to the menhir a third time, placed his palms against the surging rock and directed the power at Arngrim. There was warmth in his palms, but not heat, and there was no surge of discharge. Giles did not understand.

Arngrim then raised the sword he held and stepped forward. "It is the good Gettish power that you have forsworn that is proof against your magic. Your magic is as nothing. I will show you Gettish power now and kill you."

Giles called upon Libera in his heart. "Remember My Name," She had said. "Remember My Name."

He Remembered. And he stood helpless before the sword.

And even as Arngrim came forward, the black pig Slut, pressing close to the old man, squealed and ran beneath Arngrim's feet. He tripped and fell to the ground, which he must not have done in battle for thirty years and more, since he was raw. Giles' heart surged.

Giles said, "Your Gettish magic is all in swords. My power, which is of this land, is proof against your Gettish magic. Seek to slay me as you may, you shall not."

Arngrim rose and strove to strike Giles down for these words, but again the pig tripped him. The old man turned in anger on the pig, but it ran squealing out of reach.

"If you kill the pig, my protection will be elsewhere," Giles said. "Your magic cannot harm me."

"Do not say that my power is magic," said Arngrim in anger. "My Gettish power is not magic! My Gettish power is the true life-stuff of the Gets, and it is not magic. It is natural! It comes of our nature."

"No more than my power," said Giles.

"That cannot be," said Arngrim, and struggled to rise. Before him on the ground was the sword that Giles had from Ivor, had used, had lost, had recovered, had thrown away. "Where got you this sword?"

Giles said, "From the hand of Ivor Fish-eye."

Arngrim said, "How got you this sword from Ivor Fish-eye?"

"I killed Ivor Fish-eye with a shattered sword that I snatched from among the bones."

"Show me this," said Arngrim. "Such a one as you could not kill Ivor with a sword."

"And could not kill Romund," said Giles.

"By magic."

"Against his Gettish power, his power of Farthing. It was not proof for him as it is for you."

"Show me Ivor that I may judge you," said Arngrim. "Nay, do not fear to walk with me through the mist. If you are right, should I seek to do you harm, a rock will fall and crush me."

"That is so," said Giles. "But what you cannot imagine—that will be my protection."

They walked the corridors between the rocks until they came to the place where Ivor and Oliver lay. Giles followed his senses which were in the mist, and brought them straight.

Arngrim looked at Ivor, dead in the cold light of the moon. "I see no wound," he said. "How is he dead if not by magic?"

Giles said, "My sword of rust broke on his sword of iron and a splinter pierced his heart."

Arngrim bent to see. "And how is this shard come through his mail if not by magic?"

"It was not magic. It was but my power."

"I do not understand," said Arngrim.

"There is no magic," said Giles, "else all men are magicians. There is only each man's power. The power of the hunt for Ivor. The power of Farthing for Romund. The power of the Gets that you keep. And the power of . . . I will not say what is in my heart, not the Name I carry. But my power is the power of all this land, Nestor and Palsance. There is power here in this land that no Get may ever know because he is a Get."

"Do not say that," Arngrim said. "I know the power of the Gets as no other man. If I had given that power to Morca, he would not now be dead, but he would be the great king he dreamed to be. But Morca was a man who recked not, who ravished, who carelessly killed, a man who kept wizards, a man who walked with witches in the woods—for so it was told to me by one I believe."

"Who?"

"By Morca. In drink. In boast. I would not give that power to him because he was not the man that Garmund was, from whom the power came to me. That power was too great for Morca."

"But Get power cannot be all-in-all," said Giles. "There is the power that I hold, and that is good power which I believe as I believe my heart. If this power be the magic of witches, then the power of witches must be good." He touched Oliver's dead body. "And the power of wizards is no all-in-all, but power of its own kind, and that is not Gettish kind. There are many powers, magic only to other men."

"There is Gettish power," said Arngrim. "Which I know and keep safe."

"There is greater power than Gettish power."

"There is not better power, else why should we rule and other men not?"

"Gets rule where they rule. They do not rule where they do not rule," said Giles. "They do not rule on Stone Heath."

"What is your power if it cannot do me harm?"

"What is your power if it cannot do me harm?"

"I will not hear," said Arngrim. "I will follow after and kill you when your magic does not keep you safe."

"Nay," said Giles. "Do not strive to kill me, for you shall not."

He knew not what to say. He knew something and could not speak it. He knew it was important, but he could not call it to mind.

But it was Giles alone who could not think. Giles alone. Giles called upon Libera to help him.

Then again, in his mind, as though appearing of itself, was what he must say. He could not believe it because he knew nothing like it. But he believed in Libera, so he must speak it.

"Match your power against mine," he said. "You must prove that you have the right."

"And how shall that be done?" asked Arngrim. "Shall I use my sword against you and see if the pig dashes out of the darkness?"

He put his hand to the sword. The pig squealed somewhere close by in the mist. Arngrim dropped his hand away.

"No," said Giles. "Here lying dead is Oliver, who was Morca's wizard. Bring him to life again."

"I cannot," said Arngrim. "I cannot bring a dead Get back to life. I would not bring this wizard back to life."

"He is no wizard now," said Giles.

"Nay. He is dead."

"Not because he is dead. Because he has no book. Join with me and bring him to life again. If our powers, yours and mine, can together do what cannot be done separately, then there must be more and better magic than Gettish magic . . ."

"That cannot be. There is no Gettish magic."

". . .of which Gettish magic is only a part."

"There is only our good natural power."

"Place your power together with mine and let us see what is revealed."

Arngrim said: "I cannot. How can I do this and be a Get? How can I do this and be a Get? It is not possible."

"What is your power if you refuse? Will the power of the Gets still remain if you refuse, or will it show itself as nothing so that I might kill you then with the touch of a butterfly wing? If you refuse, will the Gets still rule in Nestor?"

Arngrim was caught between two hard surfaces and there was no escape for him.

He said, "Nothing will happen. I cannot bring the dead to life."

"Then join me and prove that my power is a false magic," Giles said.

"I will do that," said Arngrim.

Together, these two, grandfather and grandson, raised Oliver's body and carried it to the heart of rock, that ring of stones crowning the tumulus, that place within the rock thousands where the greatest power was secretly hidden. Giles knew that place, and did not know how he knew. He led the way through the mists of Stone Heath, through the living mist, until they saw before them the hillock and the stone circle, heart of rock.

There, in the place of power, they set Oliver's body down. He was a small man, a plump man. He had not yet been old, but his hair was gray. It seemed wrong for this man to be dead as he was dead, with two great wounds in his side like axe cuts. He was not a man of swords.

In death, he seemed small and vulnerable, no great man. No man for Gets to fear. No man for any man to fear.

Giles stood back. All around them were great stones, sentinels of long standing. Not sentinels, but witnesses. Not witnesses, but sources of power. No, not sources of power, but conduits for power that came from elsewhere and was gathered here for this moment.

"Blow your horn for Oliver to rise," said Giles.

Arngrim raised the horn in his hands and he blew. And it was a sound like none that had come from the horn before.

"Blow!" said Giles. "Blow!"

Arngrim blew, putting into the call all his Get-

tish power, which was not enough magic by itself
to make the dead to rise. But it was great power,
for the world seemed to rock at the sound.

Giles lost himself in the sound.

He did not think of Get or Nestorian. He did not
think of magic or power. He did not think of mother or father. He did not think of Stone Heath, or
great menhirs, of mist, of moonlight. He did not
think of Arngrim. He did not think of Haldane. He
did not think of Giles.

He did not even think of Oliver. He did not think
of Oliver, even as he leaned forward and placed his
hands on him. His head rang with the sound of the
horn. There was sweat on his forehead. There was
a gulf in his stomach. He felt the great pulse of life
and power that surged within the great pattern of
rock. He tried to focus himself, to become a con-
duit.

He thought of Libera. And in his heart, he said:
"Thy will be done." And that was all.

But that was enough. He was overwhelmed and
lost his grip on the world. He was spun dizzy. He
was twirled right out of his mind. When he returned to himself again, he was toppled onto the
ground. He shook his head in the ringing silence,
not knowing where or when he was.

"No!" Arngrim said. "No!"

Giles remembered himself then, and looked at
Oliver. And Oliver moved. He stirred! Giles rose to
his knees, and Oliver looked up at him and Arngrim. His face worked.

At last, he said, "Why am I alive?" And a tear
welled in his eye and then streaked his cheek.

Arngrim pointed to Giles, as though to say it

was he alone who was responsible. But Giles knew better. And so did Arngrim.

Giles said, "It was magic made of our power combined. We were but an instrument of higher will."

He said this believing that Oliver would not be alive again if Libera had not willed it so.

Arngrim began to cry, too. The old man who had not cried since he had left his cradleboard, he was crying. As though it was too much for him to bear, Arngrim said over and over: "I am not a Get now! I am not a Get now!"

Giles could not help himself. He, too, cried happily and helplessly. Shatterment and undoing were at an end at last, for Oliver, who had been dead, was alive again!

And Oliver joined Arngrim and Giles, crying unabashedly in both mourning and celebration. And the three cried together for what each of them had won and lost.

EPILOGUE: ARRIVAL

23

After light rain that fell late in the night, the morning dawned blithesome and cloudless. The sky was blue. The easy countryside of Palsance was green. The sweet breeze darted here and there, carrying the odors of spring about like gossip. It was the best day of the whole new year—as fine a day as you might find in any year.

On this day, two men came walking west from Stone Heath, following the morning roads of Palsance. One was a short old man with a close-cropped white beard. He wore a gray smock, ill-fitting, ornamented with rents and with bloodstains. The other was a naked youth bearing a brand on his shoulder. Both were weary. It seemed they had walked far without food and suffered much.

They followed the common roads of ordinary men. Giles' ability to follow the hidden ways within the land had not survived that great discharge of power on Stone Heath after which Oliver, who had been dead, stirred and spoke and cried, like other mortal men. Giles felt less than he had been, like a man blinded in one eye, like a man unable to think with one side of his mind. But he accepted the fact that one moment is not the same as another, that what is possible at one time and place may not be possible in other circumstances. He knew that last night on Stone Heath was an extraordinary moment. He had been touched by something great and lifted high. After soaring, he had been set back on his own two feet again—but no longer the person he had been. This new person that he was did not fret, but accepted what was.

To Giles, Libera was a river and he had cast himself into it to be carried wherever it pleased Her to carry him. That was free will. It made action possible, when otherwise he would not know what to do or who to be.

At the same time, he did not yet know Her ways. He was like a horse that has been broken to a higher will, but not yet schooled. He was like a pen that has been cut, but not yet set to the alphabet. He was like a young hawk seated on its master's wrist, waiting for the hood to be removed, waiting for a sign.

So as he walked, Giles concentrated on signs. He devoted himself to thinking on the long riddles the Goddess had set for him: Why had he been born? For what purpose was the land made? And he looked everywhere for answers in hopes of finding answers somewhere.

The first thing that he saw was that even if he lacked insight into the hidden ways today, he had not lost touch with the Goddess. There were reminders of Her presence to be seen around him in Palsance. When Giles and Oliver stopped to rest, it was close by a dolmen, a great flat rock laid across upright stones in ancient days. And here Giles sensed power like a warm hum, like a glow.

While they sat, Oliver, who had been silent all the morning interrupted Giles' thoughts.

He said, "Haldane . . ."

But that wasn't his name any longer. He said, "Say 'Giles.'"

"Giles," said Oliver. "I have a confession to make to you."

He looked at his feet. "The night that Morca died, I failed him. I attempted an Ultimate Spell, but my courage gave way and the spell came to nothing. The Pall of Darkness that brought us safe out of the slaughter was not my spell, but yours, spun by you after you had been struck on the head. There, I have said it!"

And Oliver waited for Giles' reaction. Haldane might have struck at him for these words or denied the truth. Haldane might have hated him for his failure. But Giles' sense of the necessity of the moment, the flow of the river, ruled his answer.

He said, "I remember. While on Barrow Hill, I remembered. It seems very long ago."

"My failure weighs heavily on me," said Oliver. "If things were otherwise, Morca would still be alive. I should be dead for my failure."

"No," said Giles. "Don't think that, Oliver. Accept what is. If Morca is dead and you are alive, it is not your doing or my doing merely. Other will than ours is involved."

Oliver said, "I cannot accept that. My failure was my own, and I must stand responsible for it."

"You cannot be so certain," said Giles. "As a man of magic you should know that there are other magics than your own, some much more powerful. How can you doubt it after all that has happened?

Your magic and mine may not have been the only magic in Morca's Dun that night."

"Do you think so?" asked Oliver. But then, he said, "No, my responsibility is not less. I know my failure. Whether the magic was mine or someone else's, I have been burnt by magic, and I renounce it. I've given up my book. I am not a man of magic any more. I am nothing but an old man in Palsance. An ordinary old man."

It seemed to Giles that Oliver was less than he had been, as though he had pulled himself forth from the stream of life and declared he would not swim further. Did he seem shrunken and reduced in power as he sat there? Was this responsibility?

In early afternoon of this beautiful day, they came to a village huddling against the knees of a ruined stone castle that stood on a height and shadow-guarded the eastern marches of Palsance. First they heard great tumult. Then, when they came in view, they saw many people gathered to watch boys in white and boys in green wrestling and surging in a body on the common.

"What is that?" asked Giles.

"It is the War of Winter and Summer," said Oliver. "See there, Winter is being beaten back. Soon Winter will be slain and buried, and ashes scattered on the grave."

Giles smiled at that, for it seemed to him that he had lived through a winter that was long and cold. He was ready to greet summer and make it welcome.

"But what does it mean?" he asked. This ceremony was not observed in Nestor, not even by Nestorian peasants.

"It means that we have arrived on a holiday,"

said Oliver. "Today is the Festival of Joy. See the pole?"

In the center of the common, a great Joy-tree had been erected, a bare pole stripped of branches and bark, all save the crown. In this top, there were cloths and pennons of many colors tied, and prizes of hard eggs, sausages and sweetcakes for the young to climb after.

This was the first day of Joy-month, that month when all the best flowers grow and spring is at its sweetest. On this day, throughout Palsance, men and women set their work aside and gladly played, celebrating the fertility of the Goddess. Little girls dressed their Libera-dolls in ribbons and flowers, and carried them about to show. Their older sisters likewise dressed themselves in ribbons and flowers, and on this day might dare to do that which otherwise was not done. And young boys waylaid travelers and asked them hard questions.

Giles and Oliver were seen as they approached. A little stream bordered the common. They were met first on the footbridge that crossed it by a holiday guardian, a boy with a bullock horn on a stick and a sprig of green in his shirt.

"Where is your Libera-leaf?" he challenged them. "Where is your sprig of Joy?"

"What is that?" Giles asked of Oliver.

"I don't know this custom," said Oliver. "Or perhaps I have forgotten it."

"You must be strangers," said the boy. "All who pass here on the Festival of Joy must wear a leaf like mine, grandfather, or pay the penalty. That is the custom."

"What is the penalty?" asked Giles.

"The penalty is a drenching in the name of the

Goddess," said the boy as he scooped up water in his dipper horn.

Oliver stepped back. "Isn't there something to be said otherwise?"

"Nothing, grandfather," the boy said, and whistled loudly.

Oliver dodged back off the bridge in hopes of saving himself a soaking. The boy flung water after him, but it fell short. Oliver did not escape, however. A number of other boys of the same size all armed with dipper horns came pounding up in answer to the whistle. Some ran over the bridge. Some jumped the stream. They surrounded Oliver and knocked him down, and then shoved and jostled to empty their dippers over him as fast as they could scoop them full.

Haldane, had he been here, might have run like Oliver, wary, disgusted and panicked. He would surely have fought, and fought more effectively than Oliver.

But Giles stood his ground and took his baptism with better grace. Could one who swam in the river of the Goddess refuse a drenching in her name? Wet is wet.

And by his quiet acceptance, Giles stayed relatively dry. In attempting to escape his penalty, Oliver had attracted to himself all but the first boy, the guardian of the footbridge, and he contented himself to pour three slow cold dipper horns of water over Giles. Then something in Giles' calm and steady manner made the boy cease.

Oliver's cries and the shouts of the boys abusing him brought spectators from the common. Giles heard a sudden commotion amongst the boys, and

a girl's voice saying, "Enough. Enough. You will
drown the old man." And he brushed the water
and wet hair from his face to see a blonde maid-
en driving the boys away from Oliver.

"But, Mai, we catch so few. It's our fun," the
boy beside Giles protested.

The girl looked at them. She was dressed in the
gay holiday costume of eastern Palsance, and she
wore her own Libera-leaf in her dirndl. She looked
at Giles with a frank gaze, and he did not flinch
because he was naked. He was one with the moment, and stood steady.

"Who are you, strangers?" a voice of authority
asked.

Oliver sat on the ground like a soaked gray rat.
His rent and bloody smock was now wet and muddy, too.

"We are serfs escaped from Nestor," he said. "I
am Oliver. This is my poor branded grandson,
Giles."

But Giles denied this. "He is not my grandfather. He is addled. He but says that because I
help him. Black Morca is dead and the Gets are at
war amongst themselves. In the confusion the old
man and I have made our way to safety here in the
West with Libera's aid."

One in the crowd said, "Can it be true that
Morca is dead? Did he choke while swallowing an
elk?" Great Bad Black Morca, who stood the
height of the Joy-tree and ate babies for breakfast,
was a legend even here in Palsance—nay, even
more of a legend than in Nestor.

"Why you poor folk," said an old woman. "You
young boys should be ashamed to treat them so!"

But the man who spoke for the village said, "In
Libera's name, welcome to the Festival of Joy. Join
our celebration, we bid you." And to those around
him, he said, "Make them welcome and give them
comfort. Hurry. Hurry. Can you not see how tired
and hungry these travelers are?"

In an instant, people were gathered around the
fugitives. Giles' brand was fingered by curious children until their mothers bade them stop. Giles did
not protest, but endured their attentions without
comment. He knew the meaning of the letter that
he wore on his shoulder, and it was his still center,
his constant reminder that he was the dog of the
Goddess—like Lothor's little lap-dog—ready
always to be bent to Her will.

Towels were brought to them and they were
dried. They were given new shirts to wear. And
they were brought bread and cheese to eat and beer
to drink. They were sat down on the common near
the Joy-tree. It was a perfect day for a favorite festival, and they were made part of the celebration.

They watched the games. All day, Giles saw
youths try and succeed or try and fail to lift prizes
from the top of the Joy-tree. In the evening, a great
fire was laid and lit, and there was singing and
dancing around the Joy-tree. And young couples
passed back and forth from the shadows, while
their elders lounged about smoking pipes and
savoring the end of the day.

But Oliver had something on his mind unspoken
all this day. He said, "Why did you deny that I was
your grandfather?"

Giles said, "I swore to see you safely to Palsance,

and you are safely here."

"Yes."

"Then let us take leave of each other. I am not sure we have any farther to travel together."

"No," said Oliver. "I am not home yet."

"I never promised to see you home," Giles said, and looked away. He felt responsible for the old man's life, but he also felt impatience to be free of him.

"You feel me as a burden. But listen. Since I have no magic, I need your help more than ever," Oliver said. "Bear me company home. You can do so much as that. And I will repay you. I will let you stay with me there."

"No," said Giles. He remembered the stories he had heard. Oliver's family was great. It was one thing for Oliver to call him his grandson here amongst peasants in the eastern marches of Palsance where any raid-child might bear a Gettish look. But how could Oliver pass him off as a by-blow to his noble family? Not easily.

"Listen, Haldane."

"I am not Haldane. I am Giles."

"No," said Oliver. "Let me speak to Haldane. I don't know Giles. Listen to me, Haldane. I know I am not the man I was, but do not despise me. I can be of help to you. This world is not safe for you to walk abroad alone in. There are too many who may recognize Haldane, the son of Black Morca. You need time. You need a place to be small in."

"I am not sure that is my way," said Giles. "I go where I am directed to go. As Libera wills—that is my way."

Mai, the pretty blonde maiden who had driven away the boys with their dipper horns, sought them out then. She gave Giles a look that Oliver might remember from Festivals of Joy when he was young. But it was to Oliver she spoke, and not to Giles.

She said, "How are you now, grandsire? Are you well-fed? Are you rested? Are you dry?"

Oliver said, "I am content. As you see, I have even been given a pipe to smoke. May I thank you for coming to my rescue, sweet young lady. Without your aid, I might have been drowned, and I never thought to die by water."

She said, "It is the Festival of Joy," as though that were a reason for her rescue, and blushed.

Then she said, "Since I will likely not see you in the morning, grandsire, let me wish you a safe journey in Libera's name."

Giles took that as a sign. He could not do other. Everything was a sign to him. Anything was a sign to him. And he felt ashamed of his impatience.

"Thank you," said Oliver.

Then Mai said, "May I have leave to speak to your grandson?"

Oliver pulled on his pipe and blew out smoke again. "Yes," he said.

Half-shy, half-bold, she said to Giles, "Will you come with me and sit and comb my hair?" And she drew her comb from her pocket a little way, and showed it to him.

Without a look at Oliver, Giles smiled at the girl, rose and walked away with her, accepting the moment. He did say, "He is not my grandfather. Not exactly."

"How naughty you are to deny your own grandfather," she said. "You look so much alike."

Some time later, there was a lull in the singing and dancing. In that space, Oliver saw Giles take a sudden run at the Joy-tree and swiftly shinny it. At the top, Giles seized a sweet cake from the brush, and was cheered. When he returned to the ground, he carried the cake off into the dark.

Oliver could not help but marvel at how changed this Giles was from the young Haldane he had once known. And wondered whether he would depart by himself in the morning. But he thought not.

He need not have wondered. In the night, a second sign came to Giles, a dream that he had. This was when he slept alone.

In the dream, Giles followed the white wurox of the Goddess along distant roads unknown to him, over rivers and through mountains. And Giles was not alone in the dream. Oliver was with him, one step behind. They walked for the longest time where the white wurox went, and it seemed that they wished to stop, but could not. They must follow the wurox and go where the wurox went. But then they came to a place where the wurox turned and plunged into the earth and disappeared, swallowed by the land. Suddenly gone as suddenly appeared. And in that place, Giles looked over his shoulder and saw Oliver, one step behind. And in that place, they were able to stop at last because they knew it was the proper place to halt. Or so it was in the dream that Giles had.

In the morning, there was no white wurox to be seen and followed. But Giles joined Oliver when he was ready for the road. Giles had his signs.

Oliver said, "Do you bear me company home?"

"I'll bear you company along your road," Giles said. "I will bear you company home. That, or until I see a place I know. I will take my direction as I see it. But for now I will bear you company along your road."

"Very well," said Oliver. "I am grateful for your company while I have it."

Many miles and many days later, they still kept company. It was the end of a day when there had been flowers. There was golden light, and on their left was a storm hanging heavy near the setting sun. The storm was black and the rain could be seen like threads in the sky. The storm paralleled their passage and gave them company as they walked the high road through the temperate golden spring.

They came over a crest of the hill, and a new world was revealed. Above the road on the hillside was a cottage, not unlike other cottages they had passed. Beyond the house there were sheep at graze, happy in the golden light, knowing nothing of impending storms.

"We are here," said Oliver.

Here? This was no palace or great house. It was an ordinary hut, a little thatched house. Another confession. Another failure.

Giles looked out over the valley at the gathering storm. And in that instant, his sight was whole and clear and he saw madeness once more. The farther hill had to his eye the look of an animal. In the strange light he saw the head and forequarters of a great wurox, half-sunken in the land. When he saw that great sculpture, Giles knew this was the place.

He accepted the will of the Goddess. And he

turned, and there at his elbow was Oliver, as though their destinies were linked.

They made their way up the path to the cottage door. There were flowers planted before the cottage.

"I had forgotten that," said Oliver. "So much time has passed since I left home."

They stood there in the golden glow, the first rising breezes of the storm only reaching them now. The door was painted green. It was a double door, unlike any Giles had seen before.

The top of the door opened, and a woman stood looking out at them. She was not yet old, but more than middle-aged. She held one plump hand to her large bosom.

"Yes?" she said uncertainly.

Oliver said: "Do you not know me, Berthe? It is I, Noll, your own brother, returned at last from my adventures with my grandson Giles."

"Noll!" she said. "Can it really be you, Noll? It is. It is! It is my own dear Noll, come home at last as he said that he would."

The door was opened to them and they were swept inside. As they were held and cried over and exclaimed upon, the red light of the last sun struck home in the dark storm as it overtook them at last. Thunder crashed, and the red rain fell like fire on the land.

Giles stood beside his grandfather Oliver—old Sailor Noll returned from his long travels at sea—and watched the rain fall for a moment, and then the cottage door was closed behind them and they were home.

37416	**Is Anyone There?**	$1.50
41661	**Jupiter**	$1.75
*52220	**Of Matters Great and Small** $1.95	
63120	**Only A Trillion**	$1.50
*75456	**Science, Numbers and I**	$1.50
*78456	**The Stars In Their Courses** $1.50	
83226	**Twentieth Century Discovery** $1.50	

Available wherever paperbacks are sold or use this coupon.

PHILIP K. DICK

15670	Dr. Bloodmoney or How We Got Along After the Bomb $1.50
22386	Eye In The Sky $1.25
27310	Game Players of Titan 75¢
51910	The Man Who Japed 95¢
76701	The Simulacra $1.50
86050	Variable Man $1.50
90951	The World Jones Made $1.25

Available wherever paperbacks are sold or use this coupon.

★ ★ ★ ★ ★

MARION ZIMMER BRADLEY

Ursula K. Le Guin

10703	**City of Illusion** $1.75
47803	**Left Hand of Darkness** $1.95
66953	**Planet of Exile** $1.25
73293	**Rocannon's World** $1.50

Available wherever paperbacks are sold or use this coupon.

ace books, (Dept. MM) Box 576, Times Square Station
New York, N.Y. 10036

Please send me titles checked above.

I enclose $ . . . . Add 35c handling fee per copy.

Name . . . .

Address . . . .

City . . . . State . . . . Zip . . . .

33I